When You Call My Name

Betty Lowrey

To order additional copies of this book, contact:
Bookwhip
1-855-339-3589
www.bookwhip.com

Chapter 1

"There's a storm brewing," the old man said as he passed by. "Better head to shelter. They break fast. You don't want to be hit by a flying umbrella, now do you?"

Jewel rolled to her side, as Evan did the same, to stare into each other's eyes. A slow smile began as Evans eyes shined bright with love for his new wife. "I can't believe we're here, can you?"

Her mischievous smile dawned beneath the freckles that had popped out on her nose. "When Harriet said she was sending us to the beach for a week I thought what a waste of time people laying out in the sand…"

"But you love it. Me, too."

"Yes, it's being here with you and the music they continually play that keeps the atmosphere gentle," she sighed with great contentment, "I love it and it will end before we know it." She glanced down at her stomach bare to the world. 'My parents would be ashamed of me laying out here in the sun in view of other people."

"You mean in a swimming suit but then again you would be more noticeable in those skirt and blouses, wouldn't you now?" They laughed together.

"How is it Harriet seems to know what we need?" Jewel shook her head. "It's so…extreme…that she sent us to Memphis but when that was cut short nothing do but she send us as she said, "to the beach."

"Wonderful food, relaxation and music to fill a voyager's soul," He reached across taking her hand in his. "We have lived a sheltered life, true? But from this point on we live the life our heavenly father designs for us, and if he sends us to a beach we will be glad."

"Yes, we will," She studied him with a twinkle in her eye. "Can you guess what I was thinking as we lay here in the middle of summer in ninety something degree weather? Think hard, it's pretty far out."

"Do I get a clue?"

"Santa Claus," she said with a wicked gleam in her eyes. "Let's see how far that gets you."

"You are thinking," he tilted his head and pursed his mouth just so, "hmmm. You are thinking we are going to have snow for Christmas." She made that funny expression she used when he was way off. "You want to come back here for Christmas but you know we can't afford it for another twenty years."

"No, to both of your suggestions." She stretched a slow easy delighted with the world stretch. "I have really not had a wonderful happy Christmas since I've outgrown the happy to receive anything attitude of a child." She grinned, "not that I wasn't appreciative… but we are going to have such fun, a tree, Evan. Our very own and hot chocolate or apple cider," she hugged herself. "I can't wait, Jesus birthday celebration wrapped in our love. Oh, Evan, won't it be wonderful? We will have each other."

How could he resist the thought of a Christmas so filled with love, when those he experienced as a child were sadly lacking in anything but the austerity of Jesus birthday celebrated with the most important ingredient of all missing? He closed his eyes, seeing everything she described, but most of all her.

"Love," he said, his voice husky with emotion she could not yet understand. "Love and eachother."

Nodding, Jewel raised up and leaned across to kiss Evan gently on the lips just as a boom of thunder seemed to rock the earth beneath their bodies. Jumping up, Jewel grabbed the towel she laid on.

"Wow!" Evan was collecting their paraphernalia, running behind her as she headed toward the hotel. They reached the overhang as the first large drops of rain began to pelt the ground. "That was one powerful kiss," Evan teased handing her large brimmed hat to her and watching as she pulled it firmly onto her head. Now she was struggling into the mesh shift to hide her swimming suit. "Old habits are hard to break, aren't they?"

"All old habits aren't wrong, though."

"I think you are going to be brown as a button, as they say, by the time we return."

"And freckled." She wrinkled her nose in dismay. "All the sunscreen in the world won't…"

He kissed the tip of her nose. "Who cares. I love your straw colored hair and your freckles."

Unknown to the two, they were being watched.

✳ ✳ ✳ ✳ ✳

"Those two are truly in love, newlyweds I'd say." Nina smiled the lover in her happy for them.

"Reminds me of the two we see walk past the house, holding hands best they can because he is always carrying that big old instrument case." Geri craned her neck watching them run for cover.

"That's where they store the dead bodies. They're out canvassing the neighborhood. Who knows, maybe we are next." Aldean's mouth pursed as she considered their thoughts. "We'll see."

"You watch too much television. That is an innocent couple. She was white as soap when they arrived but look at her now, she has a nice tan." Nina glanced down at her own wrinkled skin, browning in spite of the sunscreen she soaked in. "I do remember skin that had no creases, do you?"

Geri ignored both comments, thinking of home. "Why haven't we formally met anyone on our block?'

"Because you put out that do not disturb sign and forgot to bring it in. Three months. I'd say the neighbors have already pegged us as grumpy old women who don't want to meet anyone."

"I didn't mean to forget the sign, Aldean, if you saw it why didn't you bring it in?"

"Pre-occupied."

"Yeah, forgetful is a better word, huh?" She stared at her sister, "For the life of me…" she let those thoughts drop. There were better things to think and do. "Well, I'm starving. You can set here til you roast, if you so desire, but as for me, I'm going to find food."

"Waddle away, fill your gut and then wonder why you gain a few pounds."

"You are so mean, Aldean. It's a wonder the earth doesn't open up and swallow you." Geri wrapped the king sized towel around her middle and tied the ends in a knot.

Thinking to ease the conversation, Nina made her usual soothing sounds, "shh shh shh. Both of you were beautiful teens, smashing in your prime and your lovely now. So stop the bickering. We came to rest from our toils. Let's do it."

Geri did a vibrating shake from the top of her head to the tip of her toes. "I just shake her off," She gave Aldean a scathing look, "Get up. Now. We have that massage in an hour and we need to eat while the resort is serving instead of later when they're preparing the evening meal."

"All right," Aldean snapped, "If it makes you happy. I'll follow your footsteps."

Geri began to wrap the turbine around her head. "If I had any hair on my head I wouldn't have to wear this thing." The material caught on the metal clasp of her swimming suit strap. "I need help."

With all the patience in the world Nina stepped up and wrapped the material, pushed the decorative pin through and stepped back to admire her work. "Looks great, now just put one foot in front the other and let's go." Content, loving the two, she murmured, "It's a wonder that boom of thunder didn't hit us, since we can't run and we just sit there with our bad attitudes waiting for lightening to strike."

✳ ✳ ✳ ✳ ✳

While Evan checked their email, Jewel browsed the hall with its framed pictures of the Briar Cliff orchestra playing in the ball room during the week. Formal attire only. The lady sitting at the piano wore a beautiful gown, poufed on each side of the piano bench and the men wore tuxedoes. One can only wish, she thought and the grandeur, oh, I can only imagine, but we did not sign up for tonight nor do we have the proper clothes but we have each other and a night to spend together. Glancing around she saw Evan waving to her. She wondered what would he think if he had taken time to read the posters. Would he know who the fastest rising to fame director, Anclive Denario, was?

She followed him through the line, making a sandwich of choice and comfort food in snack form.

"Ummm, this is delicious. Let's figure out what's in it so we can make it when we get home."

Evan laughed. "Isn't that supposed to be dessert?" Sitting his own plate on the table he sat opposite Jewel, leaning over to spoon a bite of the lime green concoction. "Does it have coconut in it?" He grinned, "You know that goes pretty good with my roast beef on rye."

"It goes with anything." Jewel's expression was of complete delight. "I'm in heaven." She munched down on the chicken salad sandwich she had garnished with a large slice of tomato, "Will we have enough money to buy tomatoes when we go home?"

"Depends on where home is?" For a moment worry creased his brow thinking about his family's home place underwater from the dam breaking, but one thing Harriet mentioned upon their leaving was to not worry over matters at home, those situations would be there when they returned. "If the home place is too far gone, then we have to decide whether to take Britany up on her offer. The only thing about that is its farther from possible employment, Christ Church and our new friends."

"I know Britany needs a friend but she has the means to travel, I don't and if we do find employment in the Cape, we need to stay close. We just need to give it to the Lord and trust him for the answer."

"Excuse me. We don't mean to intrude but you youngsters resemble a couple we see walk by about every day. Are you possibly from the Cape?"

Evan and Jewel glanced up to three elderly women peering into their faces.

"We are from the Cape. Yes, Ma'am." Evan gave Jewel a puzzled look. "Do you know these ladies?"

Jewel scooted around the table to sit by Evan on the bench, leaving three chairs. She motioned to the chairs, and she began to see the resemblance of the three as she laid a hand on Evan's arm. "They live next door to Ellen and Daniel." To the ladies she said, "We often see you ladies out in your yard."

The three were overjoyed to join them. Introductions were made. "Geri, Nina and Aldean," Nina said, shaking hands with the couple. "We don't mean to intrude but we have a bet of sorts going on."

"Oh, my goodness," Jewel was still trying to explain to Evan, "These are the ladies that built the beautiful home we admire. We love your landscaping and we are delighted to meet you. I'm Jewel, and this is my husband, Evan."

"What?" Surprised, Evan placed his hands on the table and leaned forward to study them. "We came all the way to North Carolina to meet our next door neighbors?" As quickly as his words were spoken Evan apologized. "I apologize, I didn't live there. I only visited Jewel at the Gates home."

"That's quite all right, nothing earth shaking there, even if you didn't. I assume you live near."

"Yes, ma'am. I walk the distance every day but it might be a bit much for you."

"How may we distinguish you three apart?" Jewel found the three elderly swimsuit ladies interesting.

"Oh, that's easy," Aldean replied. "I'm the tall bossy one. Nina is soft spoken and the black hair. Geri, pronounced like J-e-r-r-y, is the smaller of us but let me tell you, she's tough, especially with me."

Nina offered her hand but Geri held back, "I may be taking a cold she said, or perhaps its allergies."

The ladies were making themselves comfortable, sharing the table, their beach bags hanging from the chair arms, all the while sorting out food they'd brought from the inside islands. "This food is to die for, isn't it?" The small one was enjoying her sandwich as much as Jewel enjoyed the dessert. "So to end our bet and I'll take home their money," Geri began, "I said you are newly weds, they say no, engaged."

Jewel grinned. "We are newlywed. Mrs. Harriet Becker sent us down here on our honeymoon." Later she would wonder if she was mistaken in thinking the expression on their faces changed at mention of Harriet's name, but maybe she was wrong.

Geri held her hand out and the two made eye contact, "You wouldn't."

"I would," Geri said, "you never have pity on me. So rake it up." The two were digging in their beach bags to produce wallets. Right before Evan and Jewel's eyes they each placed a fifty dollar bill on Geri's wrist. Stifling a cough, Geri waited, "I believe you bet a hundred."

"There you are," the two chorused. "Fifty and fifty makes one hundred. Don't push your luck."

Laughing, Geri stashed the fifties in her bag and went on talking as though it were an everyday occurrence. "Do you gamble?" She asked Evan and Jewel as she unwrapped a cough drop.

"No, ma'am, we don't have that much money and if we did our heavenly father surely wouldn't want us too."

"Not even for fun?"

"We don't know, ma'am. We've never experienced this problem before."

"Not even for fun?" Geri persisted. "Like a game?"

"Ma'am, we are Christians and we don't think our Lord would want us using his money in such a way when we have so very little to spend."

"Tch, tch, tch," Geri clicked her tongue as if in complete puzzlement. "We must discuss this." She had miraculously finished her sandwich and some of the wonderful concoction Jewel raved about. "We have massages waiting for us. I shall lay there and consider your opinion on gambling. It's very interesting."

"I want to know more about you," Aldean added, as she thought they were a bit naïve. "Perhaps you could visit us back home if we don't chance running into each other before we leave."

"It was nice meeting you," Nina said in her soft voice. "Be sure to explore nearby surroundings. The night life is said to be magnificent."

"Yes ma'am," Evan stood like the gentleman he was and Jewel gave each lady a hug.

"By the way," the tall one said. "Congratulations on your marriage. We have a young couple that has asked to be married in our back yard, in a few days as a matter of fact." The ladies looked at each other quite seriously, as Aldean continued, "we have left the landscape in capable hands, we hope, anyway, they are to mow and water according to need for the beauty of the young couples wedding."

"I'm sure it will be beautiful." Jewel replied. "We should have photos of our wedding when we return home and the Gates back yard was a fairy tale setting for us. We are so grateful." She took Evan's hand, "We will leave you now. You ladies, have a good day."

"Nice to meet you," they said in unison as they slid back rather dejectedly in their seats alone again.

"They have so much energy they tire me out," Jewel whispered. "You, too?" Evan nodded. "Let's go back to the beach and find a cabana and take a nap. How does that sound? Then we can swim again."

When they were settled inside the cabana, Evan raised on one elbow. "Talking just plain wears me out, Jewel, in my father's house we were pretty noncommittal. I don't know if it was because of my parents personal pain or if they were also raised in silence."

"You have been most patient, Evan. For weeks I didn't hear you speak to voice your opinion and then you began to talk to me and it was the most wonderful gift I have ever received that someone like you would find me interesting enough to talk with, not just talk down to me."

"No one should talk down to you, Jewel. I remember finding you fascinating in those first days we met. And now, you are my wife and I love you dearly. I pray nothing ever comes between us as it did with my parents. They lived lives of loss: The loss of human touch and sharing and caring and I suffered most."

Jewel thought about Evan's story, no she prayed that never happened to them. Evan's mother had become ill and was not thought to survive. Her sister came to help care for the home and eventually Evan's mother did live; waking to find her sister pregnant with her husband's child which they kept the pregnancy secret until the day of his birth when Evan's birth mother died and his father and the woman he thought for years to be his mother, raised him but there was never the affection normally shown a child , in resentment and retaliation for what her husband and her own sister had created against her. She swore the child would carry the shame and her rejection of him was justified. Had it not been for his father, perhaps Evan would never have known the touch or voice of love while even that morsel of care was given sparingly. Jewel shuddered, wondering how good people did such evil things to those they should love. He was a baby, her mind shouted. Evan should have known love. She vowed their life together would be strong, built on the principles of God's love toward his children. She knew he loved children because Addy had become dear to his heart. She drifted off to sleep vowing if possible she would show Evan his deserving to be loved.

Evan lay there, watching the even breathing of his new wife. A smile of satisfaction crossed his lips and his eyes brightened that she found him worthy of her affection. As a child he had wondered what he had done to be treated so casual, except as a child he had been unable to describe the hopeless hungering feeling of need he felt when he stood by his mother while she dressed him, longing for a kiss on the cheek or a smile of encouragement. He had stood there, his shoulders drawn forward, almost cowering as he wondered how to please her because he never felt he could.

Da, he whispered the name, his father had felt the constraints. Had he found his wife's sister comforting? Had she smiled and caressed him for who he was; would she have loved him, her son?

He would take the questions into eternity. What was my mother like, he asked his father and Da replied, "she was a good woman son, merriment in her soul, laughter that tinkled like a bell and hugs as warm as honey…but I took that from the one you call mother. I banished her joy by my own weak nature. Perhaps it was best your birth mother died what would we have done with the two? I was not strong enough and the good Lord knew. It is my fault, son. When you choose a wife, look for one who loves easy and feels in your heart that her love will last throughout eternity. I had that twice but I ruined the first love by taking a second. Make sure your heart beat increases when she calls your name."

He could not sleep. He must lift the melancholy by sending his thoughts to other places. He tried to think of the violin he wanted to build, special wood of a certain color…but his thoughts would not go there. He heard a trickle of laughter; looking out behind wispy curtains that concealed nothing he saw the three ladies they'd met during lunch. No doubt they were having massages, as laughter came in peals, floating across the way, chortling over the breakers that were coming in, sudsy white foam to touch the beach and recede. He reached across the foot of space to touch her hand and Jewel's fingers twined in his.

"Are you asleep, my love?" Jewel's voice asked soft and gentle.

"No, I haven't slept. I've lain here watching you."

She turned to face him, a smile on her face. "That must have been entertaining," she said as she rose to cross over to his bed. "Why didn't you waken me?" He took a strand of hair away from her cheek. "I think I was dreaming of you," she smiled. "We were dancing. Do you think we could dance?"

"You would like to dance?" He ran his hand down her arm as he thought. "I did read there's a dance in the ballroom tonight. It is formal. Do we have formal attire?"

"No. We don't." Disappointment shone in her eyes. "It was just a thought, a dream actually." Evan grew quiet. "Don't fret, Evan, I shouldn't have shared that dream."

"Of course, you should," he insisted. "Shall we swim or go in?"

* * * * *

He felt her disappointment. Though she said it was just a thought, he wished he could make her dream come true. Please God. He found himself saying a prayer before he realized what he was doing. Wasn't that what Harriet whispered they must do? Make dreams come true, she said, life is short. Jewel went up to shower, while he collected two bottles of water for the room. As he waited he overheard two gentlemen in discussion. "Where will you find a violinist at this late date? Forget it."

"Our main song will be lost without Jim. Who knew his father would fall off the ladder and break his neck. He's old. They aren't sure he'll make it." Evan listened, unable to contain himself; at last minute before they walked away he went to them.

"Excuse me, I couldn't help but overhear. May I ask what is the song and do you have Jim's violin?"

They started to brush past him. He knew. "If I could help you, perhaps you could help me."

"What's in it for you, Buddy?"

"Tell me the song, show me the violin and I'll show you what I can do before I tell you my need.'

"Are you into this?" The tall guy asked his friend who seemed to be loitering on the brink of listening. "Oh, yeah, you are, aren't you? So" he sized up Evan. "Let's go upstairs and hear you out."

Within ten minutes, Evan won them over. "Don't suppose you have a little piano player in your pocket, do you?" The business guy asked. "We never pick up a guy off the street to work with us, you understand? You have to be pretty blame good to even be considered."

"Why do you need a pianist?" They told him, most of their presentations needed a piano in the background. "But that one has to be good. No run of the mill, someone who can tickle the ivories." He began to scratch his head, as he turned to the tall guy. "Are we nuts or what?"

"Desperate."

"She's good," Evan promised. We will work your magic if you can meet our requirements. That's it."

✳ ✳ ✳ ✳ ✳

Jewel was resting by the window in the peach velvet lounger. Her hair was done in an upsweep style, she was wearing make up the way Marigold had taught her and in her ears were the small pearl ear rings he had given her the day they were married. Going to her he dropped down on one knee. "Jewel, would you trust me if I have made a decision for us to do something without talking to you first, if you knew there would be a reward for us at the end of what I decided?"

He was serious, his eyes solemn and dark as he asked and it made her heart beat faster until she was afraid it would spring out of her chest. What could he have done? He was only a little delayed in coming up. Where could he have gone to find something important that must be accomplished without asking her? But she wasn't there. He had to make a decision. Sometime she might have to do the same.

"Yes," she said, firmly, though her voice held a wisp of concern. "I will stand by you."

Tiny beads of perspiration had broken out on his forehead. "Aww." He was instantly relieved. "Are you familiar with Glenn Miller's music?" She was nodding yes, though very puzzled. "Have you heard the newest song Celine Dion has recorded, particularly the one where the piano has the opening chords?"

"Is it a television show, Evan? Name that Tune? Something similar?"

"No, my love, it is you and me performing with the Orchestra tonight in the ball room. And after we do our job, we can dance away the rest of the night." Jewel was beginning to laugh. "It's not a joke, Jewel. It's for real. Their violinist had to go to the hospital for his father and it just so happens the pianist is his wife. Since they fear the elderly father's health is in severe straits, they need a pianist and violinist."

Jewel stood and began to pace the floor along the windows. "But we have no proper attire, Evan. I've seen the photo's on the boards down stairs, they wear tuxedos and the lady wore a beautiful yellow gown." She thought for a moment. "Like in Beauty and the Beast. It is beyond beautiful."

"That's one of the songs, Jewel, do you know it?" His heart was thumping in his chest. Please say yes, he was silently praying. "Oh, I've gotten us in such a mess, haven't I?"

"No, you have not." She saw in him the little boy wondering how to make it right. "Shall I wear my robe? Will you wear your one pair of dress slacks?" She began a nervous giggle, as she threw her arms around Evan's shoulders. "Never in a thousand years would I have thought this would happen with my nearly silent always considerate love of my life. Yes. Let's do our best and pray its good enough." She turned him toward the shower. "Go. I can't wait to see you in your trousers and me my robe."

The door bell played it's little melody announcing someone was there. Jewel opened the door to find a very formal looking clothes bag right in front of her face and behind that folds of yellow chiffon draped across the arm and shoulder of a young man she had never before seen. "May I help you?" She asked.

"No, ma'm, I'm supposed to be bringing your symphony wear for the night. Where shall I place them?"

Completely taken back, Jewel stared open mouthed at the finery he placed on the bed. A tux for Evan and a dress for her. Would it fit? She was in shock. They were serious. Yes, she had reassured Evan, but had she really believed they would perform with the Orchestra? Briar Wood Symphony, originally from England now stationed in California, never in one spot long, the advertisements said, they travel the world. When they are near you don't fail to see them. It would be the greatest mistake of your life.

The boy was leaving as she tried to close her mouth. This was unbelievable. Shoes. There were shoes in three sizes. This was a fairy tale. She tried the second pair. They fit perfect. She left them on. Now for the dress. Only one dress, it had better fit. If it didn't, what then? She positioned the dress beside the lounger, zipper open all the way down, the dress gaping at the back and then she climbed on top of the lounger, standing at first to sit and scoot to the edge and place her feet inside the gown, feeling the folds touch her ankles, her knees and now she stood pulling the gown up, over her breast, her arms through the straps that would conceal her undergarments and it began to come alive to her secret dreams to one day play piano in a special setting with wonderful instrumentalists, oh, yes, dear Jesus to be part of something grand. She couldn't believe it. Really, all in one day her heart was beating so fast she feared it would spring through her flesh, the material of the dress, and land on the floor.

"Oh, oh, oh," Evan found her in front of the mirror, her mouth wide open, her eyes sparkling and happy.

"Help me, Evan." She was ecstatic. "Have you ever seen anything so beautiful? Hurry, help me."

"What must I do?"

"Zip it up, oh, Evan it just has to fit. I've never seen such finery."

"Stand still," he said, laughing. "You are like a kid. I'm trying. It likes just a smidge. Do you have to wear that slip thing?"

"I think so," her enthusiasm was disappearing. Disappointment claimed her expression.

"No, you don't, the dress is lined. Doesn't it have built into it what is needed?" His knowledge of women's garments was very limited. "Take off the slip and trust me, the dress is heavy lined, no seeing through." He waited. "Now, let's try it." The zipper slid into place. Jewel turned to kiss him.

"Now, you. Go. Go. Go. The shirt, tie, trousers, jacket, all on the bed. Do you have black socks and black shoes? They didn't send you shoes, but they did for me."

A knock on the door got their attention. "Go on," she whispered. "I'll answer the door."

"Five minutes, ma'am," the person said, leaving abruptly to head back down stairs.

"This is real." Jewel pinched herself. "I can't believe it, oh, I cannot believe it." Now her mind raced ahead to the music. "Which one will they use from Beauty and the Beast?" She had to think this through. "The one on time," she snapped her fingers. "It has to be that one. What else?"

Evan came from the bathroom into the sitting area. His long hair touched the stand up white collar. "I should have gotten a haircut," He practically moaned as he slipped the black bow tie around his neck.

Jewel shook her head adamantly disagreeing. "No, you are perfect. Trust me the reviews will say, that handsome man playing violin appeared to have stepped through time, so delicate came the violin's sound and then he was off like a roaring giant, the swells of music lifting our hearts and soul upward.

The knock on the door sounded more abrupt. "We're coming," she was able to cry out, for she and Evan were hugging each other so tightly she feared the dress zipper would tear lose and where would that leave her. Sensing her discomfort Evan apologized, going first down the carpeted hall.

"You look marvelous," he whispered. "You take my breath away," she replied. The boy was standing off stage, taking Jewel's hand, he pointed with his other where she would find the piano. "You, sir?" Evan nodded. "Two spaces away from the director, do you see them? You must take the first space and be ready when the director gives you the signal. You have the first lovely strings of introduction. The people will listen as they prepare for the official opening. But you must stay alert, sir, don't mess up."

Hurriedly, Evan studied the music. No one told him until now he had the opening notes. Jewel was studying the line-up. Now the strings were ready but they were waiting for him. He was first. It was more than he had ever dreamed. What had he gotten them into? What was Jewel going to say once it was all over? She probably wouldn't speak to him. He wanted so badly to please her; he had lost his mind! Did wives divorce husbands over silliness?

The director pointed the baton at Evan. He played the opening bar, the strings picked up; the orchestra went in to full swing. Evan's heart was pounding, so fiercely and openly was the haunting refrain, the music spoke of times past and times present, yesterday and tomorrow and his heart felt the weight of people caring, the warmth of another's breath on his cheek, the first steps of a young child and the heartbreak of the cross peering down on the room, Evan's heart was keeping time with the director's baton… and yet, time was standing still whether he lived or died today it mattered not.

Just as it seemed hearts would break the piano gave the sound of the first drops of snow, the lights from the chandeliers picked up the iridescent flakes falling as the world took on a mystical atmosphere and the flutes brought the swirl of energy to life. Evan was one with his surroundings. Jewel was playing and the audience was standing. Before they both realized, time had passed Evan was taking Jewel's hand in his own, her yellow dress flowing around her with Evan truly handsome in his tuxedo, black hair falling across his brow in a very winsome way to the delight of those who looked on as they danced by.

"I declare they are a beautiful couple," Aldean whispered and Nina replied, "In love." Geri snapped another picture of the two, her own thoughts cradling the hope she would see them more in the Cape.

"Are we alive? Is this us?" Jewel's smile brightened her face and made her eyes sparkle. "I will be black and blue if I pinch myself much more. Never in my wildest dreams was there anything like tonight. To dance with you, my dearest, to play with an orchestra, Oh…Evan, that our God would bless us so."

"How has this happened? Why has this happened. We are completely out of our comfort zone. The musicians were beyond my ability," Evan said, as they slowed for a breather. "Now you appeared to be keeping up with all of them. I'm very proud of you, Jewel." He bent to kiss her on the tip of the nose. "Do you know when we began to dance; the audience thought we were part of the program."

"Is that what the applause was about?"

"Either that or you were the prettiest girl on the floor dancing."

"Oh, Evan," she replied, wistfully. "It's the dress. If a woman wore clothes made from good material every day and her makeup, and was pleasant, the whole world would think she was beautiful. I have nothing but crudely put together clothes."

"But you are beautiful. You have an inner beauty that reveals your calm and I love that about you."

Tears filled her eyes. "Oh, Evan, I've spent all these years longing to wear a dress such as this, though I could not imagine one so beautiful and I never expected to wear one," she sighed, content. "Didn't you ever wish for a moment such as this? Haven't you ever wished to sing with an orchestra?"

"With you, yes, but," he grinned, "I have to admit the instruments tempt me more than clothes."

The director appeared as though produced by the fog machine. "Hey, you two?" He reached to clasp both their hands. "Sorry I didn't get to meet you before we began but I was assured you would be great. My name's Anclive Denaro. Call me Andy. How many nights do you have left?" Three, they said in unison. "Uh, huh. How about helping us out? Jim's dad died and now there's preparation for a funeral, and he won't return here."

"Would I wear the same dress every night?" Both men seemed to study the fact that was important to her.

Finalliy, the director replied. "I believe you can wear a different color every night."

"I'll stick with the black tux, if that meets your approval," Evan replied. "Looks like the dresses tipped the scales."

"It's a deal, then?"

"Add in Jewel a solo part singing each night and you got a deal, right Jewel?"

Embarrassed, Jewel kicked Evan's shin. "I just told you that, you're not supposed to tell."

"Well, too late now." Evan quipped, the director nodding. "She's pretty good on that I'm Your Lady Song."

A smile broke across Anclive'sface. "That one was supposed to be on the list."

"I saw it," Jewel was a bit unsure of this arrangement. "I'll let you know if I think I can do it."

"Oh, you will," Anclive replied. "The audience will love you and demand more, so be prepared."

So it was, Jewel and Evan enjoyed the day in the sun and the night living out day dreams they never expected to come true. Jewel was delighted with the mint green ball gown, the lilac and the gold but the aqua that leaned toward shades of turquoise either set her up to be the princess she felt inside for those three hours of singing, playing piano and dancing with Evan or so met her aura the audience loved her and always asked for more. Her eyes were damp with tears of gratitude and thanking her God, while her heart filled with more of his love than she could fathom. "Jesus, Jesus," she whispered. For Evan, speaking with those playing various instruments was enough. Examining the work and skill of the builder taught him more than he could read in hidden volumes of books or special manuals. That he was a handsome man in the provided tux never crossed his mind and only added to his allure.

The week passed quickly. It was time to return home.

"No matter how hard we try," Evan said, "I don't think we will outdo this last week. Do you?"

Sitting her small overnight case inside Harriet's car, Jewel backed away as he closed the trunk door. "Never." She replied as a great smile spread across her face. "How can we ever repay Harriet?"

"We can't." The outside speakers came alive to music from Beauty and the Beast. Looking quickly beyond their surroundings, Evan put his hand up as Jewel stepped into his embrace and there on the Hotel property thinking possibly only the guards were watching the two danced smiling and touching and loving each other one last time, while inside a group had gathered around the television monitor and clapped when the song ended as the two got in the long and ancient car and drove away.

'Ah," the desk clerk remarked, "Love in bloom, the couple from the orchestra, aren't they grand?"

✷ ✷ ✷ ✷ ✷

They were enjoying the scenery when they came upon vehicles sticking out of the roadside embankment.

"I've never seen anything like that," Jewel said. "Why would they do that?"

Laughing while enjoying her perplexed expression, he replied, "I guess one man's junk or should I say salvage is another man's art." He was ready to speed on home when he saw the billboard advertising Christmas every day of the year, a shop to take home. "What do you think?" He pointed to the sign. "We could find a trinket to remind us of this trip Miss Harriet gave us." He glanced her way. "It's up to you."

She clapped her hands. "Oh, yes," her smile was his reward, "I know just what we need. What would you choose?" She giggled. "Don't tell me. Let's go in and go different ways, choose an item and then come back to each other and see if we choose the same."

"Are you worried whether we think alike, or not?" He reached for her hand and squeezed it. "I think we've settled that one, long ago."

The stop was a success. When they met in the center of the store, they were carrying an ornament depicting the Savior's birth. Jewel's was a matt finish and Evan's bore a light sparkled dusting. "I chose this one with you in mind," they said together. "What are the odds of that happening?" Jewel asked.

"With us, it's most likely." Evan grinned. "Now we look forward to hanging it on our tree. Right?"

"Now the question is, do you plan to stop for the night or drive home?"

"We've had a wonderful week but I'm really ready to go back. What do you want to do?"

"I'm with you," he said. "The hours seem to slide away when we're together."

"Where are you from?" The girl checking them out was impressed with their choosing the same ornament. Evan replied that they were from the Cape. "I've not traveled outside of this state," she said. "There's always a problem with my boyfriend. It's one of those situations where if I want to go he doesn't."

"Do you attend church?" Evan couldn't help asking. "We found each other in a church and our situation was not an ordinary one."

"What do you mean?" She handed change to him and waited for him to explain. He told her how their homes were flooded and they lost all their possessions. "But," he said, smiling, "we did find each other."

"Was it love at first sight?" She asked. "My boyfriend and I grew up together, but maybe that's not always the best."

"I tell you what's best," Evan said. "May I ask what is your name?"

"Rachael."

"Here's what is best for any of us, Rachael, to know the Lord. Were you brought up in a home that attended church on Sundays and read the Bible on a regular basis?"

"Not really," she replied. "My grandmother went to church every Sunday and as a little girl I went with her."

"Was there a reason you haven't continued?" Evan was giving her his full attention.

"Well, I learned to drive and I could go where I wanted. Most Sundays I just went to my boyfriends."

"And the boyfriend doesn't know the Lord?" Jewel was examining a row of silk scarves but she was listening intently to the two in conversation; thinking how easily Evan had brought the girl to speak of her salvation. "You could be a great influence on him, Rachael, if you know the Lord."

"But I don't, not that well." Rachael sighed. "I guess I left church too soon. What if I tried to tell him about the Lord and he wasn't having it?"

"If living a life for the Lord is what you want, Rachael, and he does not, then you have a lot to think on."

"I know. Sometimes I feel that's what's missing. I don't really go to worship, I forget to pray and my life gets in a mess because what I learned as a little girl is still there. It's not exactly lying dormant."

"Would you like to get that straight in your mind and your heart, Rachael?"

"You know, it's strange you came in here, today. I've been thinking about this awhile and yes, I would."

Listening, Jewel felt a strange sense of peace as the girl and Evan went through the plan of salvation.

"I thought I accepted the Lord when I was a child," she said as they were leaving, "But now I know it's complete." She lay a hand on Evan's arm. "Thank you for that extra scripture about my boyfriend. I hope it keeps us together, rather than unequally yoked and having to leave each other."

"You did that very nicely, Evan." He glanced her way, at a loss for words he just shook his head. "I'mSerious," she said. "I couldn't have done it that smoothly and we hear people all the time saying they don't know how to lead into the plan of salvation, but you did it a though you do it everyday."

"I don't know what to say, Jewel. That is dear to my heart, if I need more training then I want it."

Chapter 2

"How do you feel?" Evan squeezed her hand. "We've held hands most the way home. Do you think we can keep this love we've experienced the last two weeks the rest of our life?"

"Do you think your parents loved each other when they first married, the way we do?"

Evan considered her question. "I've told you what happened when my mother's sister came to help when she was ill. That ruined all of our lives because of what she and my Father did, but the woman he had an affair with was my real mother and when she died I was raised by her sister, my father's wife." He shook his head. "Surely they did, why else would she have been so hurt she punished my father and me the remaining years."

"Your life was very sad because of it. On the other hand, my parent's seldom showed affection. I had a completely different view of marriage until I met the Graves and especially the Gates. Seeing Daniel and Ellen's affection, no, it's more than affection. They truly love each other and I want that. Actually, all those years, I prayed when I found the love of my life, I prayed for a marriage that would last because there was so much love."

"Then we must do everything within us, to see that it happens." He kissed the tips of her fingers. "I've already seen a change in you."

She laughed. "I hope it's a good change. I certainly have had no practice. I may be a terrible person and not know it."

"I believe you have a fierce determination to make things work. I saw that when your parents would have persuaded you not to marry me and certainly not as quickly as we did." Now Evan laughed. "I think they were pretty much right in thinking I was a good for nothing who had nothing."

"It may be that you have a thriving business if you can turn out the instruments on a regular basis."

I wish you didn't have to work. I like having you near me."

"I was wondering…don't suppose you could…nope, I know better than to ask…" She sighed.

"Well, come on, what are you thinking?"

Jewel gave him that demure look, he'd seen it a time or two when he knew she was considering something deep, like the dresses she wanted to wear but wouldn't approach the subject. "What is it?"

"I know you can't build a piano but if we had one, I could give lessons and maybe just have a part time job, instead of eight til four."

"I should know this, shouldn't I? How much does a piano cost?"

"I'm so happy you even ask, but we cannot go into that expense right now." Her voice grew a worried tone. ""What if Anne and Andrew want us to move out, now that there's no question they have custody of their children and won't need us, where will we go?"

"I've thought on that now and again as we have been away. Have you?"

"Yes," she agreed. "I have, and I've been praying about it."

"Me, too. Our prayers have already begun, now all we can do is trust in the Lord."

"Sometimes, Evan, I try to think how I can help the Lord with this…"

"Now that's trying to take it back, isn't it, now?" Evan quoted the old sea captain and they both laughed.

* * * * *

"Shall we swing by the Gates house and Miss Harriet's?"

She nodded, already unloading their possessions before they arrived, in her mind she was thinking about Andrew's special place, that he out of the goodness of his heart had welcomed Evan in to and then on their marriage, Jewel. She sighed, content and yet questioning. "How could it be, Evan that the Lord looked down on us, two different families made homeless by the flood of water, ending up at the Cape at Christ Church to meet such wonderful people?"

"You were a family; having your parents, but I was alone and boy, did I feel it."

She giggled. "You seemed to draw people to you. The Captain really liked you."

"I wonder if they did get him into the nursing home as the pastor suggested." Evan's eyes wore a troubled expression for a bit. "Seems like I'd love to work with all kinds of people, Jewel, he did interest me and touched my heart that he was willing to share his violin. I sometimes wonder if the Lord could use me on a regular basis, but I don't mean called as in a pastor's calling."

"You mean in daily life?" She had removed her seat belt and was on her knees peering into the back seat. "Isn't that what we are all intended to do?"

"But who does it? I mean it was obvious he was elderly, alone and no one there for him. He seemed confused as to what exactly he must do, you know, the day he spent trying to organize a crew and then when he was worn at end of day he asked could someone just find a bed for him."

"Oh, there it is." Reaching, she found the small satin bag pushed down into the larger beach bag that had held their towels but was used to carry home their personal hygiene kits. "Oh, my, I think your aftershave has spilt into the bag. Anyway, I found what I was looking for, safe and sound and in my hand now." She opened the satin bag and removed a small black velvet box. He watched as she removed the pearls from her ears and placed them carefully in the box. "I treasure your gift," she said.

"Why don't you wear them?"

She thought a minute. "I don't know if I should because I want them to be for special times."

"When we are able, I will buy diamonds that you can wear every day." He promised. "So here we are on the Gates Street and all is quiet. Let's drive on by the sister's house and see what they have been doing."

"I doubt they are home, yet, but I didn't ask when they planned to return." Evan circled the cul de sac, while they peered at the house that had sprung up, as generously sprawling as the Gates home and the landscaping as empowering but there was a problem. "Hmmm." Jewel said, glancing at Evan.

"Something's wrong, isn't it? Their beautiful lawn is overgrown and the shrubs have not been watered at all. Something is not quite right, but one thing is for certain their lawn service is not working."

"And they will be home by this weekend that I know. The tall one mentioned a wedding to be performed in their back yard." She felt the dismay of straggling flowers and dusty shrubs. A small sign at the corner of the house read Landscaping by Gull and Company. "Gull and Company," she said aloud. "I will guess they will arrive the day before the wedding expecting everything to be in order."

Shaking his head, Evan drove on, past the Gates, onto Main and by Harriet's house where all the lawns were thriving and green. In his mind, he wondered about the sister's landscaping service, while Jewel borrowed his phone, googled the name Gull and Company and listened to a short voice mail. "Our service is temporarily interrupted due to unforeseen personal situations. Please look elsewhere for your landscaping needs."

"What do you have planned for the rest of the week?" She asked.

"I was thinking we have friends in need and wondering if I might help them," he replied.

Jewel grinned. "How could it be, I was thinking the same thing."

✳ ✳ ✳ ✳ ✳

"Home sweet home," Evan quipped as he carried in the big suitcase. Jewel was behind him with the two small overnighters.

"Except it isn't our home. But hasn't it been nice our first nights together?"

"Yes, it has." Jewel deposited the smaller suitcases at the foot of the bed and then sank down on the side. "I love what you've done with the walls."

"I'm merely the workman. Andrew had the material." Evan was thumbing through his Bible. "I feel so blessed." He glanced to where she sit. "Don't we need scripture to bless our future?"

"We are blessed." She smiled, "but I have always wondered where I fit in on the Beatitudes. Everyone has a gift and there's a place for each of us…you know, don't you, what I'm saying? Where do you fit in?

"Let's read Luke, chapter six, I believe and see if we find our place. Verse twenty begins, Jesus lifted up his eyes on his disciples and said, "Blessed be ye poor; for your's is the Kingdom of God. Blessed are ye that hunger now; for ye shall be filled. Blessed are ye that weep now; for ye shall laugh. Blessed are ye, when men shall hate you and when they shall separate you from their company and shall reproach you and cast out your name as evil for the Son of man's sake. Rejoice ye in that day and leap for joy for behold your reward is great in heaven for in the like manner did their father's unto the prophets".

"But that is not the Beatitudes I remember," Jewel said. "There's more and a different wording in Matthew. There are more, I think nine or ten, but they do end with the same meaning that men will persecute and revile those who love the Lord." She watched as Evan thumbed through his Bible.

"Here, it is," he studied the verses, "the poor, those that mourn, the meek, the merciful and the pure in heart and the peacemakers. You are right, it does list more." He glanced up, smiling, "I'd say you fit in verse six where it says blessed are they which do hunger and thirst after righteousness, and they shall be filled."

""Verse eight for you, the pure in heart shall see God." She hugged him, her arms wrapping around his chest as she laid her head there above the beating of his heart. "I love you, Evan. I never knew God had such wonderful blessings in store for my life."

"Had I known," he answered, "perhaps I would have been a better person, as it was sometimes I became so discouraged wondering if my skill in making instruments would be recognized."

"And all the while, unknownst to you, it was." She beamed up at him. "Wow."

"Remember the verse, found in first Corinthians thirteen, "Now we see through a glass darkly, but then face to face; now I know in part; but then shall I know even as also I am known?" I think that's where I am, not understanding wholly but believing… before it is all over I will."

✳ ✳ ✳ ✳ ✳

"I plan to do a little unpacking and sorting clothes for laundry for about an hour, is there anything you need to do?"

"If you don't need my help, I think I should inquire as to when the roads will be open that we might check on the place. I don't know if we will be able to clean the mud out of the house and salvage it or not and then, too," he took a deep breath, hoping his last work before the flood would be there. "My instruments…all I could do was push them inside the old truck and run for my life with the water rushing around my ankles. When that dam broke it filled in the valleys so quickly you'd thought we were at the lake."

With a peck on the lips, Evan left. Jewel separated the items from the suitcases and surveyed the room. There was little to do and her mind was on the sister's landscape.

How sad for the couple coming for the weekend wedding, expecting a place of beauty, instead to find an unkept yard. She wondered if watering three days hence would make a difference and determined she would ask Evan. Just in case, she changed into a pair of denims Ellen had given her, found her straw beach hat and was waiting on the bench outside when Evan returned.

"Contemplating laundry, are you now?" Evan's greeting was balm to her soul. "You were only gone a few minutes but I missed you, "she replied. "Did you now?" He sat beside her. 'I've been thinking about the sister's lawn," he tilt his head and studied her intensely, "Do you think we'd be committing a crime if we went over and worked there an hour or so?" Now his eyes twinkled with humor. "Seeing as I find you sitting in the sun as if contemplating some great project, I'm thinking you and I are on the same page."

She grinned. "I've thought of nothing else, since seeing it and considering the couple expecting it to look grand…oh, my, won't they be surprised? But are there tools we will need?"

"I took the liberty of stopping by and in the back there's any number of tools, so, let's go."

"What would you have done if the alarm had caught you trespassing?"

"The thought entered my mind, and I considered my recourse, but truthfully I don't think it is on."

"I couldn't help but think how disappointed the wedding couple would be with the state of things."

It was a short drive to the street where the sisters lived just beyond Daniel and Ellen. "Do you feel you should check in with the Gates?"

"I want to," she admitted, "But they made us promise not until the eleventh and that means three more days. They have all tried so hard to give us time together." She giggled. "They don't know we like being with them, do they? I've not known this type people before."

"Nor I," he agreed. "Here we are. Come let me show you the tools on the backside of the little storage building. Beneath the overhang they are protected."

"I would guess there are larger and more powerful tools inside the building. Too bad it isn't opened. It will take you forever to mow this lawn, Evan. Had you considered how you are going to do that?"

"If I used other than a key to unlock that doors…" He sighed, "let's face it, we are trespassing and if I enter that building I think it kind of doubles the sin, don't you?"

Jewel's hand was on the knob, as she turned it ever so gently they heard a click and the door opened with a squeak of the hinge. "Oh, my goodness, did they forget to lock it?" Already she was hunched forward, hands on her knees studying the machinery in the building. "Why two kinds of mowers?"

Evan was enjoying her surprise, laughter bubbling up too, due to the mower he was itching to try. "I want to use this one," he said, meeting the dubious expression on her face. "And you?"

"I'll stick to the clippers, the hoe and those shears, if you don't mind. Just don't run over me."

Glancing toward the house, Evan wondered had the sisters forgotten to lock up before leaving.

"What's the little house for, Evan? It's built really close to their home."

"Could it be for their guests? There are three women in that one, perhaps a guest house makes sense."

"Shall we begin?" Jewel was already walking toward rose bushes that needed deheading of old roses. "If you need me, I'll be in this beautiful back yard, well, anyway, it's going to be beautiful again."

Instead of starting the mower, Evan sized the depth of cut and then chose a tool from the inner wall, checked the battery and with a whir of the motor went to work; weed eating wasn't the case but cutting away grass the mower wouldn't reach was. He was energized toward using the powerful mower next.

✳ ✳ ✳ ✳ ✳

"I've not had such fun in years," Jewel quipped as they prepared to leave. They had literally worked all day. It was Evan's opinion the sisters had no idea the state their yard would have been in, nor did they seem to understand the event they scheduled was to happen the next day and they were unavailable. "You mastered the mower," she said, grinning. "I know that was your favorite part."

"Yeah the one I have at home may run like a well oiled machine but it is ancient. This was a treat." He was studying the instructions on the lid of the watering system. "I think if I set this dial, turn that one and press this button we will have water on the lawn." Sure enough, the water came in a rush, spewing up to wet the front of his shirt and left water dripping from his chin. "Feels good," he said, throwing a handful her way. "How many years since you've had a water fight?"

"I have never had a water fight," she replied. "That would have been the devil's play, plus, wasted water runs up the electric bill."

He stood studying her. "Really?" She nodded. "Then…I think it's time you are initiated. Don't you?"

She had seen that gleam in his eye and knew what was coming. When he stooped to pick up the hose, she was closest to the end where the nozzle was and jumping forward seized it and turned it on Evan.

"Oh, no, you can't get away with that. There's another faucet right over here." He raced the length of the yard, turned on the water and grabbed the hose. "Oh, wow, this is a water stream you can appreciate." He glanced at the concrete pad in front of the storage building. "I get it, they wash the car here."

"Who washes cars anymore, they go to the car wash."

"Not these people." He was grinning. "Now that we are completely wet, what do we do about Miss Harriet's car's cloth seats?"

She gave him one last hose down. "The beach towels are still in there." She was starting to wind up the hose, when he slipped behind her and with no mercy aimed for a complete wash down. She shook herself, "now that was sneaky…if I didn't have this hose practically folded up…I would come after you…but the water is cold. Brrr." He backed away, both hands in the air. "Another day," she promised.

"I'm going to turn on the system and I'll swing back by and check it out in about an hour." He reached for her hand, leaning in to kiss her lips. "Your lips are even cold." Pulling her close, he said, "I like when we play. It's something we both seemed robbed of in our childhood…to an extent, don't you think?"

"If I hadn't sneaked off to the neighbor's house and played with Ronnie, I probably would never have known what I was missing but being an only child Ronnie had a lot of toys. Remember on the neighbor's hidden track is where I learned to drive the go cart and then the four wheeler. To this day I would be afraid to tell my parents." They were spreading the beach towels on the front seats. "Maybe we can have kids one day and teach them the importance of play. You think?"

Evan stopped with the towel on the seat, raised his head to look completely at Jewel. "Jewel, I am glad God put us in the same group of displaced persons from the dam breaking, you have made me a happy man. I pray I never fail you and that you will always know how much I love and appreciate you."

Tears flooded Jewel's eyes and ran down her cheeks. "I am completely honored to be your wife, Evan."

Leaving the three sister's property, Evan felt in the pit of his stomach life ahead was good. Someday he and Jewel would have something; if they used their talent wisely and stayed faithful to God. He glanced across to where she dozed wrapped in two or three long beach towels. One thought led to another and the conversation of the past month when the group's nemesis was named as up to his old tricks again skirting the law. Evan had to ask the meaning of the conversation. Dan said, "let me put it like this. There are things happening and we are always aware he seems to enjoy coming after us, meaning our group of friends, we think because of our faith. Walden mocks anyone having faith, yet he will act as though he is one of us in an effort to hear some little thing about our group he didn't know. Should he do a harmful act, he's protected by his chain of higher command, lawyers, judges, those who can and will bend the system, not all are for the good of the world, but Walden understands that completely and bends it to suit his need and cover his bad deeds. Have you wondered how he remains a free man?"

Chapter 3

"How in the world are we stranded in this airport, when we need to be home?" Aldean stood, hands on hips, surveying the area around them. "If you hadn't lingered, looking at those scarves we would have been on the tram, instead of lugging these suitcases clear across the terminal. Lord help us, Geri, how many scarves do you need?"

Geri went right ahead folding the scarves neatly, to tuck them in the side pocket of her carry on. "If you had no hair on your head and felt everyone was staring at you as if you were a newly hatched chick, I'd say you'd be watching for nice scarves, too." She sighed. "It's not every day you find one that turns nicely into a turban." She stopped talking as she began to cough, Aldean's phone was ringing, anyway.

"She's just tired," Nina offered, trying to soothe the rift between the sisters. "Let's get her home, back in her routine and she'll shape up. I think you better see Dr. Joe, too. Aldean will settle down."

"You've been promising that since Kindergarten." Now Aldean came fairly stomping toward them. "This can't be good," Geri said between tight lips. "She's got murder in her eye."

"You won't believe this…our yard people, you know, takes care the lawn weekly, checks the irrigation, all that baloney…he is just now getting around to calling." She was leaning toward them, her eyes flashing as her hand waved in the air in a desperate attempt to keep up with her words. "He left his wife. He's in Las Vegas, said he hit it big at the slot machines and he's not coming back."

"What about the two weeks we've been traveling, has he hired another service to take care of us?"

"No." Aldean's emphatic reply raised heads of those waiting for the next tram. "He didn't. He also forgot that he left the lawn shed unlocked and forgot to turn on the watering system after Jake's came out and replaced the heads on the lines." She slumped down beside Geri and stared into the distance. "Isn't this the weekend the young couple asked to be married in our flower garden?" She ran both hands through her hair. "Honest to goodness, we should never leave home."

"Well, that would be no fun. We worked all our lives to be able to travel when we retired."

"Some of us did, anyway," Aldean replied, her eyes squinting as she stared hard at Geri who was coughing again. "You, as I recall had a husband that doted on you; there were years you didn't work and that's when you became out of touch with the world around you."

"Yes, changing diapers and filling bottles when your baby needs you it does take you away from the world and you forget those were his children I took care of; it was a job." Trying to swallow her cough, Geri glanced down at her well-heeled foot. "These slings have held up way better than I hoped."

"Don't change the subject." Aldean's nose was definitely out of joint. "Geri, you need a good spoon full of Jack Daniels to cure that cough. Now, do either of you have the couple's phone number so we can call and tell them there's a problem."

"That just wasn't something I thought to bring along," Nina replied, "Seeing as how you like to be in charge of everything, I guess I left that to you. Sorry." Nina's soft voice drifted away as Aldean gave her a dirty look. "Well, don't you?"

"Only if we want to get something done," Aldean countered. "So what were their names?"

The tram arrived. "Let's go to our car and head home," Geri said, rising. "That's all we can do."

✳ ✳ ✳ ✳ ✳

Sutter Coleman arrived at the address Penny had scrawled on the envelope they'd found in the glove pocket of the car. He was reluctant to help set up chairs and the long canopy she insisted was a must for the wedding cake and punch to be served under. Or, she said the cake icing would melt and everything would be a mess. He'd asked his siblings to come help but both declined. You got yourself into this mess they said, handle it. They'd snickered and walked away, more likely ran to their cars out front. He was the oldest and according to them he'd brought shame to the family and not helped their popularity either.

"Let me know when you're leaving," Penny had said. "It's bad luck to see your bride before the ceremony on the day you marry." He wasn't sure if that was an old wives tale or something she believed. He loved Penny. It was his fault she was pregnant. She was a good girl, not the loose girl his parents thought, nor a slut as his friends teased. That hurt him deeply, knowing it was his fault.

Penny's father arrived with a truck load of chairs, the canopy which was more a three sided tent, and a number of small round fold up tables. Her father was cordial enough, considering the circumstances.

"Have your parents decided to attend?" Will Martin paused for a moment to study the sweaty boy who was to become his son in law. "If they are attending, we need to make the front row the correct number of seats, and if they aren't we will shorten that row so it's not so noticeable."

"I honestly don't know, Sir." Sutter felt the heat rise and settle around his neck and he knew his face had turned red. "My father wasn't too happy about it but at breakfast he told mother whatever she decided."

"And she didn't tell you?" Will's mouth settled in a straight line while his eyes held a strange glint.

"No, Sir."

"You know your folks, what do you think?"

Sweat popped out on his forehead, while his stomach tightened. "No, Sir, I don't."

"Let's get something straight, Sutter. You're going to have a hard time working with your father if they don't approve of your wife. They think you are marrying down but there's no such thing. People come from every walk of life and if they're good decent folks who do their best they have the potential to progress in this world as well as any. I've known those who thought they's born with silver spoon in their mouth and they lost it all and became near derelicts, on the other hand some really poor people have achieved a lot and don't rub their wealth in anyone's face." He paused, he hadn't meant to spring it all on the boy, "but I'm going to tell you this one time; our Penny's as good a girl as anyone would want. She made a mistake and you helped her make that mistake. Now, I'll throw this out to you. If it becomes difficult, working in your family's business I'm offering you a job on that day and I'll do right by you."

"Yes, sir." Sutter nearly fell over the small table he was positioning. "I appreciate that sir, but my grandfather expects me to stay with the family even if my own dad isn't speaking to me." He heaved a deep breath and tried to swallow. "Our Pastor's trying to talk to Mother and Dad…" his words drift away, "it's just not working." Probably because he lied, the family had no pastor nor church home.

Will tried to loosen up a bit, but the truth was he was disappointed in life over the matter. Penny had a bright future ahead until she got pregnant. Two years of college down the drain when she knew better and this boy…overgrown boy…trying to become a man had taken the wrong path and drug his child down with him. Yes, they were doing the right thing marrying for the child's sake, he'd seen to that. Mary had drug her feet on the matter. "If they don't love each other, I will not insist Penny marries him," she said.

"For heaven's sakes, Mary, we didn't raise a prostitute, surely she wouldn't just give herself away."

"I didn't say that but young people make mistakes. Would you tie her to a life of misery if she doesn't love him when he's got parents that think they're God's gift to the world and we are white trash?"

"There's a baby coming, Mary. What about the child? A child needs a father."

"Exactly." She shook her head viciously. "Will he be there if his family pulls him away? Why prolong it?" Tears smarted Mary's eyes. "If they don't want her and they're too good to give their grandchild their name, what makes you think this hurried up wedding makes a difference?"

"I can't believe you." He had studied her for a moment then reached out to touch her but she shrugged away. "Mary, don't let this come between us. I know you're worried just like me. Let's give her the wedding in the Sister's garden like she wants and be thankful we can. Our bank account doesn't match the Coleman's but we have a lot of love for our child and maybe we can love the one she has chosen as well."

"Aren't you angry, Will? With Penny and him and his parent's too, that they'd reject her?"

"I was and I am," he'd admitted, "but I talked to Pastor Joe and he said my anger wouldn't touch them it would only eat away at my peace of mind and I'm trying hard to let it go."

Now, here he was stuck in the Sister's back yard garden with an overgrown boy who thought he was a man but couldn't even vouch for his own parents attending his wedding. Will would bet his pickup truck on one thing, Old Sut Coleman, number one would be there, taking it all in, weighing the pro's and con's, not caring what his grandson thought did or said, Old Sut evidently had an influence on Sut number three and maybe that was good, maybe with the old goat in charge Penny would never starve. That's where the money was, in the old man. He was a hard task master that Will knew personally, he just hoped there was a degree of fairness left in the old guard. He wouldn't tell Mary he'd known Leona before and Sutton the athlete, too. Good at everything sports wise, but a pushover for a pretty face and Leona had a pretty face. He had known even then he couldn't maintain her life style, maybe Sutton could. She held it against him and said one day he'd be sorry. Well, he was sorry, all right, that she was mistreating his child. Twenty some years was a long time to hold a grudge.

"You can call Penny, now," Will reminded the boy. It was time to put away his thoughts on the subject, start checking the Sister's property for no surprises and send this one on his way. Penny was adamant they'd have no further tangles with fate. "If his parents don't like me, daddy, I can live with it. I love him."

Will was adjusting the hands on the garden clock, testing the chime by setting it, when Sutton left. They hadn't shook hands or done anything cordial. He was standing there when Sutton's car disappeared down the street and Harriet Becker's old car pulled in the drive. The fellow from church that sang in the choir came to meet him, holding out his hand and he shook this one's.

"Mr. Martin, from church, I believe," Evan said. "Evan Jacobs, I recognized the boy, too, but I don't know his name." Glancing at the clock, he asked, "Does that thing chime?"

"It better this evening at five o'clock." Will grinned. "You just married the girl, what's her name, Jewel?" Will glanced around. "I didn't know you knew the Sisters. They've graciously let my daughter have her wedding in their back yard." He dug a toe in the grass, seeming a bit questioning of something. "I wonder when they watered last, it's damp, some places, not many but here it is."

Evan laughed. "That's my fault. Jewel and I met the ladies at a resort Miss Harriet sent us to and they mentioned a wedding for the weekend, but we came home earlier and driving by, yesterday, we saw the yard was in a pretty rough shape, the storage unit was unlocked and the lawn was in need of a drink."

"And you did it?" Will liked this young man immediately. "Sounds like something I would do."

"I didn't tell Jewel," Evan admitted, "But I did question if anything went wrong if we would be held responsible, you know like if the mower quit or the water wouldn't turn off."

"That's a minor thing," Will replied, "In that case, you call someone to fix it."

"I was taking a big chance." Evan chuckled. "One of the sisters asked me if I gambled. I guess I did."

"The Sisters are pretty easy to work with, they have their opinions, but they're all right." Will pursed his lips, as he remembered something Penny had said. "I don't reckon you're busy this evening around five o'clock, are you?"

"You need help taking down the tables and chairs? I'll help you."

Will squirmed a bit. "The sister's said I had tomorrow if I needed to do that. They know me pretty well, I was here from day one on the building of their home, that's why I know where things are and pretty much left the list of instructions for them on how to run this place. They call me when necessary."

"So you don't need help with the clean up. If I can do it…that is if I'm qualified…is it turning things off?"

"Nah," Will scrubbed his toe in the grass again, "let me see if I can say this right. We've a little personal problem in the family, I won't go into but because of it as a daddy I know my daughter's wishes for this wedding and well, she wouldn't ask the Gates to sing or play the piano because we don't have a piano, well, to make a long story short she had your name and your new wife, Jewel, isn't it? She intended to ask you all to sing at her wedding and instead of using recorded music if you'd play the violin."

Evan was smiling. "You mean, we were gone and she couldn't ask? That is something both Jewel and I would be happy to do. Do you have a list of the music? And how about this, you don't need a piano, Jewel has a keyboard to fill in the background and yes, I'd love to do the introduction on violin." He watched Will's eyes light up. "Now, is this a surprise for your daughter?"

"I think it would about make her day….. that is besides marrying the young man she loves."

There was a line of cars a mile long that circled the cul de sac, lined up on each side of the street and came in every color, make and model. Penny's bridesmaids stood inside the attached garage, void of the sister's cars Will had removed. It resembled a fine room more than anything, it was temperature controlled, the walls were a robin's egg blue with fine white hanging cabinets and the floor was a mock stone, had It not been for the sliding door, no one would realize it was a garage. The groomsmen were a little less comfortable in the unit that housed the lawnmower but it had been swept clean and they were all interested in the array of tools on the wall, but Will had forgotten something. Like young boys, they gathered in front of the main vent and seemed to relax when he turned on the air.

Mary, the mother of the bride was ushered to her seat at ten minutes until five. Evan and Jewel had arrived by way of the back gate and were standing behind two large arborvitaes that hid a generator intended for rare times need. Jewel had sheet music placed on top of the device and was lip sincing through the songs. She had been delighted when Evan gave her the music but Evan saw the moment of confusion when a man and woman came down the aisle toward where Mrs. Martin was seated. Without hesitation, he took the two seats intended for him and Jewel, placed them on the front row by Penney's parents and bowing just so implied they were to be seated. He had only a moment before the clock at the entrance struck five to glance around and see the groom making contact with the woman and he guessed it was his mother. The young man seemed to brighten, his demeanor changed. Evan saw pride and relief and for a moment his thoughts strayed to those days he sought to please his own mother.

Jewel saw Evan breathe deep as though he had held his breath and then seem to relax. She wondered what had just transpired but the arrival of the three sisters in special occasion dress and the chiming of the clock at the garden entrance caused her thoughts to leave as Evan stepped forward and began the processional to the wedding march. The sound was warm and haunting and filled with hope as the bridesmaids came down the aisle and then the people stood as Mr. Martin walked with Penelope to where Pastor Joe was waiting with her groom. "Who comes to give the bride away?"

"I do," her father replied as he placed Penelope's hand in Sutton's with his own on top, lingering for a second. As Will stepped across the aisle to join Mary everyone was seated and Jewel began the first notes of song at the keyboard as Evan accompanied her on the violin and she began to sing. "The first time I looked into your face and saw the grandeur of your smile, I knew eternity would find us together but eternity will seem only a short while. The first time we kissed, I knew God in heaven does exist…and I can think of nothing else but that we will be blest as we make a life together..my heart I give to you…since the first time I looked into your face… your eyes brighten at the sight of me, and I ask how can that be… that you will live a lifetime, an eternity with me. God has a master plan as we walk together hand and hand…" As the song ended, the couple lighted a round white candle in the center of the aisle.

Evan began the opening of the second song…."Your people will be my people, your hopes and dreams and plans…we will see the world together…we will see the world together, and forever may we be in love…as I take your hand and your people become my family… may our hearts rest at his throne and may the Good Lord look down up on us as we become one."

Jewel could see the young couple's parents; one set wiped away tears, while the other seemed rigid, as though the words of the song seemed far from their understanding by the expressions on their face. Jewel breathed a deep breath, she could feel the animosity and she didn't even know them. Their son had betrayed them, gone against their expectations. In her own life she hadn't known other than to bow to a set of rules that shouldn't exist in today's world but it did. Yet, their young man had loved the girl and wanted to right a wrong. What would they have had him do, abandon her?

"To the back of the garage and facing the Sister's beautiful garden," Will Martin said, overhearing her ask Evan if there was a rest room. "Actually it was Aldean, the taller one of the three sisters if you don't know them yet, had us to build an outside accommodation," he smiled remembering. "She said in case we decide to tear up our garden due to our own failure and put in a pool, we'll need a relief station." He watched the bride and groom moving toward the tall columns of the sister's home, no doubt for a photo session, but then Penelope was trying to fold up her wedding dress and head for the rest room, too. "I don't think they'd be tearing out shrubs and trees,

I believe there's room for a swimming pool right about where we sit up the tables and chairs."

✳ ✳ ✳ ✳ ✳

White railroad tiles graced the walls while the floor was black and white tile and the red walls set off the white of the doors to five stalls. Such opulence, Jewel thought for an outdoor rest room but from what she had seen the sisters did everything with style. The door opened with a rustling sound of someone hurrying as the last stall down's door closed with a bang. Then there were staccato steps, someone wearing high heels stepped in quickly and closed the outer door. She heard a click and knew the lock had been thrown. Without hesitation she raised her feet off the floor, there could be a problem. She had seen the white dress through the crack in the door and knew the occupant of the last stall was Penelope, the bride. Penelope, she rolled the word off her tongue; Penny, her father once called her. She had seen the girl's face light with pleasure as she began to sing. The secret was a success. But now there was quiet; two people aware of each other. The silence grew and then a very cultured voice said, "Are you really going ahead with this, Penelope, when I ask you to drop the whole thing for now and let us all adjust to the news that you are pregnant and will deliver a baby around the holidays, meaning you will ruin Christmas just as you have L's birthday."

"I never planned to ruin your daughter's birthday, Mrs. Coleman, being pregnant I hoped to spare you some of the gossip which seems to threaten you by marrying Sutton." Penny ran her hand beneath the faucet and water splashed into the bowl. There was a pained expression on her face. "I ask, no, I begged you to allow us to be friends but you have refused and turned Sutton's sister and brothers against me."

Sutton's mother unzipped the small purse she carried and drew something from it. "Here is your last chance. Take this money and leave and that will break Sutton's heart for now but he will be rid of you and one day when the hurt goes away he will find someone else."

"And will you bribe her to leave, or is this someone you will hand pick." Penny's voice was strained.

"I do have connections." Mrs. Coleman replied snidely. "We can get this farce annulled."

"Your son loves me, Mrs. Coleman."

"But does he love you enough? Perhaps your little weekend extravaganza was not enough to keep him, only enough to snag him like a fish on a line." Mrs. Coleman started toward the door. "I'll leave this check right here and you decide what to do with it."

As the door banged shut, Jewel put her feet down, her legs had nearly gone into cramps holding them up. The lid squeaked and Penny called out, "Who's in there?"

"I'm sorry," Jewel practically cried to think she was embarrassing this new bride. "I didn't know there would be anyone else in here…"

"It's all right. Come on out…you couldn't help overhearing."

"I promise I won't tell a soul."

Penny's shoulders drooped. Then she looked at Jewel thoroughly. "I thought you and your husband were on your honeymoon." Then she smiled. "Thank you for singing, both of you and the violin music to bring me up the aisle, I loved it."

"You are welcome. Your father asked, in case you didn't know." Jewel noticed Penny was shaking. "What can I do? You aren't well, are you?"

Struggling, not to cry, Penny leaned on the marble top of the vanity that housed the sinks. "You heard. I'm pregnant and we hurried the wedding as quickly as we could thinking to keep Sutton's mother from being so upset." She lay her head back staring up at the ceiling. "They are upper class, I'm not." Tears slid down her cheeks. "I need a friend. I've been kind of cut off from my own and Mrs. Coleman's made it clear I'm not to see her daughter. She's Sutton's only sister and I can tell she likes me."

"Which threatens Mrs. Coleman," Jewel replied. "Listen, I'll be glad to be your friend." Careful of the poufy skirt of the wedding dress at her feet, Jewel leaned in and hugged Penny. "I think you should go back out and enjoy your wedding day. Believe me, when I say you can get through any diversity. You can."

"Have you?" Penny's eyes were dark with sadness that Sutton's mother found her inferior. Her shoulders were sagging and her chin nearly to her chest. "I mean…well, I don't know you and you sing like the happiest person in the world."

"I am happy. I love my new husband. He loves me. What more do we need?" She lay her hands on Penny's shoulders and forced her to stand tall. "The diversity was before I found him. Now, go out there and make your husband and your family proud of you. This is a very special day in your life."

"I know." For a moment Penny brightened. "Thanks."

"Go on." Jewel held the door open for her. "If you need me, just look around and whistle."

"You mean like this?" Penny put two fingers to her lips and whistled.

"At-ta girl," Jewel applauded her effort. "You can teach me how to do that."

✳ ✳ ✳ ✳ ✳

Jewel found Evan discussing musical instruments with the groom's father, apparently Pastor Joe had pulled him into their conversation. At the same time she arrived to hear the discussion Sutton's mother drew near. "There was an old gentleman, said he was a sailor that played the violin when we were relocating the folks who came in from the dam breaking," Pastor Joe was saying. "I never met him but I did hear him play. To my ears it sounded good."

Evan smiled, knowing it was himself the pastor heard playing the old man's violin but he didn't say anything.

"I'm surprised a river rat could be that accomplished," Mrs. Coleman said. She saw the startled look on the pastor's face. "Forgive me if that sound harsh, but you know our town is pretty well run down with all those homeless here, for only the Good Lord knows how long." Pastor Joe was squirming, his face a beet red color. "Well, you know," she continued. "We've been here all along helping to keep our city swept clean and beauty in certain places…but what will they do, loiter as they search for work? They are in general uneducated riff-raff."

"Leona," her husband reached for her hand, kissed her fingertips and smiled down on her. "We may feel a bit strong about the whole situation because of what happened to us." He sought the Pastor's attention, "Our home was vandalized by such and they destroyed a lot of expensive art. To make a long story short, no one forgets cleaning up a mess like they left to us."

"And you are saying, this happened after the dam broke and those homeless people came to the Cape?" Pastor Joe asked.

"Around Christmas," Mr. Coleman replied.

Jewel and Evan exchanged glances. It was after Christmas when spring rains had caused the dam to break. "We will be moving on," Evan said, his hand on Jewel's elbow. "Nice talking with you." Moving through the crowd of people the Sisters were just ahead. "I don't rightly know how to handle telling them what we did. That last conversation kind of left a sour taste in my mouth. Do you suppose we could sneak out and let that one ride until we are in private to talk?"

"Our instruments," Jewel whispered. "Have you already taken them to the car?" Evan nodded

Once in the car on the short drive home, Evan spoke. "I fear for that couple. To think I was afraid we would have a few problems," he shook his head, "but there's all kinds, aren't there? This couple has been brought up in two different environments, which makes one set's opinion rather shocking." They were passing the Gates home. "Do you suppose all families have problems setting guidelines for their children, but then as they grow do those guidelines fit?"

Chapter 4

On moving day someone had stuck a sign up in the Gates yard that read, Home of Dan and Ellen Gates and all their kids. The sign remained. In the Gates garden there were signs with quotes. Upon entering, one sign said, May all who enter here be blessed. Daniel had built the garden as part of Ellen's healing.

"It is a beautiful Sunday morning," Daniel exclaimed. "Come out, before we wake the kids for church. See what's happening in our back yard."

"With this drought, how could much happen?" Ellen wrapped a summer duster around her body and followed. "It's almost selfish, isn't it to water this grass when everything around us is turning brown."

"But, you my love got yourself into another wedding in our backyard and that's why we go the second mile, isn't it?" He reached for her hand and led her to the large angel. "What do you think of this?" He sat down on the bench beneath the angel and pat the space for her to sit beside him. "I think it's pretty spectacular."

"Oh, they smell so sweet." Lilies of the valley had bloomed in the last days as they were busy and now the green foliage and white flowers were in abundance. "We should get a picture." She leaned up to kiss his cheek. "You, daddy of the year, are a wonderful gardener."

"Well, you, Momma of many are busy helping every one that calls either with a book study or being a nurse for a day. I don't know how you do it." He studied her, his head tilted, his expression like a wise old doctor. "How are you feeling?"

"I'm fine. I get a little tired the long days but I try to keep my energy level up for the kids and too, there are things ahead we probably should do, if you can fit it into your schedule. I haven't told you but we've been invited to a music seminar put on by the association to help young musicians. That would be the last of August." When he was quiet she asked, "Does that interfere with something?"

"We will be short-handed at work due to the employees taking vacations." He blew out a breath of air and shook his head, "I don't see any way I can be away from the business. Can you do it alone?"

"I'd rather not and I think they wanted a man's influence for the young men attending. Doesn't that make sense?"

"It does. Remember the scripture, "All things work together for good to them that love the Lord, who are called according to his purpose, Romans eight twenty eight." She had chimed in. "So now we pray the Lord will lead them to the right person."

"I actually wondered if Evan and Jewel might apply, if you and couldn't, when the director called me he said the spot they were trying to fill was with pay but I told him if we took it you and I would decline pay. It would be a love gift from us but it's different with Evan and Jewel as they are misplaced from their home and newly married to boot. Either way I'll take care of it."

"It's *t*ime to get ready for church, Momma of many; Cereal first then dress the poppers, right?"

She laughed. "That's an accurate name for the twins. Or the two little ones might be little poopers." She wrapped her arms around Daniel's neck. "Thank you for showing me the lilies beneath our angel. I needed to stop and smell the roses this morning, excuse me, the lilies." Unwinding her arms she paused before heading down the path. "You know what I'm thinking, this is one year I'm not sure we can attend the Seminar and certainly not help, but I'm really not sure Evan and Jewel can either."

✳ ✳ ✳ ✳ ✳

Christ Church was a buzz with the people arriving. Ellen had left Holly and Noel in the Nursery and Sammy and Danny were seated between her and Daniel. Ruthie was on the far end of the pew. Ellen smiled knowing Ruthie was waiting for someone and she wondered if it would be Marigold or Jewel. Life had become quite serene with Jewel in their home helping with the children but marrying Evan and going away on honeymoon had left a void in Ruthie's life. Then there was the bond between her and Marigold, some kindred spirit of the heart where they each seemed to know what the other was thinking. Ruthie's gift had known Evan was a special person before the group recognized his caring way.

The group arrived, Harriet with Marigold and Matt. Evidently they had left the children in the Nursery; then came Anne and Andrew with Andy and little Adeline. They would try Adeline staying through the service but if she whimpered one of them would take her out. Having almost lost her Anne couldn't bear her out of sight. The Harper's filled their spot and today Jeremy and Haley were with them. Haley's pregnancy was showing. Ellen couldn't help but take a deep breath whether from relief or worry, she wasn't sure. This group of people had been through so much together they seemed more than friends, family for sure but not one's usual family, this family cared deeply about each other. And now they had welcomed Evan and Jewel into the group. She supposed the two were in the choir as usual.

The first peal of the organ sounded and everyone stood as Pastor Joe stepped up on the raised altar and the song leader took his place. The words to the song were on the screen above his head as everyone began to sing. The feeling of joy and peace in the congregation grew with each song. Pastor Joe received applause as he welcomed everyone and brought them up to date on important functions to come. By the time they had reached the last song the Holy Spirit was blessing them in a special way.

"When peace like a river attendeth my way, When sorrow like sea billows roll…whatever my lot, thou hast taught me to say, It is well, it is well with my soul. Though Satan should buffet, though trials come, let this blest assurance control that Christ has regarded my helpless estate and hath shed his own blood for my soul." The congregation sang with heartfelt appreciation it seemed of their own attendance and that of their brother and sister in Christ. Ruthie and Jewel had managed to recognize each other with a wiggle of the fingers and Ellen saw the happiness in the two smiling at each other. "It is well…with my soul…it is well, it is well with my soul."

"Beautiful day outside," Pastor Joe said as he came to the pulpit, "wonderful spirit inside our church this morning as we welcome you and pray you will feel the Lord's blessing upon you. Our scripture this morning is found in Mark, chapter nine verses thirty four through thirty six, as we stand for the reading of God's word. "Jesus called the people together and said to them "Whosoever will come after me, let him deny himself, and take up his cross and follow me, for whoseoever will save his life shall lose it; but whosoever shall lose his life for my sake and the gospel's, the same shall save it. For what shall it profit a man if he shall gain the whole world and lose his own soul?"

"How do we grow in Christ? Is it through blessings heaped upon us? When we sing the song It is Well With My Soul are we speaking of happy times, so great the writer made a song out of it? Or, is it when we walk in the valley, the shadowed times of our lives we grow? Horatio Spafford was once a prospering business man in Chicago but the fire of Chicago burned his business investments to the ground, then he was hit by further financial ruin by the failing economy. In eighteen seventy three he put his wife and four daughters on a ship setting sail for England. Out to sea the ship was hit by another vessel and sank. His wife lived but the daughters died. It was during the time the four daughters were lost at sea, from heartache and grieving Spafford wrote the song we sing; it is well with my soul."

"Today, how are you, what is the status of your soul? Are we focused on the right things in life? Are we saved? The question remains what shall it profit a man if he shall gain the whole world and lose his own soul? You look around, perhaps there's a family you are aware of, you watch that family and sometimes it seems things come their way as if they were born with a silver spoon in their mouth and then tragedy strikes, one incident after another and they hang on, sometimes by a shoe string, beat down for awhile, rising up as if undaunted but you can't see in to their heart. You don't know how it is with their soul. You see something there you don't understand and you wonder if they are people who believe in God. Then there's the poor family, scrambling to make a living, always in our midst because Jesus said the poor are always with us. Their soul is just as valuable as the next persons. Do you think they chose to be poor?" "Look closely, are they believers are they set apart. We say save, sanctified and set aside. But then there's the other side of the coin, families who profess no God, have no need for one, they say, then tragedy happens. Are these our concerns? Still, the question remains how is it with your soul? God knows. Your neighbors, friends, family are watching. Are you hanging on by a thread? Can you sing it is well with my soul in the midst of tragedy? When Spafford's wife lost the four daughters and she waited alone for her husband, she was repeated as saying, "I had four daughters that have been taken, right now I do not understand but at the end of life I will." She stood on faith and went on. How are you doing? If you don't need this message today, remember it for the time will come when you have need. Every person has a cross to bear, not the same as their fellowman, but their own cross. As we leave this place where we sing of God's love, his mercy and grace, let us examine our self whether we can say It is well with my soul and if it is not, then it is time to do something about it." Holding his bible high Pastor Joe stepped down from the altar. 'It starts here in the word of God. If you have problems and don't know how to solve them, give yourself a fighting chance, give it over to the Lord. Let Him come into your life and then you can say, It Is Well With MY Soul."

✳ ✳ ✳ ✳ ✳

Thirteen adults and nine children between them they found a restaurant willing to push two tables together to accommodate their group. Jewel was seated by Daniel on one side and Evan on the other. Sammy and Danny had rushed to wrap their arms around her and ask to sit beside her but Ellen and Daniel insisted the boys sit on booster seats between them. The boys weren't happy. It was then she glanced away to see the Martins at a neighboring table and Penny with them. Oh, no, she thought, where's Sutton. Her question was short lived when Penny saw her and came to the table.

"I thought that was you." Jewel was rising up to receive the hug Penny was giving her. "It's been a week and I meant to call you but Sut and I are just settling in. I'll call you next, how's that?" She started to move away and stopped. "Sutton wanted me to thank you for him, too. He had to work today."

"He works with his father?" Jewel managed to ask. Penny was nodding as she returned to her parents.

"Isn't that Will Martin's daughter?" Daniel asked.

"Yes, she and Sutton Coleman married last week."

"Really, and how do you know that?" Daniel teased. "I thought you were on your honeymoon."

"We arrived home early enough her father ask Evan if we would provide the music for Penny."

"I'm impressed," he replied. "I heard just last week they were getting married but not this quick."

Marigold was sitting across from Daniel and overheard. "Leona was in the shop last week and she was not happy about the matter. It is my story all over, again. The mother in law doesn't like the chosen one. I'm afraid Leona is not finished with it, yet."

"I'm sorry to hear that, Will Martin is a good man and I'd think they would be proud of his daughter."

"It's not always that way, Daniel." She reached down to Ruthie sitting beside her and squeezed her hand. "This one has been my supporter and ridden many miles with me, haven't you Ruthie?"

"How are you, Jewel?" Daniel asked, "I think you could tell the boys missed you."

"That is so nice to know. Will you need me any longer?" She leaned farther into the table trying to see if Ellen could hear their discussion, but Ellen was speaking with Anne.

"You can check with Ellen but I think she does need you one or two more weeks, it seems Dr. Lonzo likes her work and his business has increased he needs both her and Anne." He thought for a minute. "Will that interfere with your plans?"

"I just need a half day to put in resumes. The other thing, I think we are looking to purchase a piano and then I can give lessons. If that works out, maybe I can find a part time job as Evan really wants me free as he tries to build his business." She smiled. "We have a lot of things to figure out to make our life together work."

"Will you be staying where you are now at Anne and Andrew's," Marigold ask.

"Not long, I don't think." She turned to Evan. "Honey, why aren't you joining in?"

"You were doing fine," he replied. "I was just enjoying listening." He smiled at Ruthie as he looked across the table to Marigold. "I think we would be imposing to stay with the Graves. We've kept Andrew out of his mancave long enough. If our home in the country is not repairable after the water and mud, then we will have to find a suitable place here in the Cape and I will need a building or shop for the wood working part of building the instruments. It doesn't have to be huge but adequate."

"That's how I felt when I opened the shop," Marigold replied. "I will say God opened up the right spot."

The waitress came and took orders and while they were waiting Daniel excused himself to make a phone call. When he returned, "Jewel," he said, "My Aunt Georgia owns Hutson's Hotel and Social Center, and there's an upright piano that has a wonderful sound to it, that she has been wanting out of the way for some time. She said if you would like to come in and play it and it suits you, you can have it."

"Oh, my goodness," instant tears filled Jewel's eyes. "I would be so grateful, wouldn't we Evan."

Evan was beaming. "I'm sure we can pay for it Daniel." But Daniel was shaking his head, no.

"No, she wants it out of the way and there's something else, Evan. Aunt Georgia owns the small shop, it's about three buildings down from the hotel and if you recall all those buildings are painted gray with black awnings and the one I'm speaking of held an art store that gave lessons but the owner will be having twins in about two weeks and she is now in the process of clearing out the building as she feels since she already has a two and four year old that her hands will be too busy for a business."

"I don't suppose there's living space with it that would be too much to ask."

"Actually, the upper floor is equipped. There's a bathroom and the necessary accruements. But no one ever lived there. There's even an outside stair. All those shops are finished to remind one of an old time shopping area, perhaps with French taste." The waitress was bringing the food, standing at Daniel's chair, "Just give her a call or go in, she will be glad to see you whether you rent the building or not."

"I am overwhelmed." Jewel was clenching Evan's hand. "We have been praying for something to come along, haven't we?" Nodding, Evan reached behind Jewel to tap Daniel's shoulder to shake his hand.

"Thank you, I will look into it tomorrow." Evan's hand brushed across Jewel's shoulder and squeezed it. "I can't believe this," he whispered. "You a piano and possibly a place to rent would answer our needs."

Marigold leaned across to speak to the two, "Did you know Harper is a builder?" She pointed down the table to where Dorothy and Harper sit across from Haley and Jeremy. "When the time comes he could build you a beautiful home." She patted Matt's arm, "When we gain financially that will be something to think about, but for now we are happy in our big old four square that is as humble as American pie and boy do we know it when we look down the street to Harriet's spread."

For once, Evan spoke up. "We certainly don't have funds for that. Just opening a shop is going to be all we can do for the present and I'll have to make more instruments."

'I've heard they're beautiful," Marigold replied. "And you're right, nothings done easy these days."

"Did I hear someone needs a house builder?" Harper's voice boomed down the line and Marigold laughed. "Just ring me up, I'll be there first thing and give you an estimate you can't beat."

Everyone appreciated Harper, with his heart of gold and willingness to give the shirt off his back. All eyes were on his end of the table as Haley and Jeremy prepared to leave. "Hour's drive, Dad," she said as he protested. "I probably won't be able to sit through church before long; the doctor says this little one is riding on my kidney." Always patient, Jeremy tucked her purse over his arm and took her hand.

"All right then, baby," Harper boomed, rising to kiss her on the cheek. "We'll see you soon. We're going to linger here a bit and have a piece of that chocolate cake they serve here."

Marigold and Ellen glanced at each other and then waved to Haley as Jewel watched. They seemed to send secret messages to each other. She shrugged, she understood this? It was a woman thing.

"She looks good," Marigold said to Ellen and Jewel heard Ellen say, Praise the Lord."

✳ ✳ ✳ ✳ ✳

They had changed into shorts and T-shirts and were hanging up their church clothes when Evan said, "Does it seem to you we've acquired a lot of stuff, to have been married such a short time and we have to figure out how to move it all?"

"We neither one had anything after the flood of water damaged our belongings, so it had to be the gifts different one's gave to us."

"I was just wondering how we'd get everything up a flight of stairs," he sighed, "but I do know where there's a will there's a way."

For the first times since Evan moved in he heard the door bell. "Is that what I think?"

"Company?" Jewel asked eagerly. "Let's see." She rushed to open the door and found the sisters standing there. "My goodness, come in. Come in." She hugged each one as she came to them. "Please, have a seat. Evan, look who it is."

A rush of color turned Evan's neck red above the white of his shirt. He almost appeared as a little boy about to be punished. "Ladies, if I did something wrong, I'll stand good for it."

"Sha," Aldean had taken the cane bottom chair from Andrew's desk and now she rose up. "What could you have done wrong? We understand it was a dry grown up mess. Will said you two did the work all by yourself and he figured it took all day. We came to pay you."

"Oh, no, we don't want any pay," they protest together.

"But we have to and we have something to ask you, a proposition of sorts." She sat back down. "When we read our emails and listened to our voice mail, we realized our guy who normally cares for our yard flew the coop, so to speak. We began trying to find who helped us out and the first person we ask, yesterday afternoon, was Daniel Gates and he said, no ma'm he didn't even know we were gone."

"One thing led to another," Nina added, "and we found you two through our contact with Will Martin, but Mr. Gates did tell us you two were moving from the Graves coach house. I guess this is a coach house, isn't it?"

Jewel giggled, "Actually we think of it as Andrew Graves man cave."

"Well, regardless what the title," Geri commented. "We need a gardner if either of you are without a job, we'd hire you in a minute and that's not all, Mr. gates said you were in the market for a house." The speel of words made Geri cough. "I tell you coming back, my allergies are worse than ever."

"No ma'm," Jewel countered. "We can't afford a house. I think we can live up over the shop, though we've not seen it, yet."

"The shop she mentioned has not been decided on either, Mr. Gates just told us about it today."

The three sisters looked at Evan. Aldean spoke up, "Well, think about our proposition and here's the address of the house we own and the key to inspect it. Please be sure it's locked when you leave." The three moved toward the door. "Thank you for inviting us in when we came without first calling and Evan, should you and Jewel decide to take the house there's decorations up in the attic that are just perfect. They made us all so very happy."

* * * * *

"This is just too easy," Evan said, after the ladies backed out of the drive.

"Unless God's in it," Jewel replied. "Nothing ever presents itself as today. We are encouraged because we both know people who wait months for prayers to be answered."

"That we do," he nodded in agreement. "Do you want to view this house?" He held the key up, "or do you want to wait and see the building with the upstairs?"

"What should we do?" She looked to Evan to make the decision. "We have choices to make too soon."

"Let's go look at it and drive by Mrs. Hutson's building too."

* * * * *

"Do you know what I think?" He chuckled. "I do believe this house is located at the very long back side of the Sister's house. It appears almost to be in the country, because the homes are older, the yards more established, but if we walked the back yard and then through that line of trees I believe that is their home." He was amused. "The one named Geri…resembles a picture I saw of my real mother. They are a puzzle, the sisters, but they want us to learn on our own. Come on, let's see what they're offering."

It was a yellow house, the outside appeared some kind of stucco and the shutters were a strict white. There was a concrete porch with rough tiles applied in a mingled gray color on the floor and four white columns. The cut glass prisms in the storm door threw light in the evening sun and on one end was a double seat hanging swing painted a lacquered black.

"Nice." Jewel murmured. "I'm afraid to see more, I might say yes before I knew we'd have to mow the whole hillside in between." Still she leaned forward eagerly waiting to see the inside. "Oh, oh, Evan…I've never had such finery. Look at the furniture." From the entry they could see three main pieces in black laquer, a Chinese chest in the hall entry, a matching curio cabinet in the next room they supposed was the living room and beyond that a room appearing only large enough for a table and chairs with the third piece a buffet on tall legs also painted in the same design. Jewel ran a finger over the top. "It's beautiful."

"Evan, look, the table couldn't be seen, it was against the wall. Look Evan. It's a mottled yellow with a thick glass top and the chairs have black needlework seats. Why would they leave their furniture?" She began a walkthrough of the house. "A bedroom set? Evan someone has not moved out yet. Dare I open a drawer?" She did another and another and all were empty. "This is very strange." And so it continued, each room practically finished with furniture, a spread on the bed with matching curtains at the window and there the colors picked up red in the huge floral pattern, with its white background. Then they came to the kitchen, yellow with white cabinets that reminded them of the outside of the house, the appliances were white and the floors were all a dark stained wood.

Behind the kitchen there was a laundry storage room on one end and a small back porch with a huge sin. "It is a well arranged house, Evan. It has everything one would need and possibly an upstairs area." She had the distinct feeling he was not interested for it looked to be over their head.

"It's very nice," Evan agreed but I'm afraid out of our range if, in fact the occupants plan to move out."

"I raised the spread on the bed and the covers, the mattress looks new."I wouldn't want to sleep on someone's mattress I didn't know, would you?" Evan shook his head. She opened the closet. "There are no clothes but here's a vacuum cleaner." She was very perplexed. "There are no dishes in the kitchen but in the lower part of the stove in that pull out drawer there were pots and pans."

"It's complete with laundry room appliances just as the kitchen and the bathroom is fine. I've seen enough. There's no need even considering something that evidently either someone considered moving in or they haven't fully moved out. I'm as confused as you, but not as excited or verbal."

Jewel grinned. "I could never imagine starting out with furnishings in a home on this grand scale."

"Why do you suppose the living room has no furniture?" Evan asked. "There's that small area on the end of the kitchen with the leather sofa and chair and that's enough but with the rest furnished I'm not sure what to think."

"Could it be God has set this up for us, Evan? The piano could be in the front and that would be handy for students coming in."

"It's too much to think, Jewel. Who are we that we should be so blessed? We will have to make our way as all newly married couples." He saw the look of disappointment. "There, now, don't fret, one day we will have the desires of your heart. I promise. I will make you proud."

She turned into his arms. "I am proud, Evan, a pure proud because of your love but I'm not overly proud of my accomplishments for they've not been many. If there's just one thing I do that lets you feel good about our life together, then whatever it is, helps me because I'm happy just knowing we're together."

He pulled her closer. "In my eyes you outshine others and I'm not interested in anyone else's accomplishments." It came to his mind what his father said when he chose his wife. He stopped, Jewel facing him. "My father's advice is true. When you call my name, heaven and earth stand still. I listen. I know there will never be another calls my name with such love."

Side by side he walked her to the door. "Sadly, I think we should return this key to the sisters. I won't even ask the price of rent. With all this…it would be too much."

"All right, Evan." It was settled.

Penny Coleman paced the floor, sat back down in the rocking chair that had once belonged to her grandmother and after rocking a few times got up to pace the floor again. She held her hand in front to study the gold band lying next to the small diamond engagement ring. Sutton was late again. He'd worked Sunday in his father's business coming home late to say his mother insisted he have dinner with them, which meant she had eaten alone. Now, tonight, though he had promised to be early the food had grown cold, the candles on the table had burned low and she was beside herself with worry. What if something happened to him? Accidents were said to happen within five miles of home and if he had made a delivery, there could be five miles between them. Finally she snuffed out the candles and went to bed, her plate unused, and the food congealing in the bowls. She was that tired from having cooked, that now she didn't care if they lost the food. Sutton wasn't used to left over's anyway.

She didn't hear the lock turn, nor Sutton in the shower but when he sat on the edge of the bed and her body rolled she knew he was home. "Hi, babe," he said, rolling down into the sheets and pulling them over her back as he drew her close. He kissed her gently once, again and again, until she squirmed.

"Where have you been, Sutton? You promised to come home."

"Did I?" He sounded surprised, his family's southern accent attached to the words. "My parents have visitors from North Carolina and Mother wanted them to see me since I'm grown. Last I saw them I was twelve years old."

"Tell me about them."

"Well there's Lonnie, Dad's class mate he graduated with, Suzanne the wife and Kaley their eighteen year old daughter."

Penny let the news settle. "I didn't know eighteen year old daughters still traveled with their parents."

"This was a special trip for our families to reunite. Mother is big on keeping old friends."

"It's too bad she doesn't like to make new ones."

"What do you mean by that, Sugar?"

"I'd love for us to be friends but she won't make one effort to know me."

"Give it time, Penny."

She heard his voice change. "I don't have much time, Sutton. We're going to have a baby by Christmas and she is the grandmother. Wouldn't you think she'd want to know her grandchild?"

"She will."

"Not without me, Sutton. That's the one thing you need to understand. If she can't accept me, my baby doesn't go there."

"Babe, you are making too much of this. Why would you set that ground rule?"

"Because I know for a fact your mother has been spreading tales about me and talking behind my back to about anyone she comes in contact with and I won't have her putting problems between me and you or surrounding my baby."

"I'm sorry you feel that way, Babe. I didn't know she threatened your security."

"Now you know. You need to deal with this, Sutton. Don't let it go too far. I expect you home with me after work and if your mother does this a third time I expect you to set her straight."

"My mother is a power house when it comes to family, Penny. I won't be able to make a dent."

"Figure out a way." She turned on her side, her face away from him. "You decide if I'm worth it."

✳ ✳ ✳ ✳ ✳

Pressing their noses against the window they viewed the shop owned by Mrs. Hutson.

"There are two showcases," she noted. "Looks like a locked closet behind the counter. Would that work?"

"It's not bad. I think I could make it work, a few shelves on the wall, and no more depth than the wall measurement I believe there's adequate room behind that wall for working with the wood, if Mrs. Hutson has no qualms against it. But," he turned to face her. "We can't see the upstairs tonight." He walked around to where the stairs led up to the apartment and started counting. "Twenty four, Jewel."

"You look troubled. What's wrong?"

"If you have small children, they can't climb those stairs, it's too dangerous."

"I thought of that. I will have to set an age and skip the younger ones."

"But that's what it's all about. I began when I was five." He shook his head. "This won't work for us to live here if you are going to give lessons and that's part of our livelihood, should the instruments not go over."

"Let's pray about it. I can't make this decision. There are too many unknowns."

"I think praying got us here. The next step is a sound decision."

"You mean don't worry about viewing the upper apartment because of the stairs."

"Yes." He was very serious. "But the house may not be the answer either."

✳ ✳ ✳ ✳ ✳

A voicemail from Ellen confirmed if Jewel was able they needed her two more weeks. On Monday she arrived early welcomed by two hungry little boys who hugged around her legs and walked with her through the house. Ellen hugged her on the way out, saying there was a list on the table for the day.

Evan went alone to view the building and view the apartment. It wasn't bad but the appliances wore a coat of dust from sitting unused. Mostly the apartment needed a good cleaning but it was the stairs gave him the most concern. Mrs. Hutson was in meeting. He left the key, telling the manager the shop looked promising but he was uncertain about the apartment. Next he returned the key to the Sisters.

The three met him at the door, an expectant look on their faces. "Did you like the house?" Aldean asked.

"What did you think about the yellow house with its white shutters? We just got so tired of all those beige homes along the street. Yellow is supposed to make you feel happy." Geri wore a bright smile.

"The furniture? We didn't have anywhere to store it, so we left it in the house, I think they call it staging, you know, pretending someone has it furnished?" Nina sighed. "I thought it rather romantic."

"It is, I mean it must be." Evan blushed. "We thought it a beautiful home. But it appears out of our range." The sister's expressions changed. He felt the need to get out of their presence. "I mean, we can't afford much and we will continue to look, if that's all right with you."

"Young man, sit down." Aldean pointed to a high backed chair. "Now, we need to clear this up. We are offering you a house to live in, in return for overseeing our property, which was our mother's home. It's hard to part with a certain thing that had meaning to your mother and that's why we left the furniture." Aldean sat across from him in a matching chair. "Anyone who cares enough to do what you did for us concerning a grown up yard because we told you a young couple would be marrying in it over a weekend, we don't think we've judged you and your little wife wrong. You're the people we want to know if we go off spur of the moment gallivanting around the world you'll check on things."

"Now a days you don't just let anyone in your personal surroundings," Nina's soft voice chimed in.

"Of course we will fund all expenses and you will be the workmen." Geri sat nervously twisiting the tie to the scarf on her head. "We are going abroad next month; we need to know someone is here. And if you worry about the distance between, why there's a path leads straight from this back yard to where mother lived. In fact this whole subdivision was once our father's cattle farm. Mother sold it for a hefty profit after he died. She couldn't handle those cattle and we were strung around the country, then."

"There's a lot of ground to mow," Evan stated. "If I'm starting a business and Jewel gives piano lessons," he took a deep breath. They were gazing at him like three birds after a worm. "It's not that we don't appreciate your offer."

Aldean began laughing and the other two joined in. "You thought you had to mow the forty acres in between?" She slapped her hands together, making him jump, he was that nervous and he seldom got nervous. "Old man Curtis watches over the part that is still undeveloped, raises three cuts for hay on it each year and keeps it mowed with his tractor in between. That keeps it nice and green and looks pretty from the road, which entices new folks to build here."

"We wouldn't let just anyone move in our mother's home," Nina's voice was so soft he strained to hear.

"And the furniture will be very handy. But if there's a problem we can store it…but you know things go down when they're stored, just sitting there." She appeared to think for a moment. "The mattress on the bed is new. It's a mail order spread and curtains." She peered into his face. "Are you perhaps reconsidering?"

He felt his shirt collar was wet with sweat. "I haven't heard yet, the price of rent per month and there's one more thing, Jewel plans to give piano lessons. There will be children in and out of the front room."

The three met those words with smiles and clapping of the hands. "What is more wonderful than children? They are our future."

"Except," Aldean wrinkled her nose as an afterthought, "Except those whose parents spare the rod and spoil the child. I certainly got my share of reprimands."

"You were so sassy, Aldean," Geri reminded her, pausing for a moment to cough. "Nina and I learned from you to hold our tongue."

"All right young man; let's lay our cards on the table. Here's our offer and then you tell us what you want.'"

"Before you begin, it's only fair I tell you I may have to travel to present my instruments various places."

"I trust you could train a helper that could take over during those trips if you are away weeks?"

"I would think so, yes." He was warming to the proposition. The discussion went on a few minutes longer and Evan walked out with lightness to his step and the key to the house in his hand. There was only one drawback. If the farm house was in good shape there would come a time he and Jewel would move there. The sisters understood.

"We have to go out to the farm and check the house," he told Jewel when she arrived home from the Gates that afternoon. "If it's repairable we can start right away."

What they found was a sodden mess. The floor had buckled and all that was left of the walls was the studs but worst of all one side of the roof had caved in and threw the house out of line. "That's complete rebuilding," Evan said, "not just repair but rebuild. It looks like with the mold and scum the water left we just as well have Comer come up and dig a hole and push it in. If we want to build here when we've made enough money then we can but there's the drainage system to consider, they may not open this area back up."

"Do they just take your land?"

"No, they pay something, I just don't know if it's fair value price. We're talking about the government."

"It's not fair."

"No," Evan agreed. "None of this is fair, but I reckon if God has a plan for us, he will provide and help us to have even better. We're just going to have to keep our faith in Him and let him lead."

"So we will be taking the shop with the upstairs apartment?"

"Let's just pack up and be ready. How's that?" He wanted to surprise her and didn't know how. Instead he pulled the key from his pocket and said, "What do you suppose this key fits?"

"Here?" She looked around for something with a lock. "I don't know but I will tell you one thing, we need to salvage your parent's silverware and the dishes behind those doors and anything else we can clean up and make useful." She handed the key back to Evan and turned away to hide her disappointment. It would be a worry, young children climbing those stairs for piano lessons.

Chapter 6

"Did Jewel mention anything about meeting the sisters?"

Changing from her scrubs into shorts, Ellen glanced at Dan, "No, we didn't have time to talk. She said Evan had called and they were driving out to his acreage to see how the waters were receding and hoping to be able to walk through his house." She lingered, "Is something wrong? I mean, none of us have met the sisters. It seems even while they built their home they traveled a lot. I've not met them."

"Nothing's wrong that I know of, they came by asking for Jewel and Evan. I wouldn't have been here except I was working on those papers for expansion and with them spread out on my desk here I saw no reason to start all over at work. Jewel hadn't arrived yet and they were gone when she did."

"So what's your concern?"

"They heard it was Jewel and Evan cleaned up their yard and they have a proposition for them, one sister volunteered possibly a house."

"I've thought about that, Dan. They would have to leave the piano on the ground floor. There's no way to get it up those stairs to the apartment and I'm not sure Evan would want small children in his shop taking piano lessons."

Daniel grinned. "I see what you mean." Rising up from the chair he stretched. "How do you teach a child to play the piano?" Ellen put both hands in the air and wiggled her fingers. Dan yawned and stretched again. "Man, paper work is worse than hard labor."

"So, have you checked on our troop?" Ellen chuckled. "Ruthie is into MacBeth and they are all in costume practicing a play."

"I thought MacBeth was High School stuff." His eyes widened for a moment. "I forgot, our Ruthie excels." He followed Ellen down the hall and stood outside listening to the voices coming from inside the music room. "Sometimes I fear for Ruthie heading off to college at too young an age. I will probably have to go with her."

"We live in a college town, Daddy of the year."

"Still, Momma of many, I fret over Ruthie's future knowing the gift she has."

$$* \quad * \quad * \quad * \quad *$$

Evan found Jewel down on hands and knees scrubbing the kitchen floor. "Did you have an accident?"

Dismay shown on her face. "No, but I can't bring another box in of those items we brought from the farm house. I thought I could wash the dishes, but Evan, there's so much mud on them, I can't mess up Andrew's little kitchenette with our mess."

"No, but I think I know the perfect place we can clean and wash up everything without stringing things into the house. We can move Saturday if it suits you. Then I will begin in earnest setting up shop for making the instruments. My tools took a beating, too, but they are salvageable." He held out a hand to help her up from the floor. "Floor looks good."

"We must leave this place in tip top shape," she replied. "It was given out of the goodness of their hearts."

"We will." Leaning against the end cabinet, he watched as she rinsed the cloth. "If you will go with me tomorrow after work, I think we can bring the truck and it will help in the move. Maybe I could even start tomorrow while you are at the Gates. What do you think?"

"If you could take what we've brought from the house, it would help, even the boxes have dried mud on them but the dishes and silverware, all will be useful."

"You seem worried."

"Not really, but it is going to be a task carrying everything up those stairs."

He grinned. "Yeah."

✳ ✳ ✳ ✳ ✳

The next three days Evan spent transferring muddy boxes to the back porch of the Sister's mother's house. The sink was perfect for clean up. Disposing of the boxes, he would return for another load until all was washed clean and put away. On Thursday night Jewel had been noncommittal when they drove out for the truck, until she saw what was stored inside it.

"You mean these instruments have been in this truck stuck on top of this hill through the whole ordeal of the dam breaking and water covering the land?"

He nodded, "'fraid so." His grin spread across his face. "No one could get to them or they might not be here."

"I think not," she said tartly. "My goodness," she was studying the shiny backs of fine wood. "These will look wonderful on display… but Evan you must have them insured, your whole building. If you spend as much time as I think you do on each one, then you have to protect your work."

"I've not done that before."

"You were not starting a business, but then again, maybe you were and we are just now launching out together. Tomorrow, I'm calling the newspaper office and running an add for students if you think you can have the piano in place by the first of August. That would give mothers time to enroll before school starts up again."

"I would like one or two students for guitar lessons, but that's all I could justify presently."

"I can include that in the ad," Jewel replied. From Jewel's ad, Evan would receive one student.

✳ ✳ ✳ ✳ ✳

Evan spent Friday mowing the Sister's yard, trimming a few stray buses and weed eating around the flower beds. "My, my, my," Aldean's smile was wide as the Cheshire cat's. "You are making us shine."

"There are a couple loose boards on your border fence," he replied. "I'll find a hammer and secure those before I leave."

"Don't forget to stop by the house for your check," she said.

"What check?" He was confused. "Did we have mail come to your house?"

"No, Son, for doing the mowing."

"But Miss Aldean, we made a deal. The mowing for the rent."

She seemed perplexed. "Gull and Company charged us one hundred and sixty dollars a month."

"Then, Miss Aldean, are you and your sisters willing to rent your mother's house for that amount?"

"Well, certainly, our offer stands. We need to know when we travel someone is watching out for us."

"Rest your mind, ma'am, we will." Evan was walking toward the storage shed and she was following.

"Are you sure?"

"Positive."

"Are you moving soon?"

"Tomorrow if all goes well."

Aldean clapped her hands, "We will all be so relieved. Thank you, Evan."

"Thank you, Miss Aldean." He wasn't certain why but he bowed.

"You are quite the gentleman." Standing on tiptoe she kissed his cheek, laughed and fled toward the house.

Blushing and amused, Evan rubbed his cheek and shook his head. The sisters were a peculiar trio.

Saturday morning, Jewel was up tiptoeing around the house, her energy level about to pop through her head. It was going to be along hard day climbing those stairs and she couldn't wait for Evan to wake up. Finally she put the whistling teakettle on the stove and let it whistle. Minutes later Evan came into the kitchenette, to find Jewel hopping around the table, syrup and butter in the center with their plates set and waiting for pancakes. "There's strawberries in that bowl if you want with yours." She was so happy she kissed him on the lips, the cheeks and finally a big old smackeroo on the forehead. "We're moving. We're moving," she sang while Evan sat there laughing.

"Girl, what would your folks think of you?"

"Probably the same thing yours would." She grinned, pulling him down into a chair and plopping on his lap. "I never had this freedom, Evan. It feels good. The question is, what do you think of me?"

"You're the best thing ever happened to me." He pressed her close to his chest. "I get so afraid this will end too soon. I mean," his eyes took on a darkness, "Think about what happened to me when we found Addy."

"I'll never forget the doctor telling me your body was in shock from double trauma when the bullet passed through both lungs. I decided then nothing else was important but you coming out of that coma, I stayed at that hospital knowing we were penny poor but I would pay the bills someway and I would get a job when you came through." She sighed. "I've drug my feet on this, Evan, but I did place the ad yesterday and already I've received four calls and that encourages me there will be more."

"I know. It was pretty intense and there on the last I could hear the doctor talking to the staff if I didn't come around soon they would have to encourage you to take me off the support system to see if I could breathe on my own. And I wondered if you even knew what they were saying. It was kind of scary."

"Dan and Ellen were there and Marigold and Matt. They all came by and prayed with me. And they believed. When someone else believes it helps. I was pretty distraught. We'd had no time together. I couldn't believe you were going to die…but…that's what I was facing." She opened his shirt and kissed the top scar. "The doctor said you heal fast on the outside but it was on the inside concerned him."

"Well, I lifted boxes into the truck and it didn't hurt me. Let's eat and then go. I've already told the Graves we are moving today and we will clean Andrew's rooms thoroughly tomorrow."

They cleaned off the table and washed the dishes and placed them back in the cabinet. "Two people can get by with a service of six very easily," Jewel said. "How thoughtful Andrew was to make his special place an overnight stay for unexpected guests." She grinned, "Except you were here longer and added me."

"Let's go," Evan was excited to show Jewel they were going to the house, instead of the apartment. "We'll leave the car and take the old truck. That's what has everything in it. Closing the door behind them they found Marigold, Matt and Dan waiting outside. The two stopped. "What are you all doing here?"

"We came to help. Evan doesn't need to carry all those boxes by himself. Andrew would be here, too, but he had to meet a client." Matt stepped back inside his truck and Dan waved to them. "You lead," Matt called, "We'll follow."

After a few minutes Jewel asked, "Evan are you taking the long way?"

"I thought I'd show them where the sister's mother lived. You don't mind, do you?"

"No." a sadness dampened her spirit but she couldn't let Evan see it. "No, that's fine." He squeezed her hand. "Changing subjects, your new student called this morning. She is a girl."

"Come see what you think." He was fairly dragging Jewel up the sidewalk. The others followed. "It's too grand for us," he was saying as he opened the door and led them down the hall to the kitchen. One cabinet door had swung open and Jewel walked over to where there were dishes that hadn't been there their last visit. She studied the pattern and finally took one plate into her hand, then she opened the next door and the next; a whole set like Evan's mother's. Next, she pulled out the drawer at the bottom of the stove and it had pots and pans exactly like Evan's mother's. Everyone was quiet, watching her.

"Is something wrong, Jewel?" Marigold couldn't make out Jewel's expression.

"I don't know," she said, quietly. "Evan?"

"You need your piano in a place where there are no stairs. I've already told Dan and he agrees. It would be too dangerous for young children. He said they think they are so good at stairs they would probably run up them and then what would happen? They would fall and who knows how far down they'd tumble."

Dan was smiling and now Marigold and Matt joined in. "Sounds good to us. And it is a nice start. Good for both of you." The three clapped their hands as Jewel threw her arms around Evan's neck.

"Thank you." There were tears in her eyes.

"She always has tears when someone does something nice for her," Marigold pulled them into a hug.

"You probably don't know this, yet," Dan said, pointing a direction, "but Will Martin's daughter and her new husband live down the road, next house on the left."

The moving went fairly quick with Matt and Dan's assistance and Marigold helped Jewel put things in the proper place. The last item was the upright piano that Jewel had not seen. Evan had played it and was pleased and that was enough for her. It was not the ugly duckling she had imagined. Someone had cut the top down, installed a mirror over new keys and it was not the mahogany she had pictured but a sharp lacquered black. "It matches the swing," Dan offered, but the women were delighted. "It matches the oriental pieces left by Mrs. Kennedy."

"That's right, Aunt Georgia said this was the old Tifsstead before it became a development for new homes in a pricey range."

"You should know," Matt teased, "you live on the other side by the sisters."

"What do we need to bring this room to life?" Jewel's question was directed to Marigold.

"Oh, honey, I'm so glad you asked. "I know exactly and if you will bear with me about a month, the home store will have its summer sale and with my discount I can get it for you for about a third of the price." She glanced around, "How about if you have students immediately and you need chairs for them to sit on, bring in two of those wooden chairs from the kitchen."

They finished unpacking and placing furniture by four o'clock and Dan went home. "See you all at church in the morning. As he pulled away Penny pulled into the drive. She waved at Dan and came up the walk.

"Where's Sutton?" Matt asked holding out his hand to steady her as she wobbled on the bottom step.

"Oh, he works on Saturdays with his Dad in the store." Matt and Dan exchanged glances but Penny didn't notice.

Jewel all ready was leading her inside and they could hear her explaining, "we don't have furnitiure for this room. In fact we didn't have anything but Evan's dishes and cook ware."

"All right, you two, I saw that look." Marigold held their attention. "What was that about?"

"Coleman's aren't open on Saturday? We were there when Evan needed an extra roller for that bed that's a little low on one side. It's a special kind of roller that locks after you move it to keep from rolling."

Evan was in the dark as to what they were saying. "So where did you get the roller?"

"Marigold remembered there was one from a bed she had cut down to make a bench." Penny was coming back out the door, followed by Jewel.

"Leaving so soon?" Marigold asked.

"Yeah, I need to have dinner on the table. Sutton is always starving when he works on Saturdays." She wiggled her fingers and was gone calling over her shoulder, "Ya'll come see us."

Evan remembered he had left keys in the truck as they were ready to go to bed. "I'll just run out and get them," he said. "Maybe I should move the truck closer to the house too, we are new here." He was just opening the door to get in when a truck on the road honked, he straightened and looked and it was Sutton Coleman. "Hey, boy," He called to Sutton, "You worked mighty late."

"Wasn't workin'," Sutton called back."Nothin' do my mother but I have dinner with them and then she wanted to show me last year's vacation film I'd never seen when we went to the Bahamas and

I took Charlotte Green along. I can't let Penny see that, can I?" he laughed and drove away.

✳ ✳ ✳ ✳ ✳

Everyone was at Christ Church. The pews were full. Ruthie managed to sit between Jewel and Marigold. "You are my two favorite people," she said, laughing as they each hugged her and placed a kiss on each cheek. "and you can still sit by your husbands." She said the word husbands as if Matt and Evan were kings. Matt winked at her. "Sammy and Danny wanted to sit here but Momma said they had their turn last week. Are you coming back tomorrow, Jewel?" Jewel nodded and Ruthie's smile brightened.

Ruthie's joy was catching. Jewel and Evan sang out and Marigold and Dan joined in until the nursery buzzer on Marigold's arm went off and she had to leave them. The song service ended and Pastor Joe stepped to the pulpit. "Let us remain standing for the reading of God's word found in Galatians six, one through six. "Brothers and sisters," he began, "If someone in your group does something wrong, you who are spiritual should go to that person and gently help make him right again. But be careful, because you might be tempted to sin, too. By helping each other with your troubles, you truly obey the law of Christ. If anyone thinks he is important when he really is not, he is only fooling himself. Each person should judge his own actions and not compare himself with others. Then he can be proud for what he himself has done. Each person must be responsible for himself. Anyone who is learning the teaching of God should share all the good things he has with his teacher." While the words soaked into the congregation, those in the group were taking seriously what their pastor was saying. They had enough problems; they tried to settle them without calling on each other. "But," Pastor Joe continued, "There are times, should you feel led to speak with someone, maybe you ought to take someone with you. A witness as to your good intentions and not of an intention to destroy what they have."

"You may be seated. In Romans chapter eight we read use all wisdom to teach and instruct each other." He paused looking out over the congregation. "That's probably the best advice we can take when we find ourselves in a position to use Galatians chapter one. What kind of problem would we see our sister or brother participating in that we should go to them?" He laughed. "I know right now you are remembering something that could have fell into the category, perhaps you needed to warn someone not to listen to the gossip a person was telling, maybe someone was spending time with a person you knew would lead them into temptation or plain ole trouble if they picked up that person's bad habits. Now, the question is, if you found yourself in that predicament, did you handle it and if so, the scripture says to gently help make him right again. But be careful because you might be tempted to sin, too. Get the mote out of your eye before you try to remove the stick out of your brother's eye, or vice versa."

Ellen sitting to the left with Dan on her right, then Evan and Jewel, knew Ruthie would be questioning the meaning of Pastor Joe's statement. Sure enough when she leaned forward to see, Ruthie was staring at her with a perplexed expression. "I'll explain later," she whispered and Ruthie nodded, okay. Dan grinned. "That's our girl." Everyone on the row was smiling. Ruthie belonged to all of them.

Lunchtime at the restaurant brought back the statement; get the mote out of your own eye before you try to remove something from your brothers. "It means, we have to examine ourselves, Ruthie," Ellen explained, "before we go to someone else we think has a problem and tell them we want to help them, they may say, well who are you to come trying to help me when we both know you have your own problems."

"Like Sammy doesn't want Danny to fib about the rabbit, but Sammy spanked the rabbit when it pooped on the floor and it scared the rabbit, so Sammy told Danny to not talk to him because he was mad."

Everyone at the table laughed and many were saying, "you got it, Ruthie." Sammy and Danny had scoot down in their booster seats hoping no one glanced their way. Dan and Ellen were questioning each other, "What rabbit?"

"Do you know anything about the rabbit?" Evan asked Jewel.

Ruthie spoke up. "It was before Easter when Daddy told the twins to leave the rabbit alone."

"We put it back, Daddy. Really we did. Ruthie said it would smell up the house, so we did."

"Boys," Dan was looking very serious. "Do not bring things into the house, and don't pick them up, they could hurt you. And be very very sure you never pick up a snake. Do you understand?"

"We won't, Daddy." The boys were on the verge of crying. "We're sorry, Daddy."

Later, when they were home and the children were taking naps, Dan said, "dinner was interesting. Our boys held the spotlight. Was there anything else?"

"I heard Harper asking Dorothy wasn't that Coleman kid newly married and she asked why he wanted to know. Harper said, when he was checking how one of the house projects was coming along he saw the boy on the other end of town with another girl, Jim Green's daughter, and he thought if the boy was married that wasn't right."

"The day we helped Evan and Jewel with moving, Penny stopped by and it seemed she was a bit strained and Evan said Sutton came in from work around ten thirty, when the truth was he wasn't working."

"All we can do is pray for the two of them. Sutton has a doting momma that thinks the sky's the limit if her children want something. I wonder sometimes if Leona stays with Sutton one because of his money." She sighed. "I know that seems harsh but they don't seem to go together."

It wasn't long after the Sunday's discussion that Penny came to Jewel's door.

Jewel heard the knock, timid at first and then hurried. She opened the door to find Penny outside. "Come in, Penny."

"Shut the door, quick." Pennyi's words were rushed as Jewel tried to do as she ask. "I'm sorry," there were tears in Penny's voice, "but he'll be looking for me. I couldn't get in the car because the keys were in my purse in the bedroom." She was holding her hand over her right eye. "Sutton," she explained.

"What's wrong?" She reached over and lift Penny's hand away from her eye. "Did he hit you?"

Penny nodded, "But I hit him back," tears splashed down her face. "He was so angry because I had followed him all yesterday evening and when he didn't come home until late I lashed out at him. I saw him, Jewel, with my own eyes with Charlotte Green. He said his mother ask him to comfort her, she is distraught over losing him. How can that be, Jewel?" She wiped at the tears. "We were together every night the last six months until we married. She has no reason to be talking this way, now." Sitting in the one chair Jewel had moved in for the students, Penny put her head down in her hands and cried, great sobs that wracked her body. "We are married. How could she do this?"

"How could Sutton do this," Jewel wondered out loud and to her dismay, Penny's cries rose in volume. "I mean," her explanation dropped off, that was how she felt, she couldn't soften the blow. "What are you going to do?"

"I want to go talk to Sutton's mother and ask her not to interfere in our marriage and I'm going to ask her why she doesn't like me?" She glanced up to Jewel. "Will you go with me?"

Trepidation raced through Jewel's thoughts. "I don't know, Penny, I don't want to be put on the spot."

"How could you, you have nothing to do with this? You know, Pastor said there were times you should take someone with you." She stood and walked to the window. "I want to go now, while Sutton is home."

"Nursing his hand where he slammed it into the wall and not only is there a hole in the wall but he cracked his knuckles." Her tears began again, "I was shocked when he hit me and without thinking I hit him back and his lip is bleeding too."

Jewel almost laughed but Penny's eyes were round as saucers and she was worried. Berating herself, Jewel realized Penny's explanation had made her nervous too, and she was ashamed. "It is none of my business, Penny."

"If he had killed me, would it have been your business?"

"Yes, I guess, because you are my friend."

"Same thing," Penny replied. "Can we go in your car? Then I won't have to go where he is."

* * * * *

The Coleman estate set back off the highway, lighted fixtures lined the road that wound from the street up to the house. To one side a pool glistened in the sunlight. On the other, a bank of flowers colored an otherwise dismal corner and so it was as far as the eye could see opulence. "No poverty here," Penny muttered as she rang the bell, half expecting a butler in formal attire to answer the door, but it was Mrs. Coleman herself appeared, the fake smile on her face disappearing when she saw them.

She opened the door, perhaps a fourth of the way. "Yes?" She didn't invite her daughter in law in.

"Mrs. Coleman, may I speak with you?"

"If you are selling anything, I'm not interested."

"No ma'm, I want to talk with you about your son..my husband, please."

"I can't imagine anything you and I would have to discuss, Penelope. And who is this with you?"

"My friend, Jewel Jacobs. She attends Christ Church."

"I suppose that's as good a reference as you could give." She opened the door half way, "Come in." She glanced at Jewel. "You may sit here while Penelope and I use the next room." Jewel obeying took a seat.

She could hear through the opened door. "Mrs. Coleman, are you aware Sutton is seeing that Green girl?"

"Of course, I encouraged him to try to soothe the girl's disappointment. She had her cap set for him."

"That and other things such as his having dinner with you and Mr. Coleman, when he knows I prepare and look forward to his arrival, those two things added together will destroy our marriage, because it also puts Sutton on the defensive and I'm here to ask you to take what I'm saying into consideration."

"Destroy your marriage?" She clapped her hands and sounded quite happy when she said, "I hope so."

Jewel heard Penny jump to her feet, the chair scooted behind her and the tinkle of glass sounded. "I can't believe you are so cruel. Don't you care that I make Sutton happy?"

"No, I really don't believe you do and evidently you aren't happy or you wouldn't be putting demands on him." There was a moment's silence until she continued. "I'm not sure sex in your case was what made him happy, though it tied him to you for a time. There's a difference between lust and love."

"Mrs. Coleman, there will be a baby arriving in December. Your grandchild. Does that not matter, either?"

"No, it doesn't. Babies are a dime a dozen. I had three because my husband thought they proved our love. I've done my best by them but had he expected another I would have drawn the line. Two was all I agreed to, but our last one was an accident when I overly imbibed and wasn't aware of my own actions."

"You are a very cold woman." Jewel heard the frustration and anger in Penny's voice, she couldn't tell which.

"No," Mrs. Coleman was rising. "I am a very smart woman and I might add, very calculating, too." She gave an exaggerated sigh. "Let me see you to the door. I believe you've said what you came to say."

"Mrs. Coleman, I pray you do not regret this hardness. If I hadn't been brought up to fight my own battles I would be more easily hurt but in my family we are given choices and we earn them early on."

"If becoming pregnant was one of them designed to catch the most obvious boy in town, likely to succeed, then I don't appreciate your family teachings and I'll work against them with my last breath."

"My family never designs its standards on another family's principles. There's more to us than meets the eye. I'm very proud of my parents. I just can't help but wonder what happened with you that you went wrong." Lifting her head and squaring her shoulders Penny turned toward the door.

Jewel followed behind, with a trickle of fear that Mrs. Coleman might lash out at them and hit her.

They were perhaps a mile from the house when Penny leaned forward and lay her head on the dash and sobbed as though her heart were breaking. "We don't stand a chance," she wailed.

Chapter 7

Summer rolled into August and the school's began; bringing more structure to the lives of the families in the Cape. Jewel now had eight students, ranging from beginner to fifth grade progress on the piano. Evan had his shop operating physically and an online supply business. The people in Nashville that had begun selling his instruments were beginning to take orders that reached into the next two years.

"Would it help if you had an assistant?" Daniel asked, upon seeing his frustration with the long range orders. "You are one person and your business is proving your skill. There's a fine older gentleman in our church with a limited knowledge in woodworking but I would think you could teach him the steps you use in finishing each instrument. What do you think? Is it worth a try?"

Evan found Simon Nettler a worthy acquaintance before he knew the man was worth his weight in workmanship. Jewel was charmed by his soft spoken way. "Such a gentleman, Si," she would say as he always bowed to her arrival, showing her the latest thing Evan had taught him. "Tell me about your life," she would say, trying to draw him out.

"My wife has Alzheimers," he finally replied. "I go to see her every morning before coming to work and I return each evening before going home for the night. She does not know me but I know her."

"And you miss her something terrible, don't you, Si?"

"Yes." He did not elaborate. His eyes told the story. He still loved her though theoretically she was gone.

Si became used to Penny's dropping by, shaking his head sadly as she left, knowing her heart ache though she kept it to herself. His home was around the corner from the Coleman's who lived in a more affluent neighborhood, but he had known Sutton the child, who rode his tricycle down the sidewalk, chased wild baseballs to his gate and had to pay for the living room window that was broken, though Simon believed his mother assumed the responsibility when the father said, "Sutton, you knew better. I told you it was irresponsible to play near the neighbor's homes."

Si and Bertie were not blessed with children but they helped the niece and nephew through college. Now the two were adult, married and moved away and they received a greeting card each year at Christmas. He wondered if they knew they were heirs to his and Bertie's will would they stay in touch.

Penny dropped by the last of October. With a lull in the maintenance of the sister's estate, Evan accepted an invitation in Nashville. Unknownst to him, Jewel had been told Evan was to receive an award for excellence in regard to his guitars, voted by many of Nashville's famous as their instrument of choice, not only the sound but the instrument's aesthetic beauty.

"I forgot they were going." In truth, she wanted to talk to Si. She wasted thirty minutes or so, wandering around the shop, until finally she sat opposite Si as he used what looked like gauze you bound a wound with to further smooth the back for a violin. "Si, you've known Sutton since he was a child. Is there any way to break his bad habits...I think you know he keeps company with other women and I'm home by myself carrying his baby."

"Now Penny," Si replied. "I don't recommend your putting a hit out on his momma. Leona won't go down without fightin' and she usually wins."

"I was afraid you'd say that." Tears dropped onto her hands folded across her expanding stomach.

"But I tell you what, Penny. IF you love that boy, be good to him. He's not known the kind of love you have. His has been a more manipulative form of," he paused. "I don't rightly know how to describe it." He paused, his hands stopped midair, "It's not healthy, is it? I can't explain it."

Still, that night she was crying when Sutton fell into bed around one in the morning. "Jesus, Babe," he moaned. "I just gotta' few hours to sleep. Let's don't have the drama, tonight. It's all your fault, anyway, you won't go the places I go and we both suffer, so I go on ahead. My Momma okays it."

"What does she have to do with our life together?" Penny demanded.

"Don't you go bad mouthin my Momma, there's very little she don't know about."

"But she has no idea what Jesus expects of us, does she?"

Sutton gave a push and Penny landed on the floor. When she stood there was extreme pain, fearful the fall affected the baby, the next morning she went to the doctor, she had landed on her tail bone. The pain was hers alone, the baby was fine. "You need rest," the doctor said. "I know Sutton, he can fend for himself for awhile." He scribbled on the prescription pad, "Go home to your folks until baby is born."

Asking for her mother's help Penny packed her clothes, removed all the personal items from the house and left the bare necessities. When Sutton came home two o'clock the next morning, she was gone. "I'm having difficulty with the pregnancy," her note read, "the doctor said I must not be alone." Sutton fell onto the bed and slept off the good time he'd had drinkin' with Charlotte and her sister, Laurie.

When his father called him aside he said, "Sutton, there's no excuse for coming to work in clothes that look as though you slept in them. Now go home and clean yourself up. No one's going to ask you for help until you straighten up your appearance. You resemble a two o'clock drunk."

Sutton slunk home, thinking his father hit the nail on the head; he had come home at two o'clock. His clothes were all washed and folded in a pile on a chair but not the usual set laid out on the bed for him by Penny ironed that made him look good. He began to think how she treated him in regard to his disrespect of her. He called. The phone rang and rang until finally her father answered. "What are you doing home, today, Will?"

"It's noon, Sutton. I come home for lunch when I can."

'I need to speak to Penny."

"I'm sorry, Sutton, the doctor has put her on bed rest and she is not to be disturbed."

"I'm coming after her. She's my wife and I want her home."

"You should have thought of that before you mistreated her, Sutton. Penny has a restraining order against you. Don't get ideas about taking her home. Try to get your life under control Sutton. You have a lot going for you, but you forgot there are other people to consider. Penny's under our protection now."

Something ugly flared in Sutton, if a good thought flamed he cut it short and pushed it to the back of his mind. He showed the prescription to his mother Dr. Fawk had written for Penny, go home to your folks until baby is born. Immediately angry, Leona called the doctor. "Who do you think you are going against my boy?"

"Leona," Dr. Fawk's voice sounded old and tired. "I delivered that boy, maybe I have a minutes responsibility for how you have let him turn out. Now pull your head down out of the clouds and become the boy's real mother before he lands in jail or something worse. He's on a two way street to disaster." He heard the phone click as she hung up on him.

Leona's own life wasn't going well. While she was focusing on ridding Sutton of Penny, her seventeen year old daughter had something to tell her. "Momma, I'm pregnant." Leona gave up her pride and drug LeAnn to Dr. Fawk.

"Do something," she said. "She is going to college."

Dr. Fawk's looked at her in amazement. "Leona, I deliver babies, I don't kill them."

"I want this baby," LeAnn cried. "I need someone to love." She and her mother glared at each other.

"How dare you embarrass me." With a wave of the hand Leona thought to nip this problem in the bud.

"You do anything to me and I will run away. The father of my baby is rich. Do you understand? Rich."

"Does he have family…children?" Leona dreaded to hear the answer.

"Yes," LeAnn lied but he didn't and she knew she had tricked him. Dressed to the nines she could appear as a twenty something woman and she had done exactly that. Whatever it took to get away from her mother; her life wasn't that great under Leona's roof, better she get out whatever way she could. Now.

"You bring him around."

"No, you sign papers giving your permission I marry him and I'll be out of your hair." LeAnn looked to Dr. Fawk. "You are my witness. Either she gives permission or she will never see me again."

"You have learned well, LeAnn." Shaking his head he said, "I have other patients to see."

At end of day, he still remembered the scene between mother and daughter. "Did you hear any of that he asked Nurse Claire? She nodded she had. Removing his white coat, he stared into space, "That's one for the books. If Leona don't watch it, she will be left alone in that big old house by herself."

"What about Sutton number two?"

"Word has it he has found a soft spoken retired school teacher he enjoys conversing with."

"It won't last if the old guard finds out."

"That's who told me…but you're right, Old Sut said he will let him have reign for a while then pull him in." Dr. Fawk yawned tiredly. "It's a house of cards, ready to fall but there's still the youngest, Ben."

"He knows all their ways," Nurse Claire waited for the doctor's reply. "They've learned from the best."

"Ever so often, God intervenes. I see that one on a regular basis and I believe he's made of good stuff. My friend, Sut, wasn't always liberal, he had back bone and good intentions but when he made that little invention that made him rich he forgot them for awhile. Now he sees what he's let happen and it troubles him. Truly, Nurse, we are our brother's keeper and if we fail it does trouble us sorely."

She watched him, his step dragging with tiredness. She doubted he had ever failed to do his morally best. If the town took the doctor as an example it would excel but he was just one man who kept the door to his clinic open when all around more sophisticated equipment, space age designed buildings and billboards announced availability to the latest knowledge. Few knew he was a Harvard graduate with years of medical school on the East Coast in the best known facilities behind his name. More likely than not he would hang a calendar over his certificate and she knowing it must be visible would remove it.

Listening with great curiosity, the next day, to the conversation between doctor Fawk and his patient, she was surprised the young man appeared on the heels of his mother and sister's visit.

"Ben," Dr. Fawk offered his hand and Ben shook it. "What can I do for you?"

"Well, Sir. Through the years I've come to know you are a man one could count on if there was a need. First, I want to thank you for being grandfather's friend and allowing me to hang around all the many times."

Dr. Fawk chuckled. "Ben, you lent a rather amusing and enjoyable atmosphere to two stodgy old friends sharing a cup of coffee and Brummel's wonderful Cinnamon rolls. Does she still make those?" He laughed again in remembrance. "It's a delight that little café on the corner has stood the breath of time. I take it there's a reason you are here, Ben."

"Yes, Sir. I've looked into how many years of medical school I'll need to become a doctor and while it seems forever I intend to pursue it."

The doctor looking on found the boy to be quite serious, unlike his mother and maybe unlike his siblings. "That's honorable but where do I come in on this?"

"I want to be your partner. Starting now, without pay, I'm asking you to let me observe those patients who don't mind and in cases their person is not violated with me standing looking on. Is that how I should phrase that, Dr. Fawk?"

"You want to be my partner?"

"Yes. I'm asking you to lead me as I go off to medical school and when that's over I want to come back and work with you and eventually when you retire I want to become the town doctor."

"Well, Ben, how do you feel about the Hippocratic Oath?"

"Is that a trick question, Sir? I know doctors do take an oath when they graduate medical school but the original oath has become back seat. I don't think you would swear to it because of the many gods it invokes and you being a Christian, am I right, Dr. Fawk?"

Laughing, Dr. Fawk agreed. "Being a doctor does necessitate a certain degree of keeping things to one's self, integrity as in all careers is the one thing that will make or break you. It won't take long for your patients to realize how sound a person you are. Do you think you can face it?"

'You are thinking of my mother and my brother. Sutton has always been mother's favorite and some day I'll tell you why but that's all right with me and LeAnn. Grandfather may appear a gruff old man but he watches out for us and he doesn't let Mother get the upper hand the way our father does."

"I would be a little uncomfortable discussing your family with you, Ben. I will be glad to assist you in your study to become a doctor and if you swear to never discuss my patients I'll allow you to join me in my practice. You will learn more here than in a lot of books but both are necessary. I'll expect you next week, beginning on Monday and there will be task. Are we agreed?"

Ben Coleman left a happy young man. He was sixteen years old and his future looked bright.

"Did you get that, Nurse Claire?" Shaking his head, as usual, Dr. Fawk, muttered, "Wonders never cease."

"I assume that came right out of the blue?" She ask, coming from the adjoining room. Dr. Fawk nodded.

"If his grandfather knew, he didn't say a word to prepare me. He's making the boy stand on his own."

✳ ✳ ✳ ✳ ✳

"Mother," Sutton was at work. He had waited all day for his mother to make appearance but she didn't show. "Mother, I need to talk to you about Penny." I'm listening. "Her father forbids me to see her and he said they have a restraining order against me, if I should step foot on their property." Why, Sutton? Have you hit Penny? Reluctant to admit he had, Sutton ask, "Can you do anything about my seeing her?" Not if you have abused her, Sutton. That was never our intention, to hurt Penny. She just needs to take your needs to heart. But, Son, you do need to settle down on the visits to the bar. You go too often. "I thought you didn't care. Besides, it is dull and boring at home with Penny." Sutton, I tried to tell you she was not your caliber. You wouldn't listen. If you truly loved her you would look forward to time with Penny. "But she talks about the baby, we will do this and we will do that and I don't like the baby stuff." I was that way about you, Sutton. I looked forward to your arrival. "Whose side are you on, Mother?" Yours, dear. Always yours. "I gotta go, Dad's staring at me. A customer needs me." Bye, darling.

That night Sutton was ready to leave the bar early. "Why, honey?" Charlotte asked.

"I have to iron my clothes for tomorrow, no longer got a wifie to do those little chores."

"I can iron, honey. You want me to come home with you and iron your clothes?"

He was tired and cranky. Penny could be with him if she wanted. "Sure, are you ready?"

Charlotte tucked her arm through his and climbed into his truck. "I can show you a thing or two about ironing," she said. They arrived home. He showed her the nicely folded pile and the dirty clothes in another pile in the bathroom.

"I never washed clothes before in my life," he admitted. "Penny was good at laundry."

"I am, too," Charlotte said, stripping down to her panties and bra as she plugged in the iron and ironed what he needed for the next day. "Tomorrow I'll clean up this mess," she said, hoping into Penny's side of the bed. "Don't wake me when you leave in the morning. I'll get up later." She was asleep in minutes.

Sutton awoke to find his arms around Charlotte who was nestled into the curve of his body as though she belonged there. His first thoughts were, this is not right, but his second thoughts outweighed the first. Charlotte became a household word to the neighborhood and Will Martin heard quick enough. He dreaded Penny hearing the news.

"What are you going to do about Sutton?" His father asked Leona.

"I'll let it play out awhile and then I'll take care of it. Charlotte is lower on the pole than Penny was."

"Penny is having Sutton's child, doesn't that rate at all with you?" Sutton number two's features were stern, his eyes unforgiving. "That would be your lover's bloodline.

"I think I've given you enough to compensate, Sut, so don't go thinking because you have hooked yourself a little retired schoolmarm life will change. I won't be leaving your mansion and you won't be marrying her no matter how she makes you feel." She saw him blanch. "You thought I didn't know?" It was her turn to laugh. "There's very little you do, I don't know about. One fifteen Meadow Lane is another one of your elusive dreams. Do you want me to tell Miss North I know about you two?"

His shoulders sagging, Sut turned to leave for work. "By the way, Sut, your father and I hired the same detective. He knows about Elaine North. I paid for the extra info, with your money. Thank you, Sut."

He was down in the dumps all day. When Will Martin came in for supplies around three o'clock, he asked, "Are you sick, Sutton? Your color is off and you don't have much to say. It's not like you."

Sutton leaned across the counter. He was the only one in the store, the others were out on call, even the boy. "Will, I've known you since school days. You went with Leona before I did. Sometimes

I'm sorry I took her away from you, she's that difficult to live with and the boy marrying your daughter…if I could change that, I'd do it. I'm pretty much beat at my own game and I don't know how to get out of it. How do you stay as strong as you appear, or do you have bad days, too?"

"We all have bad days, Sutton. My girl is going through hell right now with Sutton shacking up with the Green girl, but what can she do? If she goes home there's a chance his temper will flare and he could hurt her or possibly the baby. It's true, for her protection, there's a restraining order against him."

"What do you know about my and Leona's courtship?"

"I'm pretty sure I know the truth, Sutton. Before you, Leona already knew she was pregnant with Charles Lander's baby. I was surprised she didn't get an abortion, knowing how she felt."

"She thought he'd come around and marry her." Sutton thought about the wealth he now laid claim to, "I was a poor boy then and she was poorer if there was such, she couldn't afford the trip and Charles had already left town. Honest to God, in those days I loved her so much I didn't care she was having someone else's kid. That love lasted through her carrying LeAnn and Benjamin. Then she became so cold, I can't tell you what our family has been through. We're a sham."

"I'm going to tell you what has kept me and Mary together. The Lord. You can't stay angry with the wife you pray with daily and attend church on Sunday's. That would be a true sham but it seems God in his mercy knows when you're trying and he blesses your united effort to stay together. Why don't you try it?"

"Church?" Sutton's eyes grew large as he thought of Leona. "She tells we belong to a church. We don't. I don't think we've had prayer in our house in ten years. Well, maybe when one of the kids was sick and we were desperate and if we've attended church it would be a special occasion."

"Sutton, this is my heartfelt invitation. Come to church, Sunday. Sit down with our family. I promise you will be blessed."

"That's asking a lot, Will. Anyway, I'm scheduled for a seminar this weekend for Universal tools."

"Sounds like you need a lot, Sutton." Will reached across and with a firm grip shook Sutton's hand.

✳ ✳ ✳ ✳ ✳

"What was that brand name again?" Sutton was thumbing through the pages of an old manuel. "We don't have it in the inventory, or I'd have recognized it." He glanced at the clock on the wall. Five o'clock.

"Rainbird." Daniel examined the head to the irrigation system he held in his hand. "It's defective because it doesn't shoot out the distance, it just spews about a three foot range and soaks the spot where it hits and leaves the intended path dry."

"Is this for your home or down the street at your business?"

"Home." Daniel replied. "I thought maybe I could get it fixed this afternoon, after work."

"How's the missus? Didn't I hear she had a health issue a few years back?"

"Last year. Cancer." Dan replied, "But she took the treatment and so far everything is good."

"Hated to hear about the cancer. The chief of Police and I were friends, Chester Mayfield. You knew him?" Sutton glanced up. "He lost his wife to cancer."

"Yes, his wife was our daughter's sitter. Bitty was a wonderful person."

"As was Chester. I hated to see him leave when his wife died. He was a solid person." He raised up with an object in a zip locked bag. "I believe I've found what you need. It's a wonder someone else hadn't needed it, seeing as there's only one." He was opening the bag. "Losing a good friend, a confidante, that hurts. There's no replacing that kind of friendship."

"Kept you in line, I bet."

"What do you know? Those are loaded words, Daniel."

Dan measured Sut's concern. "I don't know anything, Sutton. Did you think I meant something?"

Sutton studied Daniel Gates. "You seem like a regular guy, Daniel. I'm sorry I misspoke."

"You seem troubled."

"I am. This is the second time this day I've nearly spilt my guts. Could you come into the office and us talk?"

"Sure thing." Daniel stuck his wallet back in his pocket and followed Sutton.

"Have a seat." They sat across from each other. "I'm in a mess."

"Your business?"

"No, my personal family life." Sutton struggled for a moment. "It's weighing pretty heavy on me for me to bare myself to you."

"You don't have to worry about me carrying tales, Sutton. If you want confidence, you've got it."

"My wife and I have three kids, but we don't have a marriage. Do you understand what I'm saying? I've become acquainted with a lady in this town and I am thinking I will leave this marriage."

Dan was quiet.

"You don't agree?"

"I've not walked in your shoes."

"If you were facing this dilemma, what would you do?"

"I'd take it to the Lord."

"Why?" Sutton leaned forward in earnest. "What does the Lord have to do with my marriage?"

"Did you say for better, for worse, for richer for poorer, in sickness and in health, when you married your wife?"

"I did. Aren't those just words?"

"Who did you think you were addressing?"

"No one in particular, maybe her."

"Will this affect your children?"

"I don't really know. I just arrived at this decision today and it's not nailed down, yet."

"Have you prayed about it?"

"What's so special about prayer?" He was truly perplexed, this was the second man offered that remedy. "If I don't know your Lord, why would I pray to him?"

"Haven't you ever needed him? Sutton, you're close to my age, haven't you ever faced sickness or been scared? Your life, or your children's or maybe your business suffered. That's when you pray."

"I made it, all by myself," Sutton replied, stubbournly. "This was a mistake. I'm sorry to take your time."

Daniel was holding up his hand, "Lord, God, I call on you now, in the presence of Sutton. Father, if there's a feeling of distrust I ask you to remove it immediately. Let Sutton and I become friends that can share without worry. Father, I ask you to bless him this very moment. Let peace come into his heart and Father help him to seek what is best for all concerned. I pray Lord he will find you in his heart, a help to all he faces in daily life and I leave it all with you now, thanking you for friendship beyond the ordinary. In your gracious Holy name. Amen. Opening his eyes, Daniel smiled and extended his hand to Sutton. When Sutton hesitated, Daniel reached across and gave him a quick bear hug. "You looked like you needed that, man. I'll be on my way and you can bill me for the part. How's that?" Not lingering, Daniel found his way out.

Sutton's mind was in a spin. Twice in one day, two men he respected mentioned their Lord. What was this all about? They knew him, until now he hadn't strayed in his marriage and thus far he had not consummated an affair with Elaine North, though he dreamed of her nearly every waking hour. Could he give her up in the name of all that was right? Why should he?

Dan arrived home in time to change out the defective head on the irrigation system. His mind was on Sutton Coleman's personal situation. All he could do was pray for the man. Sometimes you walked into problems you wished you knew nothing about and this was one of them. He and Ellen always believed when that happened the good Lord meant for them to pray for that person because chances were they had no one else to do so. "How should I pray?" He asked quietly and the Holy Spirit replied, "Just pray."

"Ruthie, tomorrow we need to see Dr. Fawk about your immunization record. I think its' time for a booster."

"I don't like the sound of that," Ruthie replied. "What about the twins?"

"Not yet, they will stay with Jewel and you and I won't linger once we finish at the clinic."

"Does Jewel mention anything about the young lady that married Sutton Coleman?"

"Not that I know of," Ellen replied.

"They're not together," Ruthie offered. "Penny is Jewel's friend and did live down from her but Sutton became abusive and Penny had to move back home."

"Jewel told you this?" Ellen was thinking it was too much for a child Ruthie's age to handle.

"No, God is working something out in my mind. I don't know what it is so I haven't said anything. It's a process, you know."

Dan and Ellen were staring at her as though she had just read the dictionary to them page by page.

"I'll know more tomorrow and then I can tell you something. I hope it makes sense."

Daniel put one elbow on the table, his head on his hand and studied Ruthie longer. "I hope whatever you learn sheds light on any issues I might be experiencing, too."

"Oh, Daddy," Ruthie laughed. "You are teasing me again."

"No, I'm not." What he knew involved friends and what's more a fellow member from Christ Church.

"You're not?" She tilt her head and waited for him to smile but he didn't. "You're serious?" Dan nodded. "Then I hope it helps you, too, Daddy." Ruthie proceeded to eat as though it didn't bother her at all and it didn't. Ellen smiled behind her hand. Ruthie's gift seldom caused a problem. She was very mature.

✻ ✻ ✻ ✻ ✻

"The appointment is at eleven fifteen," Ellen explained to Ruthie, "But I thought we should leave early while the twins were down for a nap. That way we don't have to explain where we are going or why."

Ruthie shuddered. "Well, surely they wouldn't want a shot. I don't."

Russom's Dress Shop had a sale sign in the window. Ellen checked her watch. "Let's go in for a minute. We've neither have had a new dress this summer."

Once inside, Ellen circled the hanging racks while Ruthie took a seat at the children's corner watching another lady as she examined several pieces she had hanging from hangers in her hand. She glanced up to see Ruthie watching her. Ruthie smiled. The woman scowled and moved closer to where Ellen was standing. "I don't know about these items I've selected," she said to Ellen. "What do you think?" She held the first set up to her body and then the second. "What do you think about the colors?"

"The colors look wonderful with your coloring and your hair. And yes," she peered a moment longer into the woman's face. "Your eyes. Yes. You have made great choices. Perhaps I should put this one back; it is just like the third set which you didn't show to me. Do you plan on taking it, also?"

"That's generous of you," the lady said. "No one ever says that? It is usually dog eat dog at the sale rack. If someone likes a certain garment they don't ask if another is buying it, they take it and say who cares?"

"But there are those who don't want to chance another wearing the same garment, in church, where everyone sees each other. I try not to offend anyone." Ellen was hanging back the garment in her hand.

"I insist. Let me. I have these two and truly I don't need either but a change makes me feel better." Curious, Leona asked, "Where do you attend church?" She never cared about church. She didn't really care now but this woman's warmth appealed to her.

"Christ Church, on the corner of Main and Old Street; you know the brick lined street." Ellen smiled. "If you don't attend, elsewhere, please come visit with us and I hope you will feel at home. We love our church family." Ellen glanced at her watch. "Please, excuse me, we have an appointment and I promise if I see you at church I will come speak to you. Bye now."

"But you haven't purchased your selection."

"We will return."

After their appointment, Ellen returned to the shop on chance the lady was still there but she wasn't.

"Momma, I think that boy with Dr. Fawk was that ladie's son. He looked just like her."

"He did, didn't he?" Ellen held her hand up for a high five. "You are very astute, Sherlock." Ruthie laughed.

"There's more. I think the lady and the boy are part of what God is putting together in my mind."

"Oh, Ruthie, should I worry?" When Ruthie grinned, Ellen sighed, "With you, wonders never cease."

Chapter 8

Evan finished mowing the Sister's lawn. They were scheduled to return from visiting relatives in Tennessee. For their age, which he guessed somewhere between late sixties and early eighties, the sisters traveled a lot, in fact continuously. Aldean often said, "We don't need a home, just a tent we can fold up and carry on our back, set it up wherever we go and take it down and carry to the next place." They were spending an afternoon in Evan's shop trying to learn what he did to build a violin.

"You do like indoor potty's and showers, though, we've noticed." Geri reminded her sister.

He had hoped they would return before he left the premises but it was not to be so he headed on back to the shop. Si was to lock up before he left but he wanted to apply a last coat of laquer to the Corelli, a smaller violin at less than a thirteen inch over all measurement ordered by a private school that taught children. Their faith in him, led Evan to name the newly designed instrument after a school founded in the sixteen hundreds.

The order concerned him in the beginning. Do you have violins with an over-all measurement of possibly twelve inches? These are small children three to five year olds with an arm length possibly seventeen to seventeen and one half. It is our belief they will fall into the typical one eight violin measurement but we bow to your digression as a luthier. Many of our students are using the Mendini. The Mendini was one of perhaps five brand names for violins and Evan was familiar with the instrument.

He found the door unlocked. In disbelief he stood by the door, listening and viewing the scene before his eyes as though it were a movie reel playing out a sad story. The two buckets of lacquer previously used sparingly on the instruments had been splashed around the room. The display cabinets had been broken into and the instruments missing. The racks used to assemble had been torn apart and hacked into pieces. It was a heartbreaking scene of destruction. Where was Si in all of this? He side stepped the splotches of wet debris on the floor. Surely Si had left for home and locked the door. But they had entered anyway. Who would know about his shop? Quickly he sent Jewel a message. Come quick. Problem here. She had been home for an hour by now. He returned to the question who knew about his shop?

The write up in the Nashville paper only mentioned the state, not the town. Who would punish him and for what crime? Had he offended someone? His mind was flashing warning and searching for reason at the same time. Once, he thought he heard a noise and stood still listening. There, it came again and it seemed to come from upstairs. Choosing a two by four left over from building display cases, he raced up the stairs.

He found Si, taped to one of the poles that supported the roof, his arms hanging limp, blood oozing from his forehead, and his shirt torn in various places he guessed from being dragged up the stairs. "Si?" He spoke his name softly, half afraid his helper was dead. The way his arms hung limp was not a good sign. He discovered the sound he heard was a vent that had come loose with the wind passing through daily. Hurrying back downstairs he found a knife on the floor and went back up to cut Si loose. Si was a small man but dead weight was to be reckoned with when a man was unconscious. "Si." He laid him on the floor and was patting his face when Jewel arrived and fell on her knees beside Si's unresponsive body.

Si was in the hospital three days and during that time Jewel visited his wife in the nursing home morning and evening as Si was accustomed to doing. Waking, Si was disoriented but time brought him around. On the fourth day he was able to tell them one person came through the door interested in buying an instrument and he was completely taken by surprise when another entered and knocked him unconscious. He didn't remember being dragged, neither the stairs nor being taped to the support beam.

When the police came to question Si, Jewel was at work at the Gates.

"Please," Evan cautioned, "Watch where you step."

"Could you identify the person asking about buying an instrument?" The officer asked Si.

"I could but if they were headed to another state what good will that do?"

"Did they mention another state?"

"The one that came in last said to the other, "Are you ready to head back to New York?"

"What happened then?"

"The one I was speaking with seemed to caution him and then I was out, nothing thereafter."

"How did he caution him?"

"With his eyes and his hand; He lowered his hand as if to stop the other one from speaking."

"How many instruments did they take?"

"Seven from the cases and thirteen on stands around the room."

"Man, you run a shop on thirteen violins? That's almost unbelievable." His voice bordered ridicule.

"There are a number going through assembling scattered over this floor," Evan replied."That is why I cautioned you to watch where you step and please do not step on the pieces."

"Man, why aren't you picking them up?" In Cullum's eyes this man was a loser.

"Insurance agent told me not to touch anything."

The door opened with a swush. Harriet Becker came hurrying in. "I came when I heard, Evan, and I'm so sorry." She glanced around and saw the other two. "Well, Officer Cullum, we meet again. I do hope you are treating my friend right." She motioned for him to come forward. "Do you see what's missing? This man builds very expensive instruments." As though she had heard the officer's remark, she continued, "Unlike many who run shops, his inventory will not number high but the dollar amount is impressive. So what are you doing to help my friend?"

Officer Cullum was like a runner grounding himself before he replied. "I'm sure you've already put out an all points bulletin or possibly a road block to check contents of vehicles headed all directions. You know there are only two outlets of main interest to the Cape due to the river backing up the city on one side, and the highway the other, therefore only two are necessary. I believe you could catch the thief, unless you have dilly dallied and let him slip through already." Her eyes were piercing. "Have you done that?"

"No ma'm, I've got to check whatever I do with my Chief."

"Cullum, do you suppose you will ever want to run for Chief of Police to the Cape?"

"No, ma'm, I'm not sure I could handle it."

She shook her head and made a tch, tch, sound with her lips as she stood in one spot looking around.

"Evan, what is the next step?"

He glanced to the officer; his distrust for efficiency was growing by the minute. "The police department should put out a bulletin to all states. That would mean if anyone purchasing a violin was informed they would also be cautious. That bulletin needs to be in the hands of every instrument dealer in the United States. That is actually all the hope we have left, that someone runs onto one I've made."

"Is there anything I can personally do for you, Evan?"

"No, ma'm. I'm afraid Si and I must start all over but first we need to salvage the pieces scattered all over this floor and see how many can be saved."

"I'll leave then and you and Jewel come for dinner tonight so we can talk."

"Yes, ma'm."

Officer Cullum was scratching his head as the door closed. "Is she your aunt or something?"

For the first time since the break in, Evan smiled. "She's something."

* * * * *

The town was abuzz with news of the break-in. "I didn't know there was an instrument shop. What is the location of this shop? Did you say a violin maker is called a luthier? Is he an old man to know this? Thus went the questions and statements which would remind them Evan's business was active. The pain of loss griped his stomach but Jewell's presence always settled him down.

"You made the paper," Jewel whispered. "If you weren't famous, you are now." She buzzed a kiss on his ear. "The local newspaper wants to interview you. I will sit with you through the interview."

He caught her and pulled her close. "Just hold me tight for a minute," he asked. "I don't understand this. Just give us a minute and then you can head on over to help Miss Harriet, if you need to."

* * * * *

"Thank you for having us," Jewel finished placing the silverware beside the plates. "Evan has suffered a serious blow to his business." She paused to stare into space. "He had months of work into the finished violins but since opening the shop he and Simon were assembling the small ones for the children."

"Was he able to save the pieces that were strewn on the floor?" Harriet and Hattie were carrying in the soup tureen and matching bowls. "There now," she said. "We have the oyster soup, a salad and dessert. Do you think we can get by on that?"

"Smells heavenly and looks lovely," Jewel replied. "Oh, Miss Harriet, I'm trying to remember the special touch you put on everything and take lessons from you. I just feel some day because of Evan's work we will entertain and I do so want to do it right."

"You notice there are five place settings?" Harriet laughed. "Well, Hattie wants time with the children and Marigold and Matt will be dining with us. Let me tell you, there was a day when Marigold and I butt heads over what was proper. I learned it doesn't have to be traditional and she learned a thing or two from me…but we were at each other like…"

Hattie took it up. "It was World War Two all over again. I thought they'd kill each other, then they found out they are mother and daughter and things began to change. You just can't kill your folks."

They heard laughter. Marigold was standing in the doorway, listening. "We got over it didn't we, Ma?"

❋ ❋ ❋ ❋ ❋

They were enjoying each other's company. Marigold kept things on a funny kell and Matt was her straight man. The evening took a turn when Marigold asked, "Jewel what's new with Penny Coleman? I haven't seen her around but I do see her husband with Charlotte Green about every day."

"It's not good." Jewel glanced at Evan. "Is it all right, honey, if I tell them?" Evan nodded.

"Charlotte has moved in with Sutton. But word has it, his mother isn't happy about that either. I'm not friends with Charlotte, but she came to borrow an item and sit down and told me a lot about Penny and Sutton and his family."

"Word comes through the shop," Marigold replied, "But you have to sift through to figure out if anything is true. It seems Sutton number two now has a mistress." Marigold shook her head. "That's sad even if it is Sutton's mother and she doesn't like Penny, still she, too, was always on the prowl."

"Prowl?" Matt asked, his eyes on Marigold. "What does that mean?"

"Purrll." Marigold did a good imitation of an animal's call. "You know, she's looking."

"Poor Penelope," Harriet offered. "She seems like a good girl and I know her folks are hard working people. When I served on the maintenance board at church, Will was also serving and he did a lot of the repair to keep the church from having to call on someone else. I don't know if that's fair."

"I hope one day to be able to help in that area," Matt added.

"I was in Penny's predicament once; it isn't easy having to make all the doctor visits without your husband." Matt leaned over and hugged Marigold. They heard him say, "I'm sorry."

"I feel sorry for Penny," Jewel replied. "I try to be a friend to her but how do I tell her about Charlotte?"

"I'm sure she knows." Marigold paused, her fork midair. "This town keeps tabs on it's own. Nothing's secret. Before I left the shop, a lady told me she heard Evan Jacob studied in Italy with the masters. Is that true, Evan? She knew the exact place. She said Cremona, Italy."

Evan almost choked on a spoonful of soup. Blushing he said, "Not that I know about. I wish."

✳ ✳ ✳ ✳ ✳

Dr. Fawk sent many of his patients to The Cape's St. Vincent's Hospital. Therefore he must join the other doctors in sharing several nights a month in Urgent Care. He and his young prodigy were there when Penny Coleman was brought in by her parents. She was cramping and labor pains were intermittent. Penny recognized Ben, immediately. "What are you doing here, Ben?"

Dr. Fawk spoke up, saving Ben the explanation. "Young Ben and I have an agreement, Penny. He intends to become a doctor and I am to be his mentor. He will learn a lot working with me. Do you mind his being here as long as we keep things chaste?" Penny nodded consent.

"Are you bleeding, Penny?" He pressed on Penny's upper abdomen. "You're filling in pretty good."

"No, Sir." She glanced quickly to where Ben stood out of Dr. Fawk's way. "I'm having a few pains but mostly I'm cramping." She seemed to regret being there. "I didn't know whether to come in or not."

"You always feel free to come see me, Penny. I want to know how you are." He turned to her parents. "You two go home and get some rest. I'm going to keep Penny here with me overnight. I'm going to put her in one of the rooms next door and young Ben is going to help me check on her through the night. How does that sound to you? If anything comes up, I'll call you."

When they were gone Dr. Fawk left Ben with a child that had fallen off the top bunk of his bed and had a huge knot on the back of his head. He went alone into Penny's room. She was lying very still looking out the window. Dr. Fawk sat on the end of the bed. "Penny, what's going on? I think you are mistaking the cramps for spasms caused by the tension in your body. You are as tight as a wound clock, Penny."

"I was afraid that was it, Dr. Fawk, but my parents are so fearful I'll give up and something happen to the baby."

"You have heard the stories about your husband, haven't you, Penny?" She nodded. "So have I."

"Yes, Sir." Her voice was pitifully soft and she was on the verge of crying. "First his mother didn't like me. Then he wanted to stay out all hours of the night drinking and I can't do that, and now he's living with Charlotte Green." Penny sighed. "Dr. Fawk, for as long as I can remember Charlotte has been living with men; usually other women's husbands."

"Do you think Sutton ever loved you, Penny?"

"I'm not sure now. I guess I just loved him so much I didn't think it mattered. I thought he'd change."

Dr. Fawk reached for Penny's hand. "Have you learned anything, Penny?"

"You can't change people. They have to change."

"What else?"

"I want this baby. I don't think Sutton's family will ever want it, but my family will."

"Do you have a lot to look forward to, Penny?"

For the first time she smiled. "Yes, Sir, I do and you are trying to tell me Sutton's going to be Sutton so I better be me and do my best to stay healthy and have a healthy baby."

"I couldn't have said it better." Dr. Fawk placed her hand back on top of her stomach. "You feel that baby move and you think good thoughts; don't dwell on Sutton. He will either straighten up or he won't. It's out of your hands. But this baby…you are in control. Think good thoughts. Listen to peaceful music and before you know it you are going to be holding this baby in your arms. How does that sound?"

"It sounds good. I guess I had to hear it from you." Tears brightened Penny's eyes. "Thank you, Dr. Fawk." He was almost to the door when she added, "Dr. Fawk, Ben's the best one of all."

✳ ✳ ✳ ✳ ✳

Three o'clock in the morning, the sirens were going off. They were near enough to Jewel and Evan's home they sound as though they were inside. "What is that?" Both Evan and Jewel sat up in bed, frightened for a moment until they identified the noise. "Something has happened on our road." They dressed, locked the door and walked down to the intersection, a four way stop known for accidents.

"That looks like Sutton's truck," Evan said. "Oh, Lord, I pray not. It's bad."

"Where's the other vehicle, Evan?" Jewel strained to see. "There's only one, it can't be bad."

"It's under his truck, Jewel." Evan was gripping her hand. "Maybe we should go back."

"We can't, if it's Sutton." Their hands were locked together. "Evan, how could that happen?"

"He was going too fast. It's a freak accident, Jewel. Oh, dear Lord, what if he's dead?" Now they were advancing, their hearts beating frantically as they pushed on and came to the scene of Policemen, paramedics working and the lights on the ambulance blinking in the darkness. Three high way patrol cars had lights trained on the vehicle, Sutton's truck. Sutton was laying on the side of the road, a paramedic working with him as a second spread a blanket over his body. They watched as the blood pressure cuff went around his arm and waited to hear. "It's too low. We've got to bring it up." One of the men turned toward the people gathered around. "Does this man have family present?" No one replied. "Is there anyone here knows this man?" Jewel and Evan spoke up. "We do." The two men conferred. "Come up." They went as requested. "If you know him, we need you to talk to him. Tell him what the weather was today, whatever you can think to talk about let him hear your voice, his blood pressure is too low, we can't move him yet as we have others to check out."

"Where are the others?" Evan had seen only Sutton.

"They are cutting the vehicle loose from his truck, since he has that raised chasis, there may be life."

Jewel was talking to Sutton, holding his hand, now and then squeezing it and hoping for response.

They could hear the paramedics. "I can't tell if there's a pulse. She is so limp she appears dead. Is there another? Lord, God, help us. Her skin is stripped to the bone. No, I don't recall seeing either of them. Easy there, slide her on the board. You smell that? It's gasoline. If anyone lights a cigarette we will be goners. It has run across the road. I just didn't know it was dripping on them. The roof of the car is stuck to the underside of the truck. Thank God the wheels were knocked loose. I've never seen anything like this. Easy. Easy. This one in the back won't make it, the back of her head is hanging loose. God in Heaven help us. Bring that board closer and I'll get her on it but someone will have to put their hand at the back of her head. Buddy, Buddy. I smell smoke. Someone's struck a match. Get outta here. I'm behind you." It was as clear as a bell, their conversation. Jewel knew she'd remember it as long as she lived even while she and Evan took turns talking to Sutton. Just when they were worn thin and ready to give up, she heard a hoarse whisper. "Where's Penny?" It's not Penny, Sutton, it's Charlotte. "Is she okay?" He blacked out again. On the outer edge of the street men were beating out a fire that was spreading toward the truck. Paramedics were rushing toward Sutton's sprawled body with a board.

When he was loaded into the third ambulance, the paramedic asked, "Can you get hold of his family? Tell them we are taking him to St. Vincent's. The two girls are being transferred to Memphis by helicopter to the trauma center. You heard us talking, one of them is in worse shape than the other and the first is questionable. If you know their family, please let them know, otherwise it will be hours before the message gets to them. They have no identity on them. He has a billfold but no license."

"His name is Sutton Coleman. We didn't see the ladies but we suspect one would be Charlotte Green."

"We will see you at the hospital," One hollered back. "Thanks for your help talking to him."

Jewel called Dan's cell number. "Dan, I'm sorry to bother you, but there's been an accident. Do you know Sutton Coleman's parents? They need to be notified, but Evan and I are new to this town. In fact, we know the prayer chain needs to be started, but Dan we are at a loss to…I don't know…they told us to come to the hospital…anyway they said they'd see us there."

"Oh, thank you, Dan. Yes, yes, we will stay with the kids and you and Ellen will know what to do. Yes, we will. Yes. Sutton, Penny's husband is in bad shape..evidently he flew out the window and landed on the side of the road. Last we saw him he was unconscious and his blood pressure is low. Yes, we will be right over. Thank you."

They had been walking as she spoke to Dan. Now they were in the car, Evan taking a different road in order to avoid the accident which was now blocked off. "Are you all right with us staying over with their kids and they will go. Dan knows Sutton number two and they will call the prayer group into action."

"I'm relieved," Evan replied. "There's a lot of problem there, and I will pray while we stay with the children. I'm glad to have this opportunity if it must be, rather than go to the hospital."

✳ ✳ ✳ ✳ ✳

Morning brought the news. Charlotte's sister had died enroute to the trauma center in Memphis, Tennessee. Charlotte was in critical condition. Sutton had suffered from the fall, a broken nose, his left arm and the fingers on his right hand were broken, his blood pressure was still low but Sutton would fare better than expected. Being drunk had probably contributed to his lack of injury when ejected.

Unable to reach his parents Benjamin stayed with Sutton, going between rooms to check on Penny, too. Neither was aware the other was in the next room. Dr. Fawk believed it would only add to their issues.

Dan held information others lacked. He called Sutton who was at a Universal Tool's Weekend Seminar. Leona thinking to thwart the plans Sutton might have with Elaine went with him. "It's Sutton, Leona." Dan could hear the conversation. "Dan's on the phone. Sutton's been in a bad wreck. Two people have been air lifted to the trauma center in Memphis." Dan heard Leona's gasp of pain. "Sutton?"

"Penny's in the hospital too, Sutton. Dr. Fawk is in charge. I only know this because Evan and Jewel were on the scene of the accident and held Sutton's hand throughout the ambulance pick up. They came to sit with our children while we start the prayer chain for these young people and we will be there, at the hospital for Sutton until you arrive." Hanging up the phone, Dan shook his head. "This is terrible. They don't know the Lord and hope is beyond understanding, their hearts are breaking. Let's pray about this."

"Lord, God, our hearts are troubled, we bring that heartache to you knowing we are helpless to mend lives. It is our job to care and pray for friend and enemy and Lord it is difficult to pray for someone who wrongs us. This family, Lord, needs you. Every one of them, Father. They have hurt that goes all the way back to the day they were born. Strengthen Sutton for the news he will receive and Penny to be well. Lord you know their need in ways we cannot; now we leave them in your hands thanking you for your intervention, your authority and your love. We praise you dear Lord. In Jesus name…..Amen."

✳ ✳ ✳ ✳ ✳

The Sisters arrived the next Monday morning in full gear, all talking at once, wanting to know about the accident, that boy Sutton and why wasn't he with his wife, Penny? Evan ask them to come sit in the back of the shop, a place he and Jewel kept swept of dust with a bench and three chairs, just enough for visitors that didn't linger too long.

"Well, I didn't know this building looked out on to the city pond that is part of the old West Park," Aldean went to one of four glassed windows that bore grass cloth hangings, not pretty but worth lowering when the sun was hot. "Very nice, Evan." She sit beside Nina. Geri was left to fend for herself but she was caught in a coughing spell anyway. "Now tell us what you know about the accident."

"I don't know anything extra above what the newspaper article reads."

"Surely you know if Sutton is back with his wife and with Jewel and her friends. What about Sutton? Has anyone told him the sister died?"

"Ma'm, from the time Sutton was in the ambulance I haven't spoken with him. I don't know anything."

"But what happened to Charlotte Green and Penny, his wife?"

"You know," Geri spoke softly, "they were married in our back yard. You were there. That makes us kin." The long sentence brought on Geri's coughing, again. Evan was watching. What he was seeing on the handkerchief she held to her mouth brought concern. "Ma'm. Ma'm," She stuck her handkerchief in the back pocket of her coveralls. He risk insulting her but they all needed to know if what he was seeing was indeed what he was seeing. "Ma'm? He wanted to shake her. "Geri? Now he fairly screamed, "Miss Geri?"

"For Heaven's sakes, young man. You never scream. Is something wrong?" Geri was walking to him.

"What did you just do with what was in your hand?" They were all focused on her hands.

"Did I do something wrong?" She was oblivion to his meaning. "Did I have something belonged to you?"

"No, ma'm," Evan's voice was thick with concern. "Feel inside your pocket."

Geri did as he asked and pulled out the used handkerchief spotted with bright red blood. She began searching her body for an open wound. "Where do you suppose this blood came from, my bad tooth?"

"You were coughing, Miss Geri." He was horrified. "Come, he said, taking her to the small restroom with a mirror over the sink. "Look, there's blood around your mouth. Please, please, don't let anything be wrong."

Geri began to laugh. "I love your concern, Evan, but I think it's this bad tooth I've been battling since we went on the cruise and sometimes it bleeds. The dentist says it has deep roots and will be hard to pull. I've tried to decide to have it dug out and then I chicken out and leave it…until it bleeds again."

"It only bleeds now and then," Aldean said, seeing Evan's distress she meant to comfort him.

"But why does it bleed at all? I mean, have you seen a doctor, Miss Geri?"

"No, sweetheart. I am quite overwhelmed that you care. No one takes anything about me seriously."

"Well, we may not say it but we do, Sister," Aldean reminded her. Geri knew when Aldean used "sister" she was past irritated and there would be no excusing the next words out of her mouth. "When that renegade husband of yours took his children, that you claimed as yours," Aldean's eyes were flashing daggers at Geri, "When that happened, we stood by you, even when you paid off that good for nothing's children's maxed out credit cards, when he tried to empty your account Mother left to you and lied to the bank and tried to get into mine and Nina's."

"There's no need rehashing this, Aldean. I'm quite aware how you felt about Gerald and now I realize you were correct but I can't say that often enough to please you and if I say I'm sorry again will that make my regret any more profound than the million times in ten years I've told you?"

Aldean was standing over Geri who had slumped back into the chair and seemed to crumple up like a rotten bag of potatoes with no starch in her body at all. Nina gave a deep sigh and pulled at Aldean's arm. "you are going to have to let bygones be bygones." Her soft voice held no weight against Aldean's.

"Tell him we care, Geri, the poor man has a bad feeling about us because you are bleeding. How many times have we taken you to the dentist and you refuse to let the dentist pull that tooth?"

"So don't take me anymore. I can drive myself. Do you want me to move out of the house, Aldean?" For the first time Geri screamed at her sister. "I'm tired of hearing my history five years past. Do you understand?"

Whether her sudden movement or the rise in her voice, blood spewed from her mouth and her nose as she gagged and tried to control its source. She couldn't talk nor could she stop the flow of blood.

"She's hemoragghing," Nina cried. "Call nine one one." She had left her phone in the vehicle. "Please, do you have a phone?"

Evan rushed behind the counter, found his cell and was punching in the numbers. He gave the address. "Yes the same building where the instruments were stolen. Hurry."

Evan was in over his head. He couldn't call Jewel, she was at the Gates with five children. What could he do? He held Miss Geri until the ambulance arrived and the EMT's loaded her onto the gurney for transfer to the ambulance. "I want to ride with her." He locked the doors to the shop.

The EMT was changing pads, soaked bright red. "Are you family?" Lying, Evan nodded, yes.

"Her son." God forgive him for the lie, he had the feeling if he didn't stay with her she would die. The minute he saw the blood on the handkerchief he knew it was cancer. Why hadn't someone told them? How did he know? He just knew. She doesn't have long the words were burned in his mind. Should I tell her? No, the doctor will explain to her and her sisters. Just listen. They had given her a shot, while he was praying to cease the blood. He wondered which of the two stopped the blood's flow some twenty minutes after they arrived at ER.

It was nearing six o'clock when Jewel arrived. Evan had been in the ER waiting room all day.

"Trouble comes in threes," Jewel quoted. "What else could happen pertaining to us?"

"It has all become a nightmare," Evan said. "I've reached a point I can't make sense out of any of it."

"You are tired, Evan. Your mind, your body. You have been trying to make sense of the shop being broken into, and nothing coming from the search for the instruments. How could you be involved in this?"

"It makes no sense. She reminded me of pictures I'd seen of my mother. Then when she started hemoragghing, my mind raced back to the death of my father's wife. She had cancer and haemoragghed, blood everywhere, the bed covers, the floor…on me…" his voice dropped down to a whisper, "I didn't want her scared."

"Will they tell you when she is being taken to a room?"

"I don't think they will move her from Intensive care this soon, do you?" Evan stood, his legs were beginning to cramp. He hadn't eaten all day. "I didn't tell you why they allowed me to stay with her."

"I assumed they needed someone. Are the sisters gone?"

"They were all three at our shop when this happened." He had her attention.

"Is something wrong?"

"No, I think they wanted the latest gossip, but they will know the next time, I'm not their source." Wiping a hand across his forehead and eyes, he returned to sit by her. "I lied, Jewel. She was in such a bad way when the ambulance started to leave I ask to ride with her. They ask who I was and I said her son."

A low hum built in Jewel's chest as she looked to the ceiling, and the sound became stronger, finalliy to become a laugh of sorts. "Sorry, I tried to swallow that down but it just wouldn't go," she apologized. "That is so out of character for you, Evan. Did you really say you were her son?"

"I felt I was hers at the moment. I knew exactly what was wrong and they still haven't told us. It is cancer in her lungs and it has metastasized to her throat. I think her tonsils will literally fly out one day. When the bleeding is at its worse she can't breathe and tries to breathe through her mouth."

"You saw her tonsils?"

"No, God impressed upon me and also that she doesn't have long to live."

"Oh, no. But the sisters know, right?"

"No, God said let the doctor tell them."

"Where are they?"

He glanced at his wristwatch. "Four hours ago they said they were going to the flower shop."

"Jewel stood in front of Evan, staring into his face. "You know, my life has not been the same since I married you, nor will it ever…" Her smile was such it removed the sadness from his face for a moment. "I think our lives together are going to be…" Her words were interrupted by a message on the intercom.

"Code." The rest of the sentence was covered by a loud buzzer at the nurse station.

"What was it, Evan? Code blue or something else…It began just as the alarms went off at the Nurse's station. Do you think they are connected?" Nurses appeared from rooms and one from behind the counter walking at a brisk pace, nearly running down the hall. "Evidently it's important."

"Yes." Already he had hold of her hand and they were moving toward the area they told the sisters to wait, adjacent to heart surgery, just in case they were actually there.

"Careful," Aldean cautioned when they rushed the room. "We don't need to interrupt anyone that has settled down." She motioned toward Nina, asleep on the window seat. "Maybe we're late in knowing what's happening to our sister but.." A buzzer was going off again. Aldean stepped out into the hall. "I believe that alarm comes from Sutton's room." She was headed that way.

"How would she know where Sutton's room is?" Jewel whispered. "Things like that are kept private."

"Believe me, she would know. If she didn't she'd ask until she found out." His face was set in a way Jewel hadn't seen before. One thing she knew Evan was tired, his physical being under strain.

"Are you angry, Evan?" She was hurrying as fast as her feet would move but he was pulling her along.

"No, I'm something else, I don't know what. Why didn't they pay attention to Geri's cough?"

✳ ✳ ✳ ✳ ✳

There was a group of twenty or more medical students in a half circle around the hallway but the action or lack of action, whichever, was happening inside the room where the doctors were gathered. Two, one on each side of the bed were leaning across, removing an instrument. One said, "He's back." Another moved forward, older, perhaps wiser he took in the scene of his patient on the bed looking pale.

"It's Sutton Coleman; His heart stopped. They used the paddles." A red haired young man in a white coat whispered the words that everyone was waiting to hear. "He's breathing again. Listen." The hall was quiet enough to hear a pin drop. "That's strange." Everyone waited again to hear their spokesperson. "He said give my lungs to someone and anything else that's working. Shh, doc's talking."

"You listen to me, young man. You quit feeling sorry for yourself and pull out of this mess you've gotten yourself into. No one's getting your lungs, you need them yourself. You got a wife ready to pop with your child in the next room. Straighten up and I'll see that she comes in to see you. Otherwise, I'll send her home and you will just lay here and wonder how she's doing. You hear me? Squeeze my hand."

"He must've squeezed old doc's hand." Suddenly everyone near the door straightened and stood still as the doctor's passed by.

"That last one's Dr. Fawk," the student in the white coat informed them. "He's a crusty old guy but he'll probably make that fellow stand up and walk."

He walked straight to the desk. One nurse had run to be there when he arrived. "Find my associate, Benjamin Coleman. Tell him Dr. Fawk said collect Sutton's wife and take her in to see him."

Dr. Fawk had walked possibly thirty feet down the hall when he turned and hollered back. "Is that you Marshall MaQuire? Giving a play by play account of what's going on in Sutton Coleman's room? It took me a minute to connect your voice to the words, of course that patch of red hair on your head helped."

Hand in hand, Evan and Jewel were on their way back to the room where the sisters waited. They were listening to the nurse's chatter as they walked along beside them. "I thought we'd lost him. They said he's not out of the woods yet," the nurses were whispering as they returned to class from observing Sutton Coleman in his room. "I don't think they give much hope and they are letting him talk to his wife. You know he's under orders by the sheriff's department until determined otherwise he can't go anywhere without their escort because he caused the wreck that killed Charlotte Green's sister, and it's being investigated."

"When did he get a wife, this is the first I heard of her." The nurses turned down a different hall.

Evan pulled Jewel into the doorway of an empty room. "Jewel. I need desperately to go someplace that's quiet where we can pray. The loudness of the situation batters at my soul. I must spend time with the Lord. He is trying to tell me something but the sharpness of this situation prevents my hearing. It is as if the devil has the upper hand and only time with the Father will bring the peace we need. Presently, I feel I am one of the disciples out on the raging sea waiting for Jesus to get in the boat."

Jewel's heart swelled with compassion seeing grieving in the lines on Evan's face. Hadn't God told her he was special? His life before her had been quiet, his parents seldom talking and then they died. He was special, Evan Jacobs. Where, Lord Jesus? She asked the silent question and the Holy Spirit answered. "There's a garden beyond that wall. You will be alone. Take Evan there that he and I may speak."

✳ ✳ ✳ ✳ ✳

Jewel had not seen a garden as small but complete as this one, it reminded her of Daniel and Ellen's, except where theirs had an angel this one had a cross. The sign read simply Garden chapel. Soft music, mostly from a harp was playing, so soft one would think imagined. Two concrete benches were the only items on the stone floor. Evan sank on his knees beneath the cross. "Oh, Lord," his whispered word came to Jewel's ears as she sat on one of the benches, her mind full, her spirit doing unction for her. "Oh, Lord, my heart is heavy. You have told me Geri will die soon and that troubles me. Why does she remind me of my mother's picture, Lord? I lift her up, to you Lord, knowing Geri will find peace in you if she will call on your name. How Lord, will she call on you if she does not believe? I am exceedingly sad for her, Lord and I ask you father, give her time to come to your throne of mercy. Thank you Lord, for the mercy and grace you bestow on us when we are so undeserving. Father, there's Sutton and Penny…you alone know your plan for them, help us to lift them to you that your work will be done in their lives and his family, Oh dear God of mercy, let your grace shine on them that though they do not ask they will see their need for you. Bless the doctors who work with their patients and bless the sisters who seem not to know who you are…Father wrap us all in your love that we look to you for peace and calm in the midst of these storms of life. Lord, help us; help Jewel and me to live your plan for us, to be a witness to others. Thank you for this garden we come to to talk with you when our hearts are heavy and our mind will hold no more. Thank you father. I love you and ask your forgiveness. In your holy name. amen.

Jewel praised her God, thanked him for life its self and for Evan, asking a double portion of his love on her husband and healing on their friends. She ended her prayer and opened her eyes to see Evan standing smiling down on her and the weariness and lines of worry had left his face. Peace shined in his eyes and she prayed it was so also with her.

Returning home they fell into bed. It was minutes away from midnight and morning would come too soon. Evan would join Si at the shop on his first day back and Jewel would finish the week at the Gates.

✳ ✳ ✳ ✳ ✳

It was a time of reckoning. Benjamin padded softly toward the patient rooms. The sisters had told him they were on to his game. In other words he wasn't asleep nor awake and it was his job to see after their sister.

Checking his e-mail he found no text from his family but it was their way to forget he was part of them. He wondered about his own sister. True she was a year older than him but it always seemed he was taking her part against the parents, defending her spontaneous actions. Perhaps I should check with her he thought as he came to the Sister Geri's room.

She opened her eyes as he stood observing her. "I'm still here, son," she whispered.

"Never a dull moment," he said aloud. She actually smiled, "Yes, you're right." He listened to her heart, checked her pulse. "You are doing great." The smile faded.

"Has Evan gone home to rest?" Her eyes closed but he knew she waited for his answer.

"He said to tell you he will be here when shop closes but if you need him call and he will come immediately."

"Send my sisters home. I don't have the strength to see them. Make up something, please."

"I will," he said, patting her hand before he left. "Weren't you my teacher in third grade?"

"Yes, I remember you. You were the nice one; your sister was a hand full and your brother rotten."

"That's us. The rotten Coleman family." He would whistle a tune except he didn't know how to whistle. Taking out his cell he called LeAnn. "How are you?"

She was cross as usual. "Sleeping. It is not noon yet. If it's before six o'clock, I swear I'll kill you."

"It is six fifteen to be exact. I've been up all night and I feel great. So, how are you?"

"Pregnant. My boobs hurt. Mom's not speaking. Dad doesn't know what to do with me. I'm getting married next month. Will you give me away?"

"Breathe," he said. "Sure, and take you back when he gets through with you."

"He's the only decent person I know."

"Then why are you ruining his life?"

"I'm not, he's saving mine. I intend to live my life with him."

"For heaven's sake, LeAnn, try to mean something for once in your life, if he's decent…."

"I will." She turned over and he heard her soft pearl of breathing.

"I'm learning to pray," he said into the phone. "I listen to Sutton's visitors and I think I'm getting the hang of it. I asked Jesus to come into my heart when they led Sutton. He didn't commit. I did." He was testing her. Evidently she was asleep. "I'm serious. You need Jesus, too, before next month."

Before he left Dr. Fawk arrived. "Is it possible to accept Jesus in your heart when someone is trying to lead your brother?"

"Sounds like you were listening when the Gates prayed with Sutton." Ben nodded. "I'd say it's possible. The question is did you ask Jesus in and has anything about you changed?"

"I have hope and yes, I said Jesus, come into my heart. I need you."

"I suspect Jesus opened his arms wide to accept you, Son." He watched Ben leave. "The Gates would be happy to know about you, young man," he said aloud, "but why won't Sutton accept; the shape he's in?"

✳ ✳ ✳ ✳ ✳

Penny arrived to help Sutton with breakfast. It was his left arm in a cast and he was left handed.

Sutton watched her. She was huge with his child inside her belly and he was seeing her for the first time as a pregnant woman. While he played the town's dashing romeo, his wife had grown from a girl into a woman.

"Have you forgiven me, Penny?"

"That's a deep question first thing this morning," she replied.

"Have you forgiven me, Penny?"

She fed him and left. Sutton thrashed on the bed as much as his swollen body allowed. "You had a hard fall, Sutton," Dr. Fawk explained. "Your insides were literally scrambled by what the scan tells us. No damage we can see but it takes time for things to go back into place."

"Do you think Penny has forgiven me, Doc?" He felt the doctor was sworn not to talk about him.

"What is forgiven to you, Sutton? Forgiveness comes through the Lord."

"I speak of Penny's forgiveness, no one else."

"Have you ask her to forgive you?"

"No." Now he lay there wishing he could turn off his mind but all he had done to Penny tumbled through his thoughts and yet he couldn't bring himself to say he was sorry. He was sorry for himself; he'd been told he was now under supervision of the Sheriff's Department. They were his personal attendants. For that, he was sorry. He wondered about Charlotte and her sister. He hadn't intended the wreck that was Charlotte's fault. She stopped right in front of him less than a cars width away. By noon, he had worked his body into a complete breakdown. His arm cast was wet from the sweat. The nurse sent for Dr. Fawk.

"Bring that gentleman back that I've seen with the Sisters. No, I don't know his name." He had to suppress his inner shakiness, he couldn't think beyond what he was seeing at the moment. "When Evan and Jewel left me, this couple appeared and I guess it being a man, I remember…he said he knew my father and Old Sut."

Dr. Fawk left the room to return with a list of visitors the Nurse supplied. "There's Penny, your brother, Benjamin, Evan and Jewel Jacobs, Aldean and Nina, of the three sisters but Geri is in hospital, too." He straightened his glasses and saw two last names. "Ellen and Daniel Gates."

"That's it. Gates was the last name." He gripped Dr. Fawk's hand. "Could you ask him to come see me?"

"Have your folks not been in to see you?"

With Dr. Fawk's piercing eyes staring right through him he couldn't lie. "I pretended to be asleep. That keeps them off my back. They will blame me Charlotte and her sister got hurt when it was actually Charlotte caused the whole thing."

"How's that?" Dr. Fawk was heads up, listening, evidently he was unaware Charlotte's sister died.

"She stopped a full stop right in front of me and I ran over her little car. It was low to the ground and I have my truck jacked up and those big wheels." He noticed the doctor's expression. "I couldn't help it."

Dr. Fawk called Daniel at work and explained Sutton's request. "I'll come in after work," Daniel promised.

✳ ✳ ✳ ✳ ✳

"Sutton, I'm Daniel Gates." He offered his hand. Sutton didn't shy away. "How can I help you?"

"Are you a minister?" Sutton was disappointed when he said he wasn't. "But you quote bible verse. I need to talk to someone that can keep a confidence, you know, like a doctor or a lawyer."

"I'm neither," Daniel replied, "But I can keep confidence if that's what you want unless we are breaking the law." The room became quiet to the point the drip of water at the sink was all they heard. Sutton was thinking things over and making a decision.

"I'm going to trust you." He took a deep trembling breath. "When I start I can't stop or I won't finish." Daniel Gates nodded agreement as he pulled a chair up by the bed. "I got a girl pregnant and married her. I married her because I do love her goodness and she was a good girl. I was intrigued by that. But I couldn't live the life she thought I should, one woman, don't go anywhere without her, but she believes in God and said it was against her belief to go to bars or even nice restaurants to drink. She won't drink." He breathed deep, again, the breath seemed to go just to his upper chest and no farther. "Then I became so irritated with her I began to cut her down, make fun of her and her family and she took all this, kept on taking care of the place we lived, keeping my clothes in top shape, asking me to attend church with her and I wouldn't. Finally I got so mad I hit her. Pushed her out of bed and she landed hard and couldn't walk straightened up for two weeks…she left me afraid I'd hurt the baby inside her, so she said. I never thought much of what was inside her as being alive to be hurt but she was counting on that baby and thought it would make me settle down and I told her never."

"There's this girl, she's fast, everyone knows it, she flirts with every man, young, old, rich, poor and if there's a dollar to be made she'll go to bed with them and she always has money. But she likes me. One night I said I had to iron my clothes, my father told me to quit coming to work looking like a bum. I work for him. I think you know him but I've never seen you in our store. Anyway, Charlotte's her name and she went home with me, stripped down and ironed my clothes with me looking on. We didn't get intimate that night but eventually we did because she just moved in without asking, just took residence."

"Sutton, I believe I have the picture. Now what does that have to do with my being here? Did you need confession to clear your conscience or is there more?"

"There's more. It got worse. Her sister moved in, too and Penny heard. Occasionally I called just to hear her voice but she wouldn't talk to me. Her father started answering my calls and told me Penny has a restraining order against me." He tried to breathe but the breathing seemed to have too much time in it start to finish and he felt his head getting a dizzy feeling. "Then there's the wreck. You showed up, but my brother was here for Dr. Fawk and he said Penny was in the hospital not doing well with the baby and Dr. Fawk said to tell her about me and bring her in my room. Benjamin did that and unknownst to her parents Penny came and sit with me. I heard her praying. She said for my salvation and she sound like she cared. But she's gone again. She hasn't died has she? You'd see it in the paper."

"What did you feel when Penny prayed for you?"

"Nothing. I'm just being honest even if it shocks you. Since then, I've thought of nothing but her prayer. Over and over she ask God, let him see he needs you, let him ask you to come into his heart. Give him peace he's never known and in time let the joy that comes from you envelope his life." Sutton forgot and tried to rise up, wincing as the pain knocked him flat on his back, the mattress squeaking beneath his weight. "That struck a note. I don't think I've had peace since I was a little boy and maybe our family has never known either peace or joy she spoke of but her family does. I've seen it."

"You would like to have peace and in time joy?" Daniel asked the question as though Sutton's life depend on it. "Tell me what peace or joy are to you, Sutton. Let's see if either or both are within your reach." He noticed Sutton had turned pale from the fall back on the bed but he was breathing a bit better.

"Peace would have been me and Penny happy with each other but I had too much of the old way of life in me. Joy? Joy is what Penny looks forward to when our baby is born. It wasn't because of me; it was looking forward to the baby."

"You think your peace and joy depends on someone else, Sutton?"

"Doesn't it?" He was quiet, thinking, "I believe Penny is my first hand experience to see peace and joy."

"No, Sutton, when God moves into your heart old things move out and the feeling you experience lets you know you don't even miss them and you think Penny didn't recognize you in her joy looking forward to the baby? Why, Sutton, you planted the seed that developed into a baby that will be a part of both of you, that is a type of joy. But the joy you have that comes from God passes all understanding. It is a joy that bubbles up in your being because He has come to live in your heart. Scripture says,"know ye not that your body is the temple of the living God?" From the time you ask Jesus into your heart, the Holy Spirit moves in and stays with you until eternity."

"What is eternity?" Sutton was feeling impatient and the need to hurry.

"Eternity is our ultimate goal to be with the Lord. We don't just live out this life, die and that's it. We go on to heaven. Scripture speaks of heaven but no man can tell us the glory that awaits us through one simple act of believing Jesus died for our sins on the cross, arose from the grave he was laid in and now abides by our father in heaven."

"Do you actually believe that hog wash?"

Daniel arose from the chair. "I believe, Sutton. I wish you believed. I'll be leaving now, but if you ever need me, call me and I'll return and we can study scripture, such as John 3:16. Just read the whole chapter."

A glum countenance and a definite ache between his shoulder blades was Suttons. "I'm sorry I bothered you." Daniel offered his hand. Sutton refused. "I'll not be asking for you or anyone else," he said.

"I have a list of scripture that if you read them might help you in your search. It does require the real man in you to read them to find any kind of understanding. I'll stick it in the Bible I saw in that drawer."

Chapter 10

Dr. Fawk arrived before breakfast was served. Sutton had worn himself thin into the early morning hours and was now in deep slumber. Irritated, he fought off the doctor checking his vitals. "I thought that was the Nurses job. I already warned her."

"Young man, you have no consideration or respect for your elders. Your folks failed to spank your rear end when you were a child, otherwise you wouldn't still be acting like one."

"That's hurtful," Sutton replied. "That bears reporting, then where will you peddle your idioms?"

"I've been around here longer than the property trees. Telling anyone about me won't get you very far. No one cares and I have Seniority over the rest of these ya-whoos."

"Since you're here, how is Penny?"

"Who wants to know? That's privileged information." Under his breath Sutton called him a name. Dr. Fawk pinned a look on him. "That won't get you anything." He hung the chart on the end of the bed and left muttering. "I can just imagine after summoning Daniel Gates you probably didn't listen to a word."

* * * * *

"How was your hospital visit, last night?"

Daniel was reading the sports section of the paper. "If I were a baseball player, I'd say I struck out."

"It's not yours to make conclusion, only to spread the word." He glanced up to see if she was smiling.

"I tried but there were many road blocks. He just thought he was ready to hear. I left the list."

"This doesn't mean he won't think it over and if you left the list of scripture for him to read, it's all you can do; First Corinthians three, seven. Remember? So neither the one who plants nor the one who waters is anything, but only God who makes things grow, the one who plants and the one who waters have one purpose." She leaned down to kiss him. "God makes it happen."

"What's the news on the Sister in the hospital?"

"That would be the one called Geri. Jewel said she has cancer of the lung which has spread."

"I truly hate to hear that and we've not become acquainted before this all happened."

"It's in God's timing, Daniel. Perhaps now there's something we can do to help our neighbors."

"This is your last week with Dr. Lonzo?" She nodded. "I'm glad; The kids and I need you."

"As far as Jewel understands, the sisters don't believe in God and that's strange, I heard their mother was a wonderful Christian and practically built the church she attended."

Daniel was turning in his bible to the morning devotion. "So they are atheists?"

"I don't know if we should label them atheist." She sat opposite Dan for the reading of scripture for their morning devotional, before they both rushed off to work and Jewel arrived.

"What are they if they don't believe? Unbelievers? That sounds a little less harsh." He glanced up, "our scripture is Ephesians chapter six, beginning verse twelve. "For our struggle is not against flesh and blood but against the rulers, against the authorities, against the powers of this dark world and against the spiritual forces of evil in the heavenly realms." He was turning the pages in the Bible. "Back to chapter one, Blessed be the God and Father of our Lord Jesus Christ who has blessed us in Christ with every spiritual blessing in the heavenly realms. And finally verse twenty one, He is far above all rule and authority, power and dominion and every name that is invoked, not only in the present age but also in the one to come." He kept the Bible open as he stared into space wearing a troubled expression.

"What is it?"

"Have you considered there are young people whose lives have been shaped before they realized it could have been different than the bitterness and unrest they feel. My heart aches for this young man."

"Sutton? I was wondering about the sisters with their sweet little mother's influence. It could be the things that happen to them through the years." She yawned, knowing a full work week would bring them each day to seek God's word to help them through whatever situation presented its self. "God has given us a desire to lead others to Him. Let us pray for strength to run the race and not fall out."

He reached for her hand. "Lord, God, Heavenly Father, we need you. We are weary with concern. What if one of these dear souls died before knowing you? Lord, we pray for time for coming to know you, to accept you into their lives. For ourselves, Heavenly Father, we thank you for watching over our family, for the many blessings you give us that we take for granted. We are not entitled, Lord. We want to do our best but we ask you to strengthen us that we do not fall along the wayside. Today, Father, we ask protection on our family that the ways of the world cannot creep in to destroy the peace and calm that comes only from you. How easy it would be to look the other way and find ourselves in such unrest. Now as we face the day, dear Lord, we leave our family in your hands even as we ask your blessing on friends and your love to remain in the hospital rooms where they abide and to covet your presence. In your Holy name. Amen and amen. He waited now, his head bowed, for Ellen to finish the prayer.

"Thank you Lord for saving my soul, for being there helping me to press on even when tired and for the everlasting joy that comes from you. For blessings unnamed, we thank you. For your mercy and grace, we thank you. Now as we ask forgiveness for our sins we praise you. In Jesus name…amen."

"Could you ask Jewel to stay over that we might go once more to the hospital to see our friends?" He sighed. "There's unfinished business there, but we would not overstay to cause rift to her plans."

* * * * *

Leona stared hard at the newspaper Sutton was holding that covered his face. "Will you please put down the paper and look at me and tell me what are we to do about our child?"

He laid the paper on the table. She sat across from him. She hadn't removed her make up from the previous day, mascara had run rivulets down her cheeks, a swirl here and there where she had swiped her hand across her face, so great was her misery over Sutton's accident and one of the girls dying. She had forgotten her own vanity for a time?

"What are you going to do?"

"You go against my judgment day after day when he's a teenager, now you want me to fix a grown man's problem?" His voice was cold and cutting. "I'll speak with Bill Taylor whether there's likelihood Sutton won't be held responsible for the girl's death. If it's manslaughter, our son could be going to prison."

Her sudden wail sounded through the house. Startled, Sutton rose quickly and closed the door between the rooms. "Do you want LeAnn down here asking a thousand questions?"

"I don't care. I'm scared they will take him from the hospital and lock him up. He couldn't take that."

"He can take it as well as the next man. Get hold of yourself, Leona. You're the one they'll come for with a straight jacket. Go wash your face." He was at a loss, he'd never seen her this way.

"Is there no hope?" She walked into his arms, knowing his reluctance to touch her, still she asked, "Please, Sutton, hold me."

He had wondered what it would take to break her of her high handed ways, not caring how she treated the help, never couching her words when something went wrong and now here she was needing comfort when she had spurned his presence the last five years. Haughty, better than him, now she needed him? "I'll be going to the hospital before I go in to work. Do you want to go?"

"No." Her voice was a whisper. "I can't bear to see him there, besides he won't look at us."

✳ ✳ ✳ ✳ ✳

They met coming from different directions. Daniel was deep in thought when he bumped into Sutton.

"What brings you to the hospital?" Sutton had one hand in a pocket jingling change.

"It's a spontaneous decision to visit our new neighbors, one of them entered this week to find she has lung cancer in an advanced stage." Pausing, Daniel wondered if it were wise to mention Sutton. "How's your boy, today?"

"I haven't seen him yet but I'm told he was in a fizz yesterday. Don't guess you saw him?"

"Actually, I did. He asked for me but then he wasn't pleased I have an opinion on some of the things he's interested in."

Sutton's father laughed. "That would explain the fizz. He loses control in facing negative flow." The smile disappeared. "Do you mind telling me why he wanted to see you?"

"To understand scripture, but Bible scripture requires action few are willing to take."

"There's a table and chair around the corner, do you have a minute to sit and talk?" Sutton turned toward the table. "Here, out of the way but still where we can have some privacy."

"I have no need for privacy, Sutton. Your son asked me to help him understand but he made it clear he wants no commitment and there's little I can say after our visit together. He said he wouldn't need me."

"Then why are you here?"

"I've not been a good neighbor to the sisters who built down from us, and as I said earlier, one is ill.'

"Yes, you did mention that." Sutton pointed to a chair and waited for Daniel to settle in. One of Thursday ladies came with two glasses of ice water. She smiled and left. "I was a bit taken back by that," Sutton reflected, "I didn't know they do this." He indicated the glass of water.

Smililng, Daniel quoted, "Matthew ten, verse forty two, If anyone gives even a cup of cold water to one of these little ones, who is my disciple, truly I tell you, that person will certainly not lose their reward."

"I don't know how you do that. Why did Sutton balk at hearing scripture?"

Daniel took a pocket sized Bible from his shirt. "Let me show you rather than tell what Sutton and I discussed." Unseen by the two men, LeAnn settled more firmly into one of the two hi-back chairs by the hearth. Picking up her feet, she slipped into her real dream, to do the class anthem in front of a large audience. Her voice was wasted in the Cape. No one let her audition because she was the poor little rich girl. She almost laughed out loud, and now she was pregnant. She doubted she finished school. It was all history by the time the two at the table finished. Why exactly, did she feel lifted of a burden? She did nothing wrong. She intended to marry the most handsome twenty three year old man in the county.

"We began with John 3:16," Daniel led through the verses ready to explain their meaning "Then I switched to Romans 3:23, "For all have sinned and come short of the glory of God." We all sin. No one is innocent. Romans 3:10 speaks of all people have turned away, no one seeks God. Then I went to the consequences of sin, Romans 6:23 "For the wages of sin is death; but the gift of God is eternal life through Jesus Christ our Lord." What decision would any person make knowing the reward of sin is death but there's a better way if you believe in God and that Jesus came and died on the cross for us, we have a gift of eternal life. Romans 5:8 informs us, "God demonstrates his own love toward us that while we were still sinners, his son, Jesus Christ died for us! That means he paid the price for our sins. But how do we achieve access to all that is promised through believing. Romans 10:9 tells us, "if we confess with our mouth Jesus as Lord and believe in our heart that God raised Jesus from the dead, we will be saved." All we have to do is believe in our heart God raised Jesus from the dead and confess with our mouth He is our Lord…we will be saved. It is ours for the asking but not through works, never things we do." Romans 10:13 pulls it all together. Everyone who calls on the name of the Lord will be saved." Jesus died to pay the penalty for us and rescued us to Heaven's portals. Salvatiion starts with believing and confessing and ends with our receiving forgiveness and eternal life through Jesus Christ our Lord."

LeAnn listened. What would her father say? The man had led him through the plan of salvation just as he led her brother the day before and she heard both times. She would follow Jesus. "I ask you to come in to my heart," she whispered. "I rest on the promises and I will try to do better wherever I exist."

The days following, encountering Daniel at the hospital, Sutton decided to try the theory of salvation at home. Due to public interest in the accident and knowing Charlotte's sister had died, Sutton was not seeing the one he thought the answer to his life. By not seeing Elaine, he thought to protect her from scandal. LeAnn, knowing her time at home was short, with a wedding planned the first of October, determined the words were encouraging and she wanted to be a more loving person. Diva LeAnn was, expounding goodness to all people.

"Whatever role you are playing," Ben said, "I like it, play it to the hilt. A sweet sister is a good sister."

It was almost a happy home. Leona was in complete shock, her children behaving as adults without being threatened was a good thing. However she was suspicious of her husband and wondered what he was planning. When she asked, he replied the lawyer said they should put up a good front for their son's sake. When Sutton was released from the hospital the lawyer further insisted he rehabilitate in a nursing home. Leona visited him daily and daily he handed her the list of scripture Daniel Gates had given him.

"I don't know what to make of this."

She studied the list, collected the Bible from the drawer in the Nursing Home book shelf in the front parlor and read the words over and over. "Neither do I," she admitted. "Before long I will have some of them memorized."

"I told the man who gave me the list to not come back. Daniel Gates."

"I don't know him," Leona replied. "Where did he get your name or where does he come from?"

"I ask for him through Dr. Fawk but one of the Nurses mentioned he and his family attend Christ Church."

"What happened to your other friends, the one whose instruments were stolen?"

"I probably insulted them, too." Sutton turned his face to the wall. For him, the visit ended.

❈ ❈ ❈ ❈ ❈

"Fall is in the air." Evan propped on one elbow, smiled at Jewel. "You look peaceful lying there on your pillow. Are you tired? I counted. You fit five lessons into your schedule. I wouldn't know except I worked awhile on the back porch. We're near completion on the small violins, I can't risk another vandalism at the store."

Yawning, Jewel pat the bed beside her. "Not working for the Gates full time, I have picked up two more." She yawned again. "Oh, me, maybe I'm more tired than I thought. Anyway, the three are adults so we don't have to worry about after school hours and what child wants piano lessons before school?"

"The Insurance company called today. They won't pay coverage on the missing violins until they've done a complete investigation, thinking someone we know has them since they haven't surfaced elsewhere, or the fellow implied we might be hiding them."

"After this many months?" She sat upright. "I can't believe this world we live in. Why do people take insurance in the first place? For protection."

Evan grinned. "I've never had anyone take offense for me before. Thank you." She slid back down into the sheet and into the curve of his body. "I never had anyone love me as you do. Thank you for that, too."

"You are at peace tonight. Tell me the rest of the story." She turned to face him.

"I think the Lord is winning Miss Geri over, but," his brow became wrinkled in concern, "She is growing weaker. I try to stop by every day. Just before her evening meal is the best time…but she isn't eating much, maybe a spoonful of food per meal. Sometimes I feed her. She's so weak."

Jewel kissed his lips. "You know you are losing her and still you have peace?"

"Knowing she will go to be with the Lord is a comfort. Had she gone quickly, who knows because the three claimed not to believe in God." He pulled Jewel closer. "Now she says, Evan find that Psalms ninety one chapter and read to me, it gives me great calm in the midst of my quaking body."

"What does she mean, quaking body?"

"Sometimes the pain is almost unbearable, when the morphine plays out. Her body literally shakes. The sisters go to the Garden Chapel weather permitting, just to sit, they say, but you know those hymns are playing continually and I suspect they listen to the words."

"They leave her alone at those times?"

"I'm there and they can't bear to see her pain and don't want her to see their tears."

"What do you do, Evan?"

He was hesitant. She waited. "I pray. Or, by her request and Dr. Fawk's permission, I play the violin for her."

Jewel's body begin a slight tremor that increased until finally she said, laughing, "I should have known. There's a rumor going around, the hospital is haunted, sometimes near late evening the beautiful strains of a violin waft out over the hills that surround it."

"Are you kidding me?"

In a vine and stone walled enclosure in the center of town, a lone figure walked the boundary of a secret garden before disappearing into the interior of the stone walls. In the climate controlled rooms various treasure was displayed. Above a marble topped table that held matching candle sticks, one on each side, an oil painting of the woman at the well glowed beneath an amber light. Laughing softly that no one would suspect he was present in their daily lives, Walden walked further to study the violins, work in perfection for an owner with perfect taste. Money buys freedom he wanted to scream to the people but his was an astral life, he was there in the mainstream but unseen, alone with no human touch or voice to hear other than well paid servants who would lose their life if they told of his presence. He came to the jewels, diamonds and stones of every color, size and weight. Lost or stolen? He asked the universe knowing it would not answer. Ten years he surmised and his private and secret endeavor would grow while he underwent more surgery to change his appearance and then he would step into society in a way the present world could not imagine. There were times he caught a gleam of evil and insanity in his eyes and knew that terrible trait must be pushed down, choked out and made to disappear. It would be the ruin of all his plans. He must be sane; else it was all in vain. They thought they killed him, did they now?

He had walked the floors of Christ Church when the homeless came through. Did anyone recognize him? None but the young man had played his violin. In him he recognized a greatness of spirit. Was he the devil incarnate recognizing there was a young man with goodness pouring from his very being while he, Clayton Walden, was evil to the bone and had learned to hide the fact of his existence from the world? Ah, yes, living in quiet had its moments. Silence is golden. He laughed his strangely wild sound. Isn't it?

We all have a high priest, he let the words sift through his thoughts as his mind traveled to the times he prevailed, encroaching upon other's rights, a mere suggestion offered directly into the mainstream of their endeavors made them his, so willing to break the law or go against the Creator's will, for a mighty dollar and their moment of fame. They had no idea he quivered and shook when the Creator's eyes were directed on him. Yet, there was a rush of adrenalin through his veins when he recklessly advanced to be slammed a distance away, again. Why don't you kill me, he asked. If my people who are called by name will humble themselves and pray and seek my face and turn from their wicked ways, then I will hear from heaven and will forgive their sin. It is their choice; you are the instrument that allows them choice. But one day it will not be… the thunder rolled as Walden fell to the floor and retched in terror.

You won't kill me. I play an important part in mankind's existence.

It will not always be so.

When the storm within his mind receded, Walden slipped back out into the garden to walk and commune with his followers. Are you there, he asked aloud. Whether he heard or not, he was uncertain but he knew evil would exist as long as the world turned on its axis. His time was coming.

Chapter 11

Harriet stood looking out the window. Down the street she saw lights on in Marigold and Matt's lower floor windows. Matt was juggling the farm helping his father and trying to be home nights for Marigold.

"Don't push Matt too hard, Dear." Harriet remembered, it was the day she worked at the shop clearing out the summer items. Marigold was marking and half pricing a stack of summer T-shirts.

"What makes you think I would do that? Young men, Matt's age, have died this summer from heart attack. I don't know how Brother Joe serves at their funerals. He has had a very trying summer, now it's fall and it seems to be as bad. There, that's the last mark downs for now." She did a walk-through of the store. "We will begin fall décor next week using foliage and then Christmas can be added right on top of it. Ruthie wants to help. I miss that child. I can spend an hour with Ruthie and feel on top of the world."

Ruthie. Harriet had to smile. Ruthie was the one broke the barriers when she first met Ellen and Anne. Andrew and Anne came to mind, hand in hand with little Addie and Andy. She prayed the legal litigation had ended for them. Anne's nerves were fraught and Andrew's temper was rising. Maybe it wasn't the judge that almost cost them losing little Adeline. She thought better of him, they were old acquaintance.

"If I could lie down, close my eyes and the Lord come for me, I would be happy."

Reviewing the group's summer progress Harriet felt the need to see Ellen and Dan and the new ones, except they weren't new. Jewel and Evan were wise beyond their years. They had proven faithful to those who took them in after the flood left them destitute. Harriet had given Evan her ancient car. "I have an old truck up on the hill once the waters recede and I can drive it out," Evan protested. Now she questioned, who stole Evan's instruments; who would do that? She always defended the underdog and hadn't they all been there at one time or another? Then there was Ruthie with the love and compassion of an ancient old druid, facing the world in an eight year old body, answering their heavenly father keeping her secret safe all the while tuned in to each of them because God made her that way.

Why? She questioned, why was she remembering? And then it dawned on her. On this date she lost Bitty, who was her best friend until the day she died. Bitty. "I want to honor you my friend. I miss you." Looking back, Harriet remembered the days she thought life would never prove other than a test and how she failed. She chuckled; finding Ellen, Bitty and Anne had changed her life, put her on a new course and allowed her to help others. Thank you Jesus, she said aloud and with that drew the curtain on the past. It was time to move on, to go forward…there were things to do and tasks waiting.

God brought Penelope Martin Coleman to her mind; just like that she thought full name but no address. What, she wondered did Penelope Coleman need? The holidays were closing in. Marigold said it has to be the best Christmas ever and Harriet had replied, "Why is that, dear?"

"Ma, we've been through so much in our group of friends but one thing we had hoped for that hasn't happened was for Evan's beautiful instruments to be returned." The ladies were unaware Andrew had entered and was standing listening to their conversation.

He had his own theory but you can't beat city hall, his alter ego reminded him. No, you can't and when the world thought Clayton Walton dead, he wasn't. Walden was a master at keeping one guessing.

"My men documented their search. In conclusion on the report they wrote, it is as if the devil himself stole Evan Jacob's instruments. There are no trails leading anywhere. We believe the instruments are here in the Cape, though they may never be found. They believe there's a dark side to this."

"It reminds me of the painting stolen from Shining Light Church; the Woman at the Well. Nothing came from that search, either. Are your men saying there are people with the mindset of the devil that does his bidding or do they believe sometimes Satan does his own work? We hear things but it is hard to believe. We don't want to believe that darkness of evil has a hold in our world."

"That is the question, isn't it?" Harriet and Marigold shared understanding as each reached for a small New Testament Marigold ordered to sell in her shop but ended up giving them away. Mother and daughter shared a moment, the New Testament held tightly to their hearts.

Andrew reached back and jiggled the bell supposed to alert the shop of visitors. "Excuse me, Missus," he grinned. "I don't believe your system is working and you were on such an intriguing subject. I sometimes think Clayton Walden is right here in the Cape and I tell you with all sincerity, I know I feel his presence at times. You ask the question, is it the mindset of the devil or one of the devil's followers?

"How would you answer the question, Andrew?" Harriet welcomed his comment.

"Definitely of the devil. I remember him saying, if the devil helps me get ahead, then I will give him my allegiance. I replied, soul, and he said, "Same thing."

"Christmas celebrates Jesus birth. He probably hates Jesus. What will happen next?"

"Hate is one thing but fear is another and I know Clayton Walden feared our God. What happens next? I am not sure Clayton knows but I would think you are right. Christmas is his nightmare. He will choose a person who is so right with God and make that person miserable."

"Evan." Marigold and Harriet said, together. "Or, Ruthie." That day was etched in their minds.

As she remembered many from the group, Harriet was determined if she could prevent whoever it was from ruining Christmas, she would, but how? First they must know who was responsible. She would think on this matter as she left it in the back of her mind, for now, it was time to open the shop. Marigold had a doctor's appointment; the shop was Harriet's for a few hours. She hoped Andrew would stop by again. They needed to talk. On second thought she text Andrew, "please drop by."

The list of necessities completed, Harriet felt relieved to know Marigold still trust her to open the shop and run it. With the children attending day care in order to broaden their horizon by being with children their age, she found a number of hours simply boring. Harriet missed being in the mainstream of life. She wasn't depressed but she felt disappointed in the way some people's lives seemed filled with excitement and hers wasn't; then again maybe she couldn't live their lifestyle. Because of the children she had dropped acquaintance with Dr. Silverman and she had heard he had a new female friend, Miss Nancy Allenton from St. Louis who had moved back to the Cape to be near her children.

The door bell rang as an elderly gentleman walked in. Dressed as though ready to go out on the water, she wondered what he could possibly need from Marigold's. He seemed rather intent on looking the merchandise over before committing himself to one particular item."Interesting shop, you have," he said as she approached him. "Are you the owner?"

"That would be my daughter. May I help you?"

"I'm looking for a good pair of binoculars."

She smiled. "You missed our having binoculars by one day. A young man bought the last pair, yesterday." That seemed to interest him, momentarily. "Are you participating in the boat show?"

"Boat show?" He turned as Andrew came through the door and tipped his hat to Harriet.

"Yes, out on the river. It's an annual affair." He was dressed for the show. "You must not live around here."

"Oh, no," he said quickly. "Around and about at times to check on possessions, but I don't live here."

"Too bad," she replied. "There's a nice atmosphere in our town but with the races today and tomorrow, I'm sure people are purchasing binoculars to see how the boats do out on the water."

"That's quite all right, my lady." His eyes were on the cash register "Life is too short to squander, don't you know?" He handed her a twenty and two one's and was half way to the door before she answered.

"Yes, it is." She turned her attention to Andrew who wore a quizzical expression. "What's wrong, Andrew?" She saw the man hurrying away from their building. "I can tell something is wrong."

"Do you know that man?" She shook her head, no. "I stood right here, Harriet, cold chills literally claimed me; I can't remember where last I saw him. He couldn't possibly know me. Why the cold chills? I don't know unless he reminded me of Walden, but that' probably because he was in our conversation." Andrew leaned against one of the stools that stood on the outer shop side. "That glib remark, don't you know was something Walden said, thinking it made him sound humorous." As if to shake off an improbable theory, Andrew shook his head. "Or, he would say, do you now? That voice will live in my head forever."

"Then, let's talk about the mere coincidence and the unlikelihood of Walden having existed when he was thought dead in that last episode we all went through. How do we protect ourselves, Andrew, and what measures must we take to catch him," her eyes tightened remembering Marigold's near death experience with Walden's interference when she was in labor.

"He is a master at eluding," Andrew replied. "Yet, that type of dress the old man wore, Walden would find it intriguing to dress the part of someone he knew he would never be. I've told all of you he is master of disguise."

"You were there the day we discussed who he would choose to persecute."

"You are thinking he would find someone like Evan a candidate? Right? He thinks of Evan as weak when really Evan is strong in a sense of the word as a Christian example and knows scripture to ward him off."

"Yes. Do you ever wonder, Andrew, that our conversation we are now having has any sense to it?"

"There's something I need to run by Daniel. I'll text him that we need to discuss something important and then Harriet; I will get back to you." He glanced at his watch. "I have a case in front of my favorite Judge in exactly thirty minutes and I need a bit of time to review. He thinks of himself as my father figure and expects only the best from me; otherwise he's on my case like a chicken on a worm."

Harriet smiled. "It's good we can smile or have a laugh together, Andrew. It wasn't always that way."

Andrew hugged her. "You are a grand old girl, Harriet. I know you pray for us as though you are our mother and I thank you for that. We are blessed in so many ways but in particular by you." He tapped the counter, "wish me good luck and before I forget I'll text Daniel now."

✳ ✳ ✳ ✳ ✳

"Daniel, did you read Andrew's text? He says there's something important we all need to discuss but not where someone with alien ears could hear. What in the world does that mean?" Ellen was trying to stack dishes while the water boiled and Daniel had come in a bit later than usual.

"It's about Christmas and our children. We don't want them to hear." All the while he is talking Daniel points to a sheet of paper he is writing on. "Andrew has reason to believe Walden is active again and possibly has bugged our group's homes as he seems intent on destroying Andrew and his friends."

Ellen raised up to meet Daniel's nod of the head and then a finger to his lips. "This is scary." She wrote.

"And far out," Daniel wrote. "I agree but he knows the man, we don't."

"I'm going to the hospital, if there's a chance Sutton Coleman will see me…or maybe he would talk to you, Ellen. Isn't this the night Aunt Georgia picks up the children for a sleep over, with Ruthie's help?"

✳ ✳ ✳ ✳ ✳

Ellen found Geri sitting up in bed, reading the day's newspaper. Aldean and Nina were engrossed in a television program. "Hello, neighbor," Geri folded the paper. "I don't guess you have heard, I'm going home tomorrow."

"How do you feel about that?" Ellen sit on the edge of the bed taking Geri's hand."Oh, my, your nails are splitting and ragged, from the sheets, no doubt." From her purse she found a file and held it up for Geri's permission.

"Oh, yes, please do. I think I have everyone intimidated." Ellen began evening up jagged edges and pushing back the cuticles. In a short time she had Geri's nails looking splendid. Geri beamed and said, "thank you."

The nurses arrived to prepare her for bed. "I think I'm all ready, and that's no pun. However, if that gentleman is out in the hall, please tell him to come in and talk to me if he doesn't mind doing so."

Laughing, Ellen said, "You know that's Dan, my husband."

"Of course, but there's a little fun in it, don't you think? He was here and tried to explain a bible verse to me but I am pretty hard headed." She grinned. "I'm pretty sure he will agree."

"You know, Geri, it doesn't matter how hard our head, the main thing is whether we believe Jesus was born of a virgin, died on the cross for us and rose again on the third day. Victorious. It's what is in our heart."

Geri clapped her hands. "In other words the beautiful story we hear at Christmas and Easter is not just a classic tale, it is true. For real?" She leaned forward in the bed, her eyes questioning. "Is it really true?"

Putting away the fingernail file, Ellen brought the little New Testament she always carried. "Geri, you were a teacher. Tell me, has the scripture been with us long?"

"Oh, my dear, it has lasted for two thousand years. The people in the Bible are so real it is as if they could step right out of the page."

"Who wrote the Bible?"

"I know the answer," Geri clapped her hands. "It was written by inspired men. Inspired by God."

"You believe there's a God?"

"Oh, yes," she replied reverently.

"Then," Ellen turned through the pages of the New Testament, "John, three, sixteen, reads For God so loved the world He gave his only begotten son that whosoever believed in him should not perish but have everlasting life." With solemn attention she peered into Geri's eyes. "Do you believe?"

"I do." The brightness in Geri's eyes only led to a huge teardrop slowly falling out to run down her cheek.

"Tell me what you believe, Geri, and please tell me when did you decide to believe?"

"I'm so ashamed," Geri began. "Our mother believed. She raised us to believe. This is the God of our mother." Geri placed her hand over her heart. "I know he lives in our hearts. I'm sure he has protected me all these years from only He knows what…and I went blithely on my way ignoring him. You see, as children we suffered to be in church every time the door opened and we vowed when we left we would do exactly as we wished."

"You were saved and baptized as a child?" She watched Geri nodding her head.

"We did that for our mother."

"Was everything you thought outside of being a Christian worth it?"

"I went on as was normal and I didn't find those tidbits outside of Chritianitiy were worth my time of day." She lay back and pulled the sheet up. "Let me think what I'm going to do with this new found religion. I feel pretty certain it will move right in, take over my life and let me know I have everything at my fingertips." Geri held her hand up, admiring the nice evenness of her nails. "Thank you."

"When did you begin to believe again?"

"Ending up in hospital, was not my plan. Now they say I'm stage four lung cancer. When the doctor said, "You have cancer, I knew I wanted under loving care, not someone who thinks of patients as someone you take under your wing and it's all just make-do until it's over. Right then, I said, Jesus please come back into my heart."

"Did you tell your sisters?"

Geri began to laugh. "They know. They've seen the difference in me."

"You, my friend, are a revelation." Rising, Ellen said, "I'll leave for today but I'll be back." Their smiles locked in on each other and their hearts spoke. "Is there hope for your sisters, Miss Geri? I know you love them more than life its self and vice versa."

"There's hope. Where are you going?" Geri held her arms open and Ellen swooped in for a hug. "You're not getting off this easy. As I understand it, the kid next door is a hard boiled egg. March in there with your little red testament in your hand and tell him the Lord sent you to do business."

Ellen leaned back to look into Geri's face. "Do you mean this, or are you teasing?"

"I've never been so serious and if you don't get the job done, send that boy in to me. Let me tell you something, if you think he can't walk…" She gave a delightful laugh. "He walks around that room all night long." Exhausted, Geri leaned back against the pillows. "Leave his door open just a crack."

✳ ✳ ✳ ✳ ✳

Daniel sat with Sutton number two at the table out of the way but in the corner, adjacent to his son's room. He watched Ellen march by, go into the son's room and leave the door open a crack.

"What's that all about?" Sutton's father asked. "Wasn't that your wife?" Daniel shook his head.

Within five minutes, there was sound of raised voices. They heard young Sutton saying, "Get out. I didn't invite you into my room. I don't want to hear your Jesus stuff and no, nothing about my wife or child."

"Daniel. Daniel." He was so wrapped up in what was coming from one door, Daniel barely heard what came from another. Surprised he went to Miss Geri's room. She pointed to a wheelchair, only the backend of its silver wheels showing from behind a door. "Bring that to my bed, Son. Then close your eyes while I flop down into it. That's right. Are the wheels locked? Then close your eyes and here goes." All Daniel knew was the chair was a bit heavier, covers were hanging off the bed and Miss Geri was in the chair. "Now, go next door. I have something to say to the young man."

"Who are you?" Sutton stood by his bed addressing Ellen in the corner. "What is this rush on Sutton Coleman day?" He whirled, nearly stumbling as the woman from the room next door wheeled in.

"Young man," Miss Geri began. "Get back in your bed and prepare to listen. Yes, that's it. You will be over tired tonight when it's time for a bath. Now, young man, I am seventy years plus, I have lived a good life but three months past they told me I have stage four cancer of the lungs. Now at my age I don't know your life background, but I know this, you need the Lord." She coughed and then asked for Daniel to pick up where she was leaving off. "Tell him he had a close call and next time he may be dead."

"What do you know about anything?" Sutton glared at Geri, then turned his hateful face to Daniel.

"I'll tell you what I know," Geri put the tissues over her mouth momentarily, then continued. "I was afraid I'd die and go to hell. You better think about that and the pitiful mess you've got yourself in, that young girl dying and you don't know if they'll blame you or not. I heard you crying in the night and I cried with you, so don't you tell me something's not scaring you because it is."

"What girl died. Charlotte?" Sutton sank onto his bed. "No, oh, no." Then he felt his dad come stand by his bed, he knew when his father laid a hand on his arm, that feeling when he was little and Dad kissed him good night. "Dad, is it true? Charlotte's died?" There were tears running down his cheeks. "Dad, Penny doesn't come anymore. She did come and pray for me. Then she quit and Mom doesn't come. Why, Dad?" The cocky young man they all knew now sit there a broken little boy

"Son." Sutton Coleman was a broken man. "She comes, but you tell her to leave."

"But she shouldn't leave, Dad." A sob broke as Sutton's shoulders shuddered and his dad pulled the sheet over his son. "She's my mom…..Dad…did Charlotte die?"

"Charlotte's sister died in Memphis."

"Can I go home, Dad?"

"I ask, Son, they said no, you are up on charges of manslaughter. They have a state facility preparing for you."

"I'm in prison when I leave here; is it out of state?"

"No, it is state run."

"Isn't that unusual?" Sutton was coming out of the shock of everyone jumping on him.

"Lie back, Son and think about it. How else do you think you'd be treated? Drunk, in a wreck and one of the girls already has died, the other not responding to anything."

"God help me," Sutton exclaimed, pulling the covers up to his ears. "Everyone, please leave."

"No, Son, I think you need to listen to something. These fine folks are going to clear out, except me, you and Mr. Gates. I want you to listen to what he has to say. It may be the difference between life and death."

"Not without you, Dad."

✻ ✻ ✻ ✻ ✻

Ellen was unsure whether to wait for Daniel or return for him since they were together but Sutton having the temperament known to clear rooms; she decided perhaps she should stay. She found the corner table and was sitting there when Leona recognized her as the lady in the dress shop.

"Well, hello," she said in greeting. "you did go back to the dress shop, didn't you? Wasn't what you are wearing one of the dresses we were fond of?"

Extending her hand, Ellen said, "I don't believe we had time to introduce ourselves. "Ellen Gates."

Smiling, Leona took her hand. "I'm Leona Coleman, Sut Number One's daughter in law. Everyone knows him. The next two Sutton's haven't made a name for themselves until this summer, now they are." She shuddered. "It wasn't part of our plan. I've heard your name mentioned Mrs. Gates."

"You've come to visit your son?" They were appraising each other. Ellen decided she could like Mrs. Coleman.

"Yes, if he will see me." She fingered the ends of her hair, a tip off she was stressed. "Do you have children, Mrs. Gates?"

"Please call me Ellen." Ellen smiled. "Yes, we have two sets of twins and our oldest daughter, Ruthie."

"Is Ruthie a teenager?" Pulling her hands away from her hair, she said "If I am to stop fiddling with my hair, I nearly have to sit on my hands." She tried to laugh but the laugh had an almost touch of a sob to it. "I ask about the teen stage because, truthfully, you may have heard, I have a seventeen year old that is to be married next month. A sixteen year old following Dr. Fawk around at the hospital and then there's Sutton who is responsible for an accident that killed a young woman." A tear rolled down her cheek. "I have this terrible fear Sutton will spend years in prison, it depends how he is tried."

"First, may I say I'm sorry your mind is so troubled at this time. Has your son given his version of what happened? Sometimes when one is injured and can't talk for self rumors are spread that are not true. As for your second son, I did see a young man with Dr. Fawk and I would say my impression of the doctor is that he is a wonderful man, a good example for your son and lastly, congratulations on the wedding."

"No, she's pregnant. Our daughter probably planned the whole thing to get out of our home." Leona fell back into her old ways temporarily and said, "I doubt you in your chaste Christian world would understand such a worldly family that seems to delve in sin. For that matter, my husband is having an affair with a good little Christian lady, also." She flicked a piece of lint from her skirt. "If I sound bitter, I am. My world fell apart while I wasn't paying attention."

"What were you doing?" Ellen found Mrs. Coleman studying her from squenched eyes, almost closed.

"I was doing what other rich women do, watching out for myself, though I ran a beautifully clean home, placed three delicious meals on the table daily whether they come home or not, and I kept my body toned and well groomed. Is that what you wanted to know?" She saw only kindness in Ellen's expression. "Well, I do have help. I organize, they do the jobs. All of them." She sighed. "I hope you have help. And if you don't I'm truly sorry, you must have days you don't know which way you are going."

Ellen laughed. "That might be most days, but I'm getting close to being home full time again." She leaned toward Leona, "Mrs. Coleman, it seems our husbands know each other, we should be better acquainted. When I return full time as my children's mommy and Daniel's everything, please come see us." Her smile was so genuine and the inflection in her voice and words, kind, Leona was moved.

"I apologize. I don't think I even asked you to call me by name, Leona. And Ellen, it has been years since anyone has wanted my friendship. I feel honored. When your life settles down, perhaps we could do lunch."

"And yours. I will be praying for you Leona, as mother during two very trying situations. May God strengthen you and give you peace through each time of need. I hope you look down the road and see the love the new baby will bring to your lives. You know in the Bible it says a little child shall lead them."

"What do you think it means?"

"I've always considered, first it meant the love and innocence of a child will keep us in line with Jesus, but further than that, we love our children so much we want only what's best for them that we can afford, and they make a better person of us."

"Oh, Ellen, I'll think on that. Sut is waving for me to come see our son. It has been delightful speaking with you."

"A blessing, Leona. Good evening."

Chapter 12

Struggling from the deep sleep, patting the bed beside her, he was gone she had known. She found him sitting at the table, the Bible open, his hands supporting his head. Taking a moment Jewel thought this is as I first saw him, in faded blue denims, his hair in need of a trim, but his eyes were so intensely alive taking in everything around him and I felt he was someone I needed to know. Head bowed, eyes closed, did he know she was there?

Her heart skipped a beat. What if he had not felt the same about her? Life had been very strict, a box with four sides and only one door she could leave when given permission, at her age it was almost unbelievable and yet she had lived that life. These last months with Evan, the freedom was exhilarating. He was concerned about the supply of violins made for the school. It was time to put them on display and yet, he could not, losing the first violins had left its mark and made him cautious.

The time had arrived for Jewel's student's first piano recital, and she was hesitant. Few would understand the lives she and Evan lived previously. They were living freedom in a way she and Evan would never take for granted but with that new found treasure came responsibility.

"What shall we do?" Her arms around his neck as she stood behind him, she kissed his neck and then lay her head on his shoulder. "We have decisions, don't we and I know you've been praying about them." Reaching around, he pulled her to sit on his lap.

"When I pray I see this place, similar to the Garden Chapel at the hospital but I'm mystified why it shows up in my prayers. Do you understand? Like if we pray for Penny and Sutton their picture might be so vivid in our minds but this is a building or a wall I've never seen."

"Are we to build a wall, Evan?' Her forehead to his she looked through distorted eyes to his.

He smiled. "I don't think so, but what are the chances we find this one? The Cape flowers and spreads over places and they disappear like the secret garden."

"It probably is someone's garden you've passed by. Can you sketch what you've seen in your mind?"

"I did." From beneath the place mat he pulled a gray leaded sketch. "I felt silly doing it."

"Why, Evan, isn't that right down town, you might say the center of the shopping district they tried to make more appealing? Why would you feel silly sketching this? It's wonderful. You are very talented."

"Be positive, if it brings results try to remember the Lord is behind this. Now," she squirmed on his knee, "where shall we hold the children's first piano recital?" He had that look of needing to say something. "May I help you, Sir? I can tell you need to say something."

"Hmmm, oh, yes, what about my one guitar student?"

✳ ✳ ✳ ✳ ✳

"What?" LeAnn shrieked. "Did I forget I would be asked to do concert? Well, no. When?"

"Don't overload with items, because it is too humid to have to carry around excess baggage."

"Today?" LeAnn jumped from the bed, hopped into the shower and in fifteen minutes time was fully dressed and ready to join the thousand other teens who have nothing of worth but an expensive collection of singers committed to making it big in the world. LeAnn had once hoped to play guitar in one of those successful groups but now she was dedicated to becoming mother of the year.

"Where are you headed", her mother asked as LeAnn struggled with her arms full and the guitar hitting against her legs.

"Recital. I had forgotten."

"I'll go with you."

"Really?" She was suspicious of her own mother. "Why are you already dressed and want to go with me?"

Leona shrugged. "I'm trying to be a better parent."

"Then come on. You can drive."

"Where to?"

LeAnn read the instructions on her phone, from messages and Jewel Jacobs. "From one hundred Old Brick Road turn right on Heaven's Way Street and it is number seven at Christ Church Boulevard."

"At a church, how quaint." Their arrival was a sweet tip off of good things to come. A gentleman offered to park their car or show them where to park. "You have my permission to park it," said Leona. They left the car in his hands, following the pairs of foot prints on the concrete, right up to the portico of the church where well dressed ladies came for them and ushered them to the musician's room.

"You may leave your instrument and I will walk with you to the make up room." She smiled a brilliant welcoming smile that belied anything other than kindness when she spoke.

"How can a piano teacher do all this?" Leona spread her hands. "It is almost a wedding, not a recital."

✳ ✳ ✳ ✳ ✳

Evan saw LeAnn arrive with her mother and waited for LeAnn's return from make up. "How do you feel about the two pieces, traditional and religious, being combined?"

"I like it," she grinned and winked at her instructor, "and this shinding so decorative is not bad, either."

"I had nothing to do with it. But, maybe I should prepare you, Jewel ask that I begin the Recital."

"Cool," she replied. "Does that mean you are playing violin?" He nodded and she exclaimed, ""Very cool." Turning to her mother she said, "Mother this is Evan Jacob's my instructor. My mother, Leona Coleman." Evan's natural kindness was shining through in his delight for Jewel's success.

"Happy to meet you, Mrs. Coleman. Your daughter is a delightful student, very talented."

He was leaving as Ellen gates came toward them. Leona stood and the two embraced to LeAnn's surprise. She couldn't wait for the lady to leave. "How do you know her? She's Mr. Gates wife." LeAnn wrapped her arms around her body. "It was Mr. Gates trying to lead Sutton to salvation that I listened to and received the Lord into my heart."

"You did?" It was Leona's time to be shocked. "You and Ben? Sutton needs it but refuses?"

The lights dimmed. Jewel took her place at the piano. Evan stood to her right, some three feet away as she began Chopin's Nocturne Op. Approximately five bars in, Evan positioned the violin and raised the bow. The lights dimmed further as the candles on the piano created shadow. The students on the front row leaned in with their audience and listened as they were transported through time and each heart knew the desire to be accomplished as were their teachers but too soon it ended.

"Welcome," arms outstretched with a warm smile, Jewel stood before them. "Welcome, to our very first recital showcasing three months of the world's love of music coming into our own hearts. I promised the children, yes, we, the teachers would perform, but briefly, for they are the showcase of today, their hard work, patience and showing up for a very important step up the ladder of learning their instrument of choice."

"We have taken the liberty to use the screen to capture each child as they arrived and played each weeks selection. I think you will recognize the determination to learn and their pride in accomplishment. That said, the screen unfold from above and a perfect likeness of little Melonie Camp appeared.

"Our first star is Melonie. Melonie is three years old. We help her on and off of the piano bench. Right now, Melonie plays mostly two octaves, her scale is center of the piano and she does it very well. I won't tell you the name of the piece she is playing because I know you will recognize it, immediately."

Whether it was the private insight of Jewel into each child now shared with parent and friend or their child's performance the audience supported and encouraged each child and when little Kenny Hornsby seemed to momentarily forget what he was playing for a full five minutes, the visitors clapped hands and chanted you can do it, you can do it, Kenny, you can do it. Kenny became so tickled he put his hands on the keys and finished with wild abandon. He then bowed and waved to all.

It was LeAnn brought the Recital to a successful end. She began the first piece entitled Country as scenes of country roads, hills and streams and mountain filed behind her silhouette. There would be a photo of her and then a majestic view as the Song entitled Country ebbed into How Great Thou Art. By the time LeAnn finished the audience was standing in silent appreciation. There were tears in the people's eyes as LeAnn stood. "Thank you." She said.

An older gentleman spoke from the mid section of pew. "Young lady to what do you attribute your great talent?"

"Sir," LeAnn looked around as the lights were slowly brightening. "Mr. Evan Jacobs has taught me to recognize the value of each piece of music but I need to tell you, in the last week I gave my heart to God. I ask Jesus to come into my heart and even I see a greater depth to my guitar ability."

"Was your decision or knowledge of your choice pressed upon you by your instructor?"

"No, ma'm," Le Ann stepped forward to see who was speaking. "It was never mentioned. My brother was in the hospital and we were not certain how severe his injuries. What happened is this; a man came and quoted scripture to my brother. The man knows my brother rejected the scripture. What he does not know is that I was saved to eternity." The lady turned and left the pew and the room while one by one the others came to congratulate the students and several thanked LeAnn for her contribution of music and her testimony.

✳ ✳ ✳ ✳ ✳

Dan stopped in to congratulate the two on their first recital.

"Oh, man, it's all Jewel." Evan's pride in his wife was showing. "I only have one student and truthfully I've not taught her guitar, she already has her own style but I was able to show her a few insights."

Dan chucked Evan on the shoulder. "I hear there was a moment of sweating drops of blood. Right?"

"Truly. I haven't discussed anything with Jewel yet, but it was heart stopping. LeAnn cleared us." He thought a moment. "Actually, Dan, LeAnn was very brave. I didn't see it coming and I don't think she did."

"God works in mysterious ways, his wonders to perform." Ellen gave Evan a hug. "It was marvelous. The parents are surely pleased with the still life video and impressed with their child's performance. Now, we are collecting our five from the Nursery and going home. God bless you both." Evan was smiling and thanking her for her help all the way to the doors that separated sanctuary and church class activities.

✳ ✳ ✳ ✳ ✳

October moved into November. Geri was growing weaker each day. "I don't know if I'll make it to Christmas," she said. She walked very seldom now. The wheel chair had become a friend. Nina had made a small carrying bag from canvas with straps that buttoned over the side bar for Geri's tissues, cough drops and paraphernalia. The scarves fit her head more like a bandits each day. She had become so small and thin it was her bone structure you saw first and then the magnificient smile.

"I wonder if the Gates would come sing for us tonight? Seems I'm bored to the bone and it's making me figidty. She peered down the street to the Gates property. "I'd love to see their fountain once more. There's something about that angel settles my longings."

"Tell me about your longings," Nina's soft voice encouraged.

"I don't know much about heaven, do you?" Shaking her head no, Nina came to sit in the chair opposite Geri.

"Are you thinking about Heaven a lot these days?"

"Afraid so," Geri agreed. "There's not much else to think on, except I do wonder about that Coleman boy that was in the room next to me in hospital. He cried and when he cried I cried."

"Why do you think he was crying, Geri?"

Geri liked watching Nina. She had the innocence of a child. It was no wonder she spent her life teaching Kindergarten students. She fit into the seat, could look them in the eye and her voice took them by surprise. They listened afraid they would miss something she said in her soft way. "Sister, he was scared. You know, his wife is Will Martin's Penelope. But Sutton is such a terror, feeling entitled to having a girlfriend while he has a wife with child on the way. Still his crying made me sad."

"He lost the case. They're sending him to the State facility at Jefferson City. He leaves next week."

"I've seen it from the Interstate, I believe, when we went there as a group of teachers." Geri coughed, swallowed a bit of red liquid from a bottle in the side pocket and waited for the cough to quit. "Do you remember going there, Nina? I would say from his location he will look out on the Capital and then there's that magnificent church steeple. I do believe Thomas Kincaid used it in his paintings."

"I don't know," Nina replied. "Old towns have churches with steeples. Thomas may have used another place."

"Want to bet on it?" Geri smiled. "Use to, we would have bet for the heck of it. Where's Aldean?"

Tears spiked Nina's eyes. "What will we do without you?"

"Don't you worry. I'm leaving you things to take care of so you won't remember I'm gone."

"What do you need right now?"

"Nothing. You can rest but later…I'd like to call Sutton at home and talk to him before he leaves, then if you'll ask the Gates if they'll sing for me…and I guess I have to give up on seeing their backyard, don't I?"

Nina laughed. "Probably yes on the mobility, especially if it's cold outside. The rest, I'll work on." She hurried into the kitchen where Aldean sat hovered over a cup of coffee. "She's looking for you."

"I can't do it. I'm not strong like you and I don't intend to keep her upset with my crying."

"You have to. She's still here, Aldean, Who knows we may not have her in another week."

✳ ✳ ✳ ✳ ✳

Jewel's five o'clock lesson was canceled. "She's running temp," the mother informed Jewel. "I think she needs to stay in." Agreeing, Jewel started dinner. It would be nice for her and Evan to have time to discuss the week's business and she had found pictures she wanted to show him. She was browning meat for Spaghetti when he arrived, washed up and found her in the kitchen. His eyes lit up seeing dinner was almost ready but most of all that they had time together. "Here," she said, "you do this, I'll make salad and the spaghetti is ready to drain. How's that?"

"I stopped by to check on Miss Geri, probably five minutes, but she had tired out and was asleep. It is sad what she has asked Miss Nina to do, but I understand completely."

"What's that, Evan?" Finished with the salad, she crossed the room for the pictures on top of the black oriental chest. She laid them out on the table side that bore no dishes. He was draining the grease from the browned meat. Emptying the package of mix into the meat he added a half cup of water and stirred. "Umm, that smells professionally done, like a true Spaghetti kitchen. Hmmm." She sat the bowl of spaghetti in center of the table, by the smaller one holding shredded cheese. "Wonderful."

Taking their seats, they held hands and Evan said the blessing. "Thank you, Lord for another day of blessing and your protection.

We pray for others in need, Lord, and especially for lost souls. Now we ask your blessing on the food. May we use it to strengthen our bodies that we might better serve you. We love you and praise your Holy name. Amen.

"Now," he said, helping Jewel with spaghetti before he filled his own plate. "Miss Nina said Miss Geri spoke of Christmas today, afraid she won't be here and the sisters are sad. She ask me when the Gates decorated for Christmas as they were gone last year during the holidays. It seems Miss Geri has a longing to celebrate Christmas with her sisters and friends. I truly had no idea to answer the question."

A slight smile worked across Jewel's face as she listened. When he was finished she pointed to the pictures. "I found these today."You must look at them when you are finished."

"You have spiked my attention, why not now? He arose and went to the other side of the table. As he studied the pictures he glanced her way, a smile on his face and in spite of his body feeling the day's work the pictures inspired him. "Jewel this is wonderful. Where were they?"

"I pulled the bottom drawer free from the oriental chest and they were beneath the drawer lying on the dust panel at the bottom. I'm sure leaving them behind was unintentional."

"It is the sister's Christmas with their mother. They are decorating the house." He sat back down to his dinner. "If we could do the same for them, Jewel, what a special gift of love. Did you notice the love for their mother so evident on the sister's face, in those pictures?"

They were quiet for a spell, only the sound of a fork on a plate. "Have you been in the attic, Evan?"

"No," he smiled. "Now I remember…what did they tell us?"

"There's decorations in the attic." Spontaneously, their hands went up in a high five.

Hurriedly, the dishes were finished. Evan pulled the ladder from the ceiling down to the garage floor. Jewel waited and then the boxes came down, four in all sealed tight but labeled Christmas. They were excited as two children, smiling, going through the boxes and then the call to Nina.

"Can you come for five o'clock dinner Saturday? I'll come for Miss Geri and carry her to the car. Miss Harriet's car will accommodate her very well. Yes, a surprise and a bit of work to follow. See you then."

✳ ✳ ✳ ✳ ✳

"I like your new sign." Daniel watched Evan fit the back to an instrument front. "Man your wood shines like a new penny. I suppose that's a secret?"

"Yeah, it is," Evan replied, holding his hand on the violin while glancing at the one Daniel was studying. "it's gauze, like a doctor uses I'm told, fine gauzy material that takes down the last little bump. It works for me but it might not the next person. Some finish with the lowest abrasive sandpaper but I find it leaves a slight marking."

"There's a call on my phone from you. Anything I can do for you, Evan?" Evan relayed his visit with Miss Nina and Miss Geri's comment. Dan listened and began to smile as he learned what was in process. "we would love to come. Why couldn't we all sing? That's the night Aunt Georgia spends time with our troop. Perfect." Extending his hand, he said, "come out and look at my newest product, you may need one. I can get you the sample for nearly nothing."

The conversation away from Evan's shop was not Daniel's newest product but plans the group were sitting in action geared toward the holidays with hope in their hearts to recover Evan's stolen violins.

It was mid-morning when Evan heard the door buzz and came from the back to give assistance. He thought he recognized the lady but couldn't place when he had met her. She was elderly, dressed a bit warm for the fall weather, a scarf on her head and a shawl around her shoulders, but then the elderly were often cold when others weren't. "May I help you?"

She seemed to be studying the room, not the instruments but she said, "I would like to see your violins, please." Her voice. Her voice. He must bring her into conversation. "Do you play, madam?"

"No," she replied, "my children are quite ept, but I do not." Pointing to one, she asked, "Could you?" While he played the violin she closed her eyes with her head tilted back and he saw emotion wash across her face. As he lingered with the bow on the last refrain, Evan remembered where he had seen her. "I need to think on this," she said. "You play beautifully, I'm sure I will return."

Her visit left him shaking as fear pressed through his very being. It made him afraid to leave his shop.

Andrew was investigating areas he would not know how to navigate. That gave him a degree of comfort but with the completion of the smaller violins for the school, Evan worried. He needed to get the message out. Dialing Andrew, he asked, "Could you refresh my memory on where you sent your copier when it needed repairs? Yes, I do still have the box it came in. I'll pack it up. Thanks, Andrew."

Leaving the shop that evening, straining beneath the weight, Evan carried the box with the copier in it to his truck, sitting it in the bed next to the cab. With no one following he drove to Dan and Ellen's home. The box was transferred to Daniel's work truck he had pulled inside the garage. Clicking the lock to the truck, Daniel said, "I'll have your copier to the company tomorrow and you should hear from them in a couple of days. How's that?" The two clasp hands in a firm hand shake. Evan nodded, greatly relieved.

The next day, Si helped him load the saw horses into the back of his truck. "I'll take him the tool box, when I leave this afternoon. That way, he can return it Monday morning for our use. We won't be needing those saw horsed for awhile, will we?" Si shook his head that they wouldn't. Evan gave a slight chuckle. "You are a man of few words, Si. They used to say that about me, but this group of people from Christ Church, Si, they are something else. If loving you one way, doesn't work, they love you another. It is truly the love of God in action."

As he had done the day before, leaving the shop Evan drove to Andrew and Anne's home. Andrew met him on the curb. "Come on in and see my finished project, well…you did more here than I ever could and you knew what you were doing." Evan picked up the tool box and carried it into Andrew's private space. Before he left, Andrew transferred it to his Suburban parked in the garage and clicked the lock.

The next day the UPS truck made a stop at Andrew's office before it made the run by the Gates Building where it picked up an order going to an individual in another state. Strangely, the truck had been followed from Andrew's office to the Gates building. An elderly woman stood on the corner watching the proceedings. Grave's package appeared to be a box the size legal documents were stored in and true to their conversation, the box from Gates was the copier. The old lady breathed deep and smiled. "No one would send precious instruments so loosely wrapped in a copier box. It was a copier."

"Don't go trying to fool me, boys. That won't work, don't you know."

✳ ✳ ✳ ✳ ✳

Officer Cullums felt the sweat form in his arm pits and knew it was making circles on his good shirt. Miss Harriet insist she pick him up at home and he was to wear plain clothes. No uniform. He would never have gotten involved in this secret tryst but his commanding officer said he must. The recovery of thousand dollar instruments stolen from Evan Jacob's shop would put his name in the paper. He wished. Cullums wasn't so certain and he'd rather be anywhere but here. The limo came to a stop and then they were walking up the stone path to Daniel Gates home for a sit down dinner. That was what he was told. There was to be no discussion of the project that would take place in the back yard garden. Yes, sir, the plot thickened. He supposed people with wealth could do what they wanted, why follow police regulations when they could make their own.

Putting his hand in the pocket of Sunday trousers, he wiped the sweat on the lining and forced himself to put on his best non-committal facial expression. It scared dogs in his neighborhood, he hoped it had an effect on these people and he hoped there was a decent dish of food he would recognize.

He knew the people from articles in the newspaper, except there was a time he was buddies with Harper Gipson but the man wouldn't remember. Families Gipson, Graves, Gates, Langly, Jacobs and Pastor Joe from Christ Church were present. Add him and Miss Harriet and there was a table full. Thirteen people to be exact and the food was delicious. The food served to loosen his tongue. They were no longer as reprehensible as he suspected. He was in. Whatever their project, he was their man.

The group adjourned to the garden to the sound of the water fountain and the piped music that flowed from the Angel. It was when the group settled, it seemed a great calm came over them. Cullum glanced around. True, he was apprehensive but calm in the Cape? If they could bottle the feeling he now experienced, then they were on to something.

He left with a broader idea of who they were. He tapped his forehead; it wasn't all about money not these people, their next idea wasn't to fill a spot with something expensive but to help another who was in need and maybe it wasn't a material thing, maybe it was encouragement or just listening to a lonely soul who had no one. There was where his instructions lay when his commanding officer cross examined him with all those questions, barking his superior self over lowly Cullum, man oh man was he going to be surprised. It was simple, their plan and now he saw it, felt it even. First steps first. The city must get a listening device down through three feet of soil into the garden façade where Walden was holed up. Walden again. Unbelievable to think he was alive.

Even now he could hear Andrew Graves saying, "Never forget, he is a master of disguise. He enjoys it. Nothing thrills him more than to have been within two feet of you, rubbing elbows and you don't realize he's there. All the while he is laughing his way back home. Why does he never die? Because many times he has made up his paid henchmen and they are doing whatever he asks because he pays well, no one beats Walden. Remember, he is an expert. He has probably walked beside us and we never knew."

What could he tell the chief? He wasn't Chester Mayfield, he didn't listen when he heard the answer. They would waste precious time under his watch. Cullum might be the low man on the pole but he had Miss Harriet. She wouldn't let anything happen to him. He would do his part for those good people.

The plan was made. Pieces of paper were passed around as though the instructions were part of a game, then all pieces were put in a can to take inside. An on-looker would think they enjoyed the game. If Walden was there, surely he was confused. Plan A and Plan B, would play out in the shoe department. Cullum sighed. He was tired and needed sleep before facing the chief.

Chapter 13

Accompanied by her father, Penny was there. Sutton saw her when she came through the door. Oh, man. She was huge. For such a tiny person she was all protruding belly, all baby. His child. His face remained without expression, austere to say the least. He turned his head and studied the state seal. The Judge entered from his chambers and the Bailiff called out, "All rise." It was hard for Penny to rise.

"Young man are you aware of the laws you have broken and that you're responsible for the death of your friend?" When Sutton failed to answer, the Judges voice rose a notch. "Do you understand the severity of the charge against you?" This time Sutton raised his head and gave a muffled, "yes, sir."

"You have been found guilty of Manslaughter in the life of Caroline Green. Now the responsibility lies on your shoulders to serve a term of imprisonment in the Department of Corrections of the State of Missouri for a period of seven years."

"Seven years?" Leona's legs would not hold; she slumped down into the chair. "My boy," she sobbed. "My boy." Sutton in his own misery gripped her hand. "Do something," she pleaded with her husband.

The Judge spoke, "Young man you may say good bye to your family."

Penny was leaving with her father with tears streaming down her face. Somehow she knew Leona would be clutching her boy to her breast and begging the Judge not to send him away. Would she ever take part in the blame? She stumbled and felt her father's firm grip on her elbow.

Sutton remained stoic, but he kissed his mother and LeAnn, as his eyes lingered on the door Penny had exited while he shook hands with his father and brother. It was as he turned away, his father grabbed him in a hug he knew he'd never forget but the Officer in charge pulled him away. He was in for a long ride if they were taking him tonight. He could not imagine the freedom he had known taken away. It was as if his life flashed before his eyes.

✳ ✳ ✳ ✳ ✳

Aldean read about the trial. "It made the front page," she explained to Geri. "He will be thirty if he serves the complete time the Judge gave him. Did you speak with him yesterday, Geri?"

"Yes," her voice was soft, barely above a whisper. "I told him Jesus loves him and I do, too, but that I won't be here much longer so I can't write him letters." She started to chuckle but it caused coughing."You know what he said?" Aldean walked over with fresh tissue. "He said all the stories you told me about your growing up as a child in the Cape, I'll always remember them. Then, I said, you will remember me. His voice became husky as he said, yes, ma'm. You see, there showed the real man beneath the spoiled boy. There was longing in his voice and he said one last thing."

"Will you feel up to going to the young couples tonight?"

"To Mother's home? Our home?" She went into a round of coughing. "I wouldn't miss it."

✳ ✳ ✳ ✳ ✳

"Oh, my goodness," Geri's eyes were wide as a child as she rode into the house in Evan's arms. "My, my, my, Aldean, look at the tree in the window. We are having Christmas at Mother's house."

She squeezed Evan's neck. "Young man, you and your wife are so thoughtful. Thank you."

Grinning and as happy as she, Evan replied, "our pleasure but there are a few items we didn't know where to place, so there's still a job for you three." He heard Nina's giggle but Geri was coughing. Aldean's long legs on the steps were first as she opened and held the door.

"This way," Jewel was leading them to the new sofa, decked out with a new sheet and a warm blanket solely for Miss Geri's comfort. "Tell me if this spot is all right, if not we will move the sofa. Marigold was able to have it delivered this afternoon. You know we've been waiting for it all these months to go on sale." Everyone laughed. They were happy to be together and bring joy to this one who was ill.

When she was settled, Evan moved three cardboard boxes closer to where she lay. "Door number one, two or three," he teased. Geri pointed to the larger box. "You think you know what's in it?" She nodded.

"Our Nativity set. Where did you find it?"

"You told us there were decorations in the attic. Remember?"

"But we looked for it when we were moving," Geri explained. "It simply wasn't there."

"I hid it," Aldean confessed. "In those days Nina rid herself of way too many items for change and I didn't want just anyone having it, so I hid it in the farthest corner."

"It wasn't in the farthest corner," Jewel said, mystified. "It was at the side of the stairs."

"I moved it," Nina admitted. "I had a bad quarrel with Aldean over it, but I finally decided she was right."

"Why did you leave me out?" Aldean and Nina dropped down beside Geri.

"We knew you would make one of us take it and we didn't deserve it…but we were selfish and didn't think you deserved it either. So it's sit here all these years waiting for this couple and tonight."

Geri tried to clap her hands. "It was meant to be. It's a God thing that they have it."

One by one the familys arrived while gradually through the stories of their youth the sisters placed the remaining items. The dancing Santa went on top of the Oriental chest of drawers, the glass Christmas tree with fifty tiny lights was the center piece for the library table in the hall way and the assortment of tiny animals, each exquisitely formed were placed beneath the tree the girls had kept from toddler stage, the bristles nearly bare on the branches with a tiny star at the top. "On the buffet," Nina offered, "because father gave her an additional piece each year and she didn't want one to be broken so she cleared the buffet and kept them under her watchful eye throughout the season."

"Come, it is time to eat. Daniel, would you and Matt push the sofa near the table so Miss Geri will not feel stuck off in the backroom alone." She watched as they began the slow move across the floor. "You don't have to worry about scratches, guys. See under each leg is a piece of carpet so you can push it right on in with ease."

Storing the food and clearing the table was a quick task. Everyone had helped Jewel by bringing a dish and they had discussed how to keep the meal a true celebration without the chaos of too many casseroles and instead a traditional Christmas feast. Geri was able to eat perhaps two teaspoons of potato and gravy but she dare not try the turkey Dorothy had cooked, meat was to heavy to digest.

Now the guys were moving Geri near the piano as Ellen took her place on the bench and Daniel handed out sheet music they had copied. "Don't tell, we don't want problems. Okay?" Everyone made a statement for Daniel's benefit, of course, that he would be severely punished for copy write reasons.

"I have to ask, where are your children?" Aldean was rather taken by the little girl Ruthie and the twins were fun to watch. "You have the boy and new little girl, Addie," she addressed Andrew and Anne, who were nodding, affirmative. "I was fearful when your child was taken but then Evan rescued her."

"They are all at our home," Daniel replied. "We have a wonderful lady from church being entertained about now." He laughed.

"Because they will do anything to stay up late. She has her hands full." He glanced around at the group and Miss Geri on the sofa. "We gathered to honor our sisters, tonight. Someone said Miss Geri made the statement she wouldn't be here much longer. We face her statement with the knowledge we will miss her, we are sad, but when we consider she will be happy, shining in heaven with Jesus, perhaps sitting at his feet worshiping him and he will hold out his hand and she will rise, free of pain, glowing in the happiness of seeing her parents again and she won't remember the agonies of her health issue here on earth…that means we are to realize in a short while we will see her again but tonight is a happy night of celebrating our love for one another. You know Jesus gave us the gift of his love in a way we can never repay but we can share his love with others. Now what song should we sing?" He smiled and remember, "we will save the Christmas carols for last as we sing praise."

"How Great Thou Art." It was that way, after each song, another was mentioned and then noticing Miss Geri's weariness, Daniel ask, "Miss Geri would you like to say anything as we come to a close?"

"Today my sister ask me a question, but we were involved in conversation to the point I didn't get her question answered. She was reading from the newspaper about Sutton Coleman's incarceration. She asked me when last he and I spoke by phone, what did he have to say? Sutton had told me he would always remember the stories I told him about growing up in the Cape, but his voice became husky when I said Sutton I won't be here much longer and I don't know if I'll make it to Christmas." She swallowed to keep down the tears that threatened each time she thought of his reply. "You have to," he said, "make it for both of us and have the best Christmas ever. Sutton has not yet confessed or accepted salvation, but his heart is changing. At this point, if prison doesn't harden him, Sutton will begin to see there is a better life and he will meet the one who laid out the plan for his, please, keep Sutton in your prayers." Andrew dropped down to look straight into her eyes and she smiled. "I know your question, young man. Yes, this has been our celebration for the best Christmas ever."

* * * * *

Outside the window, the old woman walked past. From viewing the activity behind the window his summation was, "They are the partyingest people I've ever seen. What could be so important to decorate a house and have Christmas early?" He really didn't care, his plan was to bring an item of worth to his collection. He had thought to take the lady's harp when she came to perform but in view of the missing objects of worth and value missing in the Cape, she canceled her tour. A plan began to form in his deranged mind. He knew exactly what he would take and he knew when.

Rearranging the shawl on her shoulders, the old woman walked to the corner and entered the shiny black limo. "We can go now," he said to the driver. "I'll get out a block from the wall."

* * * * *

On Monday Geri asked Nina to write a letter. My sister has been kind enough to write for me, Sutton. I wanted to say goodbye. You have enlightened my life, allowing me in my last days to communicate with you. Sometimes life seems very lonely, so much so that in a room full of people one feels a void. I pray you are well and that you will give your heart to the Lord soon. You've already had one close call; another could take your life. God bless you, Sutton Coleman, until we meet again. Your friend, Geri.

Later, having rested, Geri ask for Evan. It was late evening when he arrived and Geri was too weak to speak, but when he took her hand he felt her try to squeeze his own. "I think from the moment I met you there was a special bond," he said in a voice so low it was a wonder she heard, but she must have for she smiled. "You resemble the picture I have of my birth mother. Oh, I wish I had known her." He stayed but an hour. It was the last visit between them. Geri died quietly in her sleep that night, two days before Thanksgiving.

Pastor Joe met with Evan and Jewel, Daniel and Ellen. "Here is the list Geri requested and Evan if you will, she wants the violin for her last viewing." He smiled, "she has written, let Evan play as they do the viewing of me, just before the lid closes on the casket." Shaking his head, he said, "She could be morbid but always with humor." He placed a second list inside his bible. "Please, ask me at end of day if I remembered to give Geri's letter to Penny Coleman."

As the large clock in the foyer chimed three, Thanksgiving Day, Pastor Joe took his place behind the podium." I'm honored to lead in Miss Geri's final hour. She had a simple reason she said where I was to read the scripture that was dear to her heart and in the chain of life's happening share special moments with you." He glanced down at the notes Miss Geri had given him. "She loved the song Give Thanks. And it was Ellen and Dan Gates she asked to sing for her."

"Please stand for the reading of God's word that Geri chose for us today. Psalm fifty seven, verse seven through eleven. "My heart is fixed O God, my heart is fixed. I will sing and give praise. Awake up my glory; awake psaltery and harp; I myself will wake early. I will praise thee, O Lord, among the people. I will sing unto thee among the nations. For thy mercy is great unto the heavens and thy truth unto the clouds. Be thou exalted, O God above the heavens; let thy glory be above all the earth."

"This is Miss Geri's philosophy. Be glad and praise the Lord. I'm sure she had down days too but what we see now is a person freed from sadness and strife and from pain. She pointed out to me verse one of the same scripture speaks of the hard times one has. "Be merciful unto me, O God, be merciful to me for my soul trusteth in thee; yea in the shadow of thy wings will I make my refuge until these calamities be over and past." And calamities she did have, One evening as she labored in breathing, between bouts of coughing she asked, "Pastor, do you realize chapter fifty seven of Pslams sounds a lot like Psalm chapter ninety one?" He that dwelleth in the secret place of the most High shall abide under the shadow of the almighty. I will say of the Lord, He is my refuge and my fortress, my God, in Him will I trust. And verse four," she said, listen, "He shall cover thee with his feathers and under his wings shall thou trust; his truth shall be thy shield and thy buckler." Doesn't that sound just like verse one of fifty seven? In the shadow of thy wings will I make my refuge." Miss Geri was so sincere in what she was thinking she would lay it right out in front of you, no matter what it was. If she could help someone else have a better life, then that's what she wanted. In these last days she would say, "What a mighty God we have. I've not been true to the God my mother taught when I was a child, but I've always known He was our Father, and wanted the best for us and his word was dear to me."

"A sweet life has ended. Her living testimony is this; to love the Father, to seek salvation now because if you wait you may miss the opportunity and then you leave yourself open to hell, tormented with no relief throughout eternity. I was always amazed at Miss Geri's insight into a person's problem."

Miss Geri was laid to rest in a private cemetery, not far from the house where she was born. Aldean and Nina were at a loss for words that many people came in spite of the fact the weather had turned cold and a light rain began to fall. The celebration of their sister's life had been painful but pleasing and though they had never attended Christ Church they felt God's love spread through the people.

The church furnace seemed unable to keep up with the need. Due to the young children, the group decided there must be other arrangements for the time they would spend together. "Come to our house," Ellen invited. "Surely it will be warm." She looked to Daniel who grinned and nodded. Aldean and Nina were hesitant, not understanding if others beside the group were included. "Daniel will drive you ladies to be with us and then take you home when you wish to go." She saw their shoulders lift. "You don't need to be alone, tonight, until bedtime then I bet you sleep."

"Have you adopted us, Daniel?" Nina climbed into the second row of seats. "Come on, Aldean."

"Why not, Miss Nina?" His smile was infectious. "If you don't have family here, then yes, definitely."

"We don't have anyone anywhere, dear. That's why we could travel. There is one set, from Tennessee, says they are far off cousins...but I don't believe there's any way we could be related." Aldean was more subdued than he remembered. Or, perhaps losing her sister was a terribly traumatic event.

* * * * *

Friday morning, Evan slipped quietly from the bedcovers. The hands on the clock seemed to be at three and for a moment he hesitated but he was anxious to see how the last coat dried. Jewel was sound asleep and that was unusual, but she might have had something on her mind and couldn't go to sleep last night. He would hurry down to the shop, check on the small violins and be right back for a breakfast of pancakes, bacon and eggs. He kissed her lightly on the cheek and was gone. As he reached the back door and thought he heard her call his name, he stopped and listened but there was no further sound.

Dressed in black jogging suits, full face hat covers over their face, the two were late, but the woman stayed up past midnight and he didn't want them in the house if the occupants were awake. She was certainly awake, doing this, doing that. She ironed for an hour, scrubbed the kitchen floor another and when they thought she was going to break she spent the last hour dusting every place one could think of and a few they never considered worthy of dusting. Now, they were to gather what he called antiques, very valuable on the market and he had told them where to find each piece.

Why would anyone want a spiral tree that had few branches on it? That was item number one. Next they looked for the set said to be on the black oriental chest. It wasn't there. Wrap each piece he said, which meant it would slow them down. Why would he want someone's nearly tattered old piece of time when he could afford to buy them out, lock, stock and barrel? Huh? He must be coming closer to the tall chest of drawers he described as holding the dancing bear? His kids had better toys. He wouldn't let them play with Walden's collection for nothing. Most of it was filthy, anyway. His partner was supposed to be looking for hidden instruments. He wondered if the man knew what an instrument was.

It was crazy and he was crazy being drawn into this mess, with Christmas a month away. What if they got caught? Then he felt something glide past him. "Evan," she called out. That's when her gown got caught in the Velcro of the slip over rubber boots he was wearing. Last time it rained so heavy he lost his jacket. Don't worry, he thought, it's a long story. "I oughta hire someone else, you're too funny to believe." People willing to work at this level were either all brawn or brain, never both. All the junk circulated around in his head. There was one that worked nearby he bet wouldn't be such a groaner but then Walden did the choosing, and he only came in by a hair.

She was coming back. He saw a reflection of her white gown in the mirror only seconds before she ran pell-mell into him, bounced back and slid. He heard her head hit that heavy piece of furniture and her gasp of surprise. As she went down she whispered, "Evan." He forced himself to stand still, while his heart roared and drummed against his chest. Lord, he asked in silence am I having a heart attack? But the drumming slowed, eventually, and he'd heard no noise out of her. He stooped down, found her face in the dark and bent to listen to her heart. It was beating at a regular pace. If he could place her head on something, he was sure she'd come around in a minute. A small pillow was within his grasp and he reached to raise her head thinking to slide the pillow home but something sticky was on his hand, running between his fingers. He smelled his hand. He knew what it was, metallic, mind boggling, Evan Jacob's wife was unconscious from the fall where she hit her head on a heavy piece of furniture and blood was oozing from the wound.

"You got everything?" He hissed, so great was his terror of being found in this house and blamed for the lady's fall. "Come on, we have to go." He'd broken the rule. They were not to talk or call names. The old woman was a block or two away, walking and star gazing. "Let's get out of here." When the clouds covered the moon, those items they took from the house were transferred to the walled enclosure.

At four fifteen, the text to nine one one came in. Woman down, head injury. Door unlocked. Husband at work. Address as follows. Yellow house in the new division that used to be a cow pasture. Greenwich.

✳ ✳ ✳ ✳ ✳

Evan felt good as he locked the door. He and Si had worked hard to recover the loss. Money wise impossible, still they were building inventory for the Christmas holidays. The school out West had received the shipment. There had been one hold up when he received a call from the company saying an elderly lady had come to their facility to claim the contents but the address on the box was to a repair shop. Satisfied, Evan knew each item inside the box was addressed to the school and when they called to confirm their order had arrived, he and Si breathed a deep sigh of relief.

The sale of instruments by the shop in Nashville was keeping this business going. Jewel's giving piano lessons was the means by which their personal lives were fed. Heaven help them if another disaster appeared. The day had started with anticipation; he could not let the downside of the business affect his feelings. He and Jewel had too many blessings for him to get hung up being negative. Backing out onto the street, he headed home to Jewel.

He pat the steering wheel, feeling the old truck glide along. Some country tune cropped up in his mind, "I got no problem with you, let's say I got no ax to grind, just leave my sweetheart alone, or else you'll be like the rollin' stone." Evan threw his head back laughing. It felt good going home to the woman he loved knowing she loved him, maybe more, she was better at everything she did. The country song left his memory, the one he was working on filed through , When you call my name…all heaven and earth stand still….just call me call my name. "For you, Jewel," he whispered.

Turning onto his street he saw the lights blinking. "Great, someone's run out of gas. My blessing." And then the full effect hit him. There was an ambulance and it must be the driver standing outside making a call to someone. His cell phone rang. It was there all the time and he wasn't aware he brought it.

"Mr. Jacobs? "I regret to tell…"

He was trying to advance and they were holding him back, "Don't use those words," he screamed. "Let me in there. Let me go." He doubled over in pain. His sobbing could be heard down the road.

Daniel came bounding across the lawn; pushed the EMT away to take his place, one arm around Evan's neck, the other around his waist, holding firm. "There's no beatin' on him, fellow. He didn't do anything."

"Why can't I go in?" Evan's words brought tears to Daniel's eyes. "She can't be dead, Daniel."

It was an hour before they were able to carry her out on the gurney. Both EMT's swore they had never seen so much blood for a head wound and no doubt that much loss was what threw everything out of kilter. When they arrived they couldn't get a heart rate, BP, nothing. A third EMT trained policeman used two rolls of paper towels sopping up blood from the floor. He knew Dan and said, "It wasn't something a family member should see."

"Any idea what happened?" Evan was hovering over Jewel as they were loading. "I got a call from someone downtown saying the ambulance was headed to my buddy's house so I came right over." Dan was watching as they closed the doors to the ambulance and excused himself. "I should close up the home and drive him to the hospital; he's slow moving all of a sudden. It may be this last thing has put his body on overload. It's been a long hot summer."

"I'll give them credit; my kid takes piano lessons from Miss Jewel. They appear to be a hard working couple ready to get ahead honestly. I'm all for that. But this injury could set them back. It doesn't look good. They will leave here in about five-ten minutes if your friend needs to check on anything."

Deciding to do a walkthrough of the house, Daniel noticed a few things were either in different locations or had been taken, The Nativity set, they claimed one hundred fifty years old was gone and there were three other empty spots he remembered. He was wondering whether to say anything to Evan. The man was in shock and rightly so, but there might be something of importance missing. "Evan, I think you need to do a quick walk through the rooms before we leave and see if everything is all right."

Evan returned, went straight to Dan's vehicle and sat down. "I can't believe there are people that low, but there's several things missing so I guess that proves they are." Evan buckled the seat belt and ask LeAnn if she would like to go, to which LeAnn replied, "no, Sir." She didn't bother to tell him she had her own transportation down the alley. For some reason, tonight she wanted to tell him thank you for helping her with the guitar. Therefore when she finished helping with the clearing away after the family meal she had free time. "Would you like for me to do anything for you?"

"No, LeAnn, but thank you. Right now, nothing is more important than medical attention for Jewel." LeAnn hugged her instructor and closed the passenger door of the Suburban. They both gave an embarrassed laugh over the tears running down their cheeks. The ambulance left the drive with Daniel staying close behind.

"Jesus, I've never done this until Sutton and now I'm doing it again. Please heal Miss Jewel." She drove careful going home when she wanted to speed as usual but seeing Jewel's unresponsive body concerned her and the other thing was, she desperately needed to see her Momma. "Oh, if she would just throw her arms around me. Please Jesus."

She ran up the steps and let the door slam behind her. "Mother." She listened. "Mother?" Leona came out of the chair in the next room. She had dozed but she knew that tone in LeAnn's voice. Hurrying, she met her daughter; arms outstretched pulling her in. "Sweetheart, what's wrong?" LeAnn was crying again, "Hold me, Momma, hold me. It's so awful." Now, Leona was guiding them into the next room falling into the chair, LeAnn on her lap, head on her shoulder just as she did when she was little.

She began to tell the story. "My instructor's wife, the one at the piano, at recital, you saw her?"

"That's Penny's friend, isn't it?" Leona looked down into her daughter's face and bent enough to kiss the top of her forehead. "How is Penny? You do stay in touch, don't you?"

Almost a giggle escaped LeAnn as she straightened and slid down onto the floor between her mother's knees. "She's about to pop. If that baby doesn't come soon, Penny will blow up."

"Really? What is she going to have?"

"A boy and his heart beat is so fast on the ultra sound you'd think it would fly out of his chest."

"You're sure it's a boy?"

"Gotta little water spout to prove it." LeAnn laughed so joyously for a minute she forgot Miss Jewel.

"Oh, Momma, you can come to the hospital with us when Penny has your little grandson." She saw sadness cross her mother's face. "Penny won't care, Momma. Penny doesn't hold on to bad stuff."

"Tell me the whole story. What happened to your instructor's wife?"

"No one really knows except someone called nine- one- one and she was alive when the ambulance left."

"They have a group of friends that will rally around them and help take care of Miss Jacobs."

"Would our friends…."

"We have no friends."

Within the hour across town Ellen's phone was ringing. "Yes, we will keep you informed by Facebook. Thank you."

✴ ✴ ✴ ✴ ✴

Daniel finally glanced at his watch around midnight when his stomach rumbled so loud the people across the room smiled when their children giggled. "Guess you heard that," he said. They nodded. "Evan, I'm going down the hall and see if they have any sandwiches. I think they close around midnight." He was gone maybe ten minutes, and returned with a bag of chips, two sandwiches and two bottles of water. "I didn't make it home for dinner. We had a truck load of supplies come in just at closing.

"You need to go on home, Daniel. I'm grateful for everything but I'll be all right now."

"I'm staying until you see Jewel and I know where you'll be sitting the rest of the night."

At two o'clock in the morning, Andrew tapped Daniel on the shoulder and sent him home. As he settled down by Evan, the doctor came into the waiting room. "Mr. Jacobs?" Evan sat up with a rush.

"Can I see her, Doctor?" The doctor rubbed his hand over his face as he heaved a deep breath.

"It will only disturb you, Mr. Jacobs while I don't think she will waken. I know you have all these questions but we don't have much to go on yet. She has been unconscious seven hours and it will probably last three to five more hours before she rallies. We don't know if she can hear us, nor if she will be able to speak. I'm sure there is a lot of confusion if she is able to think, but we can tell by her unsteadiness she has no idea what that's about either. I'd say we all need to get some rest and give Mrs. Jacobs time."

"I can't leave." Evan's shoulders drooped, his countenance just as heavy.

Andrew laid a hand on Evan's shoulder, "I understand when Andy was hit by the automobile and we didn't know if he would live, I stayed. Come on, buddy, let's find a couch long enough for our legs and we'll be right here." Andrew left briefly, going down the hall, to return with a pillow and a blanket for each. "It gets cool in here of the nights." He motioned for Evan to lie down and then practically covered him with the blanket as one would a child. That was their first chuckle. "It's not cold, yet," Evan sputtered. "You are doing a good job, Andrew, but I'm not cold." They ended up laughing.

"There's a lot of noise in this area they call quiet, isn't there?" Andrew checked his watch. "Near Three. "

Evan swung his feet to the floor. "I've been watching the door. Is there another way to get to other parts of the hospital? There's been no one coming through these doors."

"Yeah, there's a whole corridor, nothing but beds, nurses stations and a few rooms for patients with the most problems, though if not in demand they situate someone with dire problems in there."

✳ ✳ ✳ ✳ ✳

It was five in the morning, Matt dropped by. "Go home, Andrew. There's a rain and I don't have to go out to the farm. I'll be here with Evan. He handed Evan a cup of coffee and a small brown bag. "I know you will say you don't feel like eating but I'll say this, you have got to take care of you, there's a lot lies ahead and it is imperative you are well."

'How do you come to the conclusion a lot lies ahead?" Slowly Evan was peeling the paper down from the sausage egg sandwich.

"Man, twice with Marigold. It doesn't matter whether the situation is large or small, there's so much involved but you wouldn't have it any other way, as long as your loved one is getting better."

There was a shift change at six o'clock. Evan caught up with two of the nurses. "Please, may I see my wife?" They glanced his way. "Who might that be?" one asked. "Jewel Jacobs," he replied. The two gave each other a glance he didn't understand. "We have orders to bathe your wife and then we'll see if you can come in." The big door closed. Evan returned to the sofas where Matt had folded the blankets.

The nurses intention to bathe Jewel were not in her favor. The movement brought on vomiting with Jewel clutching her head while one of the nurse held the basin and the other spread towels on the floor to catch the over spray. Hearing the retching, Evan bolted into the room. "Let me hold her," he said, "She's too weak to do this by herself."

Dismayed, the nurse looked around for her superior. "One good thing has come out of this. She moved her arms, is that good?"

Evan sent Matt home. "I'll be in Jewel's room. You don't need to sit in here by yourself. Go home." Exhausted, he was relieved when the doctors said there would be no visiting his patient but the husband could stay in the room if he wished. The doctor was beginning to wonder what was coming next.

At the end of the second week, Evan asked again for the doctor's opinion on the test they had run. "We are prone to think there might be brain damage if a person stays unconscious more than twenty four hours, I've actually refreshed myself on this, since your wife's arrival. But there was that time she moved her arms and clung to you. And though the action was pure reflex, it still dismisses brain damage. A new CT verifies the bleeding has not stopped and anytime there's bleeding of the brain there's also swelling. Have you noticed?"

Harriet arrived to find Evan head between his hands sitting in a chair, feet widespread, staring at the floor. The nurses had run him out. "Hello, Evan?" He stood and he looked so forlorn, Harriet opened her arms and hugged him. After a spell of small talk which was going nowhere, Harriet said, "Evan, I've come to offer you advice. You have business to take care of, not only overseeing your violin shop, but I understand from Si, orders are piling up and there are also invitations for violin workshops. If you don't reply now, those dates will disappear and those soliciting your appearance will think you are not interested. This is what builds business. Now what should you do, Evan?"

"I can't leave her."

Harriet would always remember Evan's tormented expression. Now, she said, "Evan, you are grieving and Jewel is alive. When you pray thank the good Lord she is alive and expect the best not the worst." Evan sunk down into his chair as though he had not heard but his mind was racing. What must he do?

He supposed Harriet was calling her driver when she used her phone, but within seconds the doctor stood by her side. "Harriet Becker." There was a handshake and then the doctor said, "Harriet, I will escort you in. You have my permission to speak to Mrs. Jacobs and then I wish you a safe trip home." He bowed and took her hand and led her into Jewel's room where he left the two alone.

Harriet pulled her chair near the bed. "Jewel, honey, you are going to have to come out of this fog. Evan's beginning to look like a sack of bones and he's not going to work. I'll let you In on a little secret; Daniel and Ellen are seeing to your children's lessons. Who knew Daniel also played violin. That aunt of his recognized as a boy he had the skill and it was she who pushed all those instruments into his life."

"Now. The committee met and everyone's home will be decorated for Christmas and you remember our topic. Time is moving on and you don't want to miss Christmas. Think the strongest thought possible and we will see how you are doing in the morning and I'll tell you right now, Ruthie is all set to come see you she has a very contrite heart just thinking about you. There are things I feel sure you want to know. The Police are searching through paper files I've never known about, as to why anyone would take those antiques from your home which would be easy to trace and if they find the burglar then possibly that is the answer to how you fell and who called in to nine- one-one. You may know this, but Penny has delivered a little boy, well he was a nine pound boy so that's not really small, is he? Squeezing Jewell's hand, Harriet rose up and kissed her on the forehead. Remember, Ruthie will be here tomorrow."

✳ ✳ ✳ ✳ ✳

The group that met at the Gates house before Thanksgiving to enjoy the late fall foliage in their garden returned to help decorate. The decorating was beautiful and enjoyed by all but in truth it was a cover for the discussion they had earlier in the year that strongly believed Clayton Walden was alive and intent on destroying them. For all the hurt he put on their group they wanted his foolishness to stop.

"We know the person creating this mischief or in Evan's case, down right destruction and loss, that person has money to carry out such well planned schemes. Why would he do all the damage? He is a man of a warped mind. I can't imagine he has ever lived a regular life where you kiss your child and tell them you love them on an hourly basis. Something must have happened when he was a child. However, that is not relevant to what we watch for as Christmas approaches. Law enforcement showed their weakness when little Adeline was the taken and again vandalism of Evan's home but worse is the fact they have done nothing to find who hurt Jewel, which makes us wonder if someone at the Police station is in his pay. Let's take a moment and review what has been different about this year and the aggrivation he has shown on our lives."

Matt spoke up; "I have wondered the same, why would an obviously wealthy, intelligent and educated being, get caught up in the lives of everyday people, I mean, for instance, stealing the painting from the church. No one has seen any thing pertaining to paintings in the news or otherwise, which means it was not stolen to end up in some art gallery or famous place but to some private collector."

"What about the violins? That was pure greed. It is uncaring about children as a whole. This person scoffs at men who must work an hourly job. The thing is, some weary truck driver has more integrity and care for the inner workings of common people and their belongings, and we will do well to remember that."

The Sisters had been listening. Aldean spoke. "First, let us thank you for including us tonight. Geri was the more articulate of us, but I'll try. Where does the Police Department stand in all this investigation?"

"I'm afraid that's it," Daniel replied. "Nothing is ever done, Walden is never caught and this time it was one of our's again. The last time Marigold was in labor when the dirty work was done and she was taken from the hospital. If we don't stop him, who will? The question is, why is he targeting us?"

"I'm afraid I don't understand what you mean about the violins?" Aldean questioned further.

"Evan had an order for a private school of music that teaches violin. Before the violins were shipped they were taken and not a trace of their existence has been found by the police. Sometimes, we are afraid one of their own gives the information to Walden and that is how he does whatever he wishes successfully."

"If, he is alive," Aldean persisted, "Where would he hide that no one sees him? That's a bit unusual."

It seemed all eyes turned to Andrew. He shrugged, "don't look at me. It's true, I worked for the man and for a while his culmative wealth intrigued me, I almost fell into his footprints but for the love of a good woman who found Christ." He paused, thiking what was important. "It may be in his warped mind he still knows the difference between good and bad or in his case we might say evil. I've told you, he said he sold his soul to the devil in order to prosper, I don't know if the Lord stops speaking to a person beyond that point, I don't know why Walden trys to ruin or destroy good people, it seems he has a passion towards a good person like Evan and isn't that what the devil does, moves in, little by little and takes over. So where does he hide? In plain sight, looking good. Have you encountered someone lately that appears so good or kind or helpful.

You choose your own situation…if he's alive, he is active, he loves disguise and the art of pretending he is someone else…I honestly don't know about Walden, any more. I do know the devil moves in and little by little he changes a person's mind set as he uses who ever he wants, the thing is we must be strong because of our God and stand against him. Are we strong?"

A great boom of thunder shook the ground as rain drops hit the window and the door bell rang. Daniel hurried to let the person in. Beyond the curb he saw one of the city Police cars and stepping out of the shadow of the overhang that shielded him from the rains's onslaught, Cullums in full rain gear handed him a large envelope as he smiled, saluted and returned to the car.

Daniel hurried back to the group waiting to see who would venture out in such a rain storm.

"It was Cullum," he said. "He brought this." Daniel opened the envelope and then the page within. He read, "You cannot win, not now, nor eternity. There's nothing says you can win. I am legion in high places and on the lowly street where you walk. I am found in beauty though I turn it often to squalor. Remember, since time began I have been here. You are but a leaf blowing in the wind. You can't win."

"It wasn't Cullum," Daniel's dismay reflect in every face. "Andrew, could it have been him?" Everiything was on pause, there were people's feelings of despair, some who felt an isolation from the others, a mix of emotion flailed before their eyes. Harriet thought to express regard to Geri's sisters found them cold and unreceptive. Before the people they rejected her offered hand. Harriet was immensely relieved when Daniel, Matt, and Andrew brought the meeting back to order for dismissal.

"Ephesians 6:12 has taught us we do not wrestle against flesh and blood but against the rulers, against the authorities, against the cosmic powers of this dark world and against the spiritual forces of evil spirits in the heavenly places," Dan quoted as he stepped to the piano and reached for his bible, "verse thirteen of Epesians reminds us to arm ourselves against evil. Here it is. "Therefore put on the full armor of God so that when day of evil comes, you may be able to stand your ground and after you have done everything, to stand."

"Yes, we must stand firm and last but not least verse sixteen tells us to take up the shield of faith which can extinguish all the flaming arrows the evil one throws against us."

"How would one such as you describe obtain a police car, when they are suspicious of everyone?" Aldean persisted, calling out to Daniel. "I don't understand your faith. This is hard for me."

"We must stand firm in our faith. That is our message. Now as we prepare to dismiss, let us hold hands and pray a praiyer of faith that Jewel will recover with no side effects and very soon."

"Like tomorrow," Marigold exclaimed. "Because it is possible. The last verse of that reading tells us to "pray in the Spirit on all occassions with all kinds of prayers and requests. With this in mind be alert and always keep on praying for all the Lord's people." Marigold smiled. "It can happen folks, it has happened for me. I am living truth. God can heal Jewel quickly or in time as he wishes. Right folks? For the effectual fervent prayer of a arighteous man availeth much."

"James 5:16," Daniel added. "Thank you all for coming. Now, before we leave let's pray. Harriet?"

"I've not led in public prayer, Daniel."

"But you pray, Harriet and we all serve the same God. I think we could use your wisdom."

"Father," Harriet's voice trembled with emotion. "Lord, let us come before you thanking you for all that you do for us, when our hearts are breaking for others, when our minds are consumed with the endless problems life brings and we forget to say thank you, Lord we thank you for friends and family that care and come together but most of all, Lord, we thank you for salvation we receive when we believe on you and ask forgiveness and you come into our hearts and we become your child as surely as you become our father. Father, we ask healing on Jewel and we ask peace in hearts that are distrubed over what's happening in our lives now. Sometimes, Lord, our fear is that what happens next will be more troubling and heartbreaking if that is possible and we are growing weary not being able to stop the turmoil. Lord, help us to put it all in your hands, to abide by faith while doing our part, faith that you are there wherever there's a need watching out for your children. Lord, we don't understand why Jewel is not conscious, perhaps we needed to ask when our hearts were combined, and we are asking now. Father for families torn apart, for those who are alone, those who grieve the loss of loved ones, we ask your peace and comfort into their lives and now as we go our separate ways, Lord, lead and guide us and keep us safe from what would destroy us. We love you, dear father and thank you for your son. Amen.

✳ ✳ ✳ ✳ ✳

Daniel hugged Harriet. "Thank you, Harriet. I know there's a lot of goodness in your heart and I know through the years you have learned lessons from heart ache that we cannot fanthom You mean a lot to me, Harriet and I just wanted you to know."

"Thank you, Daniel. It seems this year we've not had just one large happening to deal with but many. I think in our group of friends we strengthen each other because we hold each other accountable to do what is right."

"Harriet, there's something else, in regard to what happened here tonight. We have to be careful where Ruthie goes and who she is with. Do you understand what I'm thinking?"

Understanding dawned in Harriet's eyes. "I had not thought… oh, yes, Daniel, if he would disguisde himself and come here, then he can be anywhere and should he realize Ruthie's gift, she will be targeted same as Evan. It is the untainted innocence and goodness he strives to snuff out." Sadness replaced the light of understanding. "Daniel, talk to Ellen and be quick to explain to Ruthie about strangers. I will pray."

Chapter 14

There was one light on in the sanctuary. The old woman saw this as she walked slowly past pushing the four wheel carriage she had salvaged from the dump outside town. The dump was becoming an eyesore to the entrance of a prosperous mid-sized town that had about all the amenities a town needed. The past town fathers thought to put it behind a row of pines that interlocked from close plantings, still the dump had enlarged faster than the growth of the trees and like a kid with dirty fingers parts of the dump were shining through and no one had time to amend the problem. She chuckled. It was pleasing.

What to do about the two that messed up at the Jacob's. What to do, when to do anything would blow her cover. What do you mean, she hissed when the one said he had called nine one one because he feared the woman would die, the blood was pouring out of her head that fast and he didn't want it on his hands. Her death, he alreadiy had her blood on his hands, his shoes, and he hoped that was all while he held onto a stupid nearly bare Christmas tree. She heard his thoughts and was not happy with him.

She hadn't like that remark. If she'd had her cane she'd beat him severely. It wasn't his to make a remark about anything he liked but to take his pay and buy what pleased him. She didn't care. He had a decision to make before they reported in after midnight tonight. True, agravattion was going well of these lily white christian brother and sisters. She laughed, stepping inside the wall that felt seamless. Removing the scarf, the headband, the long woman's coat, he let out a roar of satisfaction. The walls shivered but didn't break. No one knew his whereabouts. That was his only protection.

Like that in the flip of an eye, he became himself. He did feel comfortable as she seemed to. That's why he took a painfully long time applying the make-up, allowing his former dead self to come alive. He had actually gone to the couple's home. Tonight. There were moments of delusionment but presently his mind was clear as a bell. Again, he roared.

Brother Joe stopped to listen. There it was again. The sound gave him goose bumpst from the tip of his nose to the top of his toes, it was a roar not unlike a lion but highlighted with great timbre. In his heart he knew the roar of the devil would be loud and strong but "My God," he whispered, "is stronger, my God is bigger than any other, My God." His attempt to sing the praise song his congregation loved was feeble, for though he believed his god would defeat the devil, he trembled to think what the devil was capable of doing, Hadn't he tried to prove time after time he could out do the God of the Israelites?

"Father." Pastor Joe fell on his knees. "When will this endless battle stop? When will you show your power and authority that all will know you are the King of Kings and Savior of mankind."

"Joe," the voice chided, "how many good men would we lose along the way because they have not yet learned the lesson and accepted my son? Trust me, Joe."

✳ ✳ ✳ ✳ ✳

Matt and Marigold walked to the house with Harriet. "Ma, I have a question, in your prayer you ask God to bless us, I think I can say this correctly, that sometimes we fear what will happen next could be worse than we have already experienced. What did you mean, Ma?"

Harriet motioned for them to take a seat. "I think you will agree this has been a hard year. It began with the flood, many people of our area were left homeless due to the dam breaking from Spring rains and most of us either support or took in those homeless. I chose to support the cause. Andrew and Daniel's homes housed Evan and Jewel. Their problems became ours. You know the rest of the story, Addy taken, Evan's hard work down the drain when the violins were stolen, then the break in at his home."

"But Ma, our group drew together, closer, we have been since little Andy was hit by the car, I almost lost another baby, Ellen has had the cancer treatments." She draped her arm around Harriet's shoulder,"I think for all everyone's been through we've come out stronger because we had to go through it."

"I just have this feeling, dear that we aren't finished. We are fragile at this point with Jewel in the hospital and Evan doesn't know if she will be…" Harriet stopped, her mouth pursed in that funny way she had trying not to cry as she bowed her head.

"Oh, Ma," Marigold led her mother to the two chairs everyone sit in when they came to visit. On her knees she peered up into Harriet's face. "Mom, I know there's more you aren't telling me. I think I know what it is…so I'll just jump in here. I don't know if you had met the sisters before. The one was cordial enough but I noticed…the tall one was almost cold or maybe haughty to you and on our one other encounter it was the same. So what goes there and is that it? Because I know it hurts when someone snubs you, but you know what, Ma? I got enough tinkerbell in me, I just don't give a rip. If I've not hurt them then I don't owe them the time of day. Ain't that right, Farm boy?" She turned to Matt. He was grinning. "That's why that big hunk loves me."

"She's tough all right," Matt said, while his thoughts were on his mother treating her badly and not acknowledging her, she was strong to take that and he knew down deep it did hurt, a lot.

"I don't know the sisters, Marigold. Was she really cold to me? I had other people on my mind and I know I told the dark haired one I was sorry in their loss of the other sister, but we didn't talk beyond that. Oh, my, must I be concerned over that, too?"

"No, ma'm, you're my mother, I'll handle it."

"Well," rising to leave, Matt said, "that's scary. I think I'll see if Hattie's ready to turn loose the kids."

Later, climbing into bed beside Matt, Marigold said, "Ending of another day we've been given. The wee ones were so tired. I bet Hattie wooled them around all day. Good thing we had Harriet with us."

Matt laughed, "Since when does she let you call her Ma?"

"When she's too worried about something to notice." Marigold yawned as his arm drew her near.

"Someone else seems a bit tired," he kissed the top of her head and pulled her into the hollow of his body. She was asleep. Silently he spoke to his Savior. "Thank you, Lord. I know others are hurting and I pray for them but thank you, I'm a happy man."

✳ ✳ ✳ ✳ ✳

Penny was in and out of the bed. It was nearing ten o'clock but there had been little rest the last hour. Finally her mother heard the baby crying and came in to see what was wrong. "Mother, please hold him, I'll call doctor Fawk and see what I should do."

"I think it's colic but I don't' know what they give babies for colic these days." Picking up little Colton, Mary asked, "Is it all right with you if I take him in where your dad is sitting?"

Penny waved her on, as doctor Fawk answered and she told him the problem and that her mother suspected the colic. "I'm at the hospital making rounds," he replied, "But a sales rep was in the other day and left samples he said would stop colic in babies, if you want to try it, I'll send Ben after it. Just come to the hospital."

Colton was wide awake listening to his grandparents talk. "He's still having little stomach pains," her mother said, "I hold him firm against my body and that comforts him a little but you will need it later."

When she arrived at the hospital, Dr. Fawk was speaking with an elderly lady who had brought in her husband. When they finished talking he came to where she waited. "Ben's not back yet, but he won't be long. You might want to peep in on LeAnn. She's in that second room down there. She went skating with a group and some kid tripped her and she's waiting to see if the x-rays say it's a fracture or a sprain. She can't bear to put her weight on that foot…so I'm guessing. But a sprain can be painful."

"Oh, no, her wedding is in two days."

"She may be wearing a cast under the wedding dress, huh?" The doctor smiled and moved on.

"Oh, my, LeAnn." Her sister in law was sitting against the head of the bed, the foot badly swollen was propped up on pillows. "That looks angry." Le Ann nodded as her mother stepped from behind the curtains. "I'm here to pick up medicine for Colton. My mother thinks he has the colic."

Leona smiled. "So you named him Colton? Sutton told me that was what the two of you had chosen."

"Yes, ma'm. He's a fine baby and that name suits him. Sutton wanted a name that bore strength."

"Well," Leona stumbled for words. "I hope the medicine works. Sutton had colic for three weeks when he was born. I thought it was for older babies but he had it and his grandmother said his father.."

"I never heard that before, that dad had colic as a baby. Are you sure, Mother?"

Leona fumbled with the bed sheet. "I'm sure." There was such an expression of pain crossed her face that Penny felt sorry for her. She was turning to leave when she knew what she must do.

"Mrs. Coleman, you are welcome to come see the baby, if you want to."

"I'd like that, Penny." A tear formed and ran down her cheek. "With Sutton gone, it would be comforting. Behind her back, LeAnn was rolling her eyes and mouthing don't trust her.

Ben caught up with her in the last hall before the entrance waiting room. "Penny, wait up. Listen, if you've got five minutes, how about going in and saying hello to Jewel. It's a sad situation, Penny."

Hurriedly, Penny glanced at the clock on the wall. Her mother hadn't called. "Can you show me to her room, Ben?"

"Let me prepare you, Penny. She hasn't spoken and still unable to do things for herself."

"Have her parents visited her?" He shook his head and she asked, "why?"

"Last I heard they said she brought this on herself, marrying that good for nothing fellow." He opened the door to Jewel's room. "Her husband just left. I like him, Penny, but I got to go, now. See you later."

She walked over to Jewel's bed. They had changed her to her side and pulling up a chair, Penny could look right into her face. She took Jewel's hand into her own. "Hi, it's me, remember me? I was your next door neighbor until my marriage fell apart." She was silent, thinking and then she said, "Remember when I came to you and Evan, Sutton had struck me and I said I was leaving. I had to tell someone, Jewel and you both were nice to me."

"Jewel, you are talented and such a good person. I know God has a plan for you, but you're going to have to do your part. If you hear me, Jewel, squeeze my hand. You can't lay here wishing to die because so many things seem wrong with your body. What you have to do is understand He will take care of it all. Our God is more powerful than any problem the devil lays on us. I had to think that one out, and it took me a few days. Now I don't know if my and Sutton's lives are tied together or not, him being in the State prison system doesn't help, besides that we aren't communicating but we have the sweetest little baby boy. I want you to meet him, maybe you'd want to be his god-mother, do you think?"

"I'm coming back, Jewel and I'll hold your hand and wait for you to squeeze it, but I do wish you'd try hard to do it now. You see, Christmas is just around the corner and I want you and Evan to be together. Me and Sutton can't. Well, with Colton I"ve got a small piece of Sutton with me, haven't I. Could you squeeze my hand, Jewel? If it's possible I'll see you in a few days and I'll be praying meanwhile that you are coming out of this coma, I don't rightly know what to call it. So I'm going now to take medicine for my baby. Remember, Christmas is almost here and we said we prayed for a good one. Well, I'm still praying. Bye now." She squeezed Jewel's hand and waited for a response but there wasn't any.

✳ ✳ ✳ ✳ ✳

Evan appeared at four o'clock the next morning. First thing he noticed a new tube running from Jewel's body and the oxygen was back. "No, no no," he cried out, beside himself that they would do that while he was away and they were supposed to call him. "I didn't leave until two, why didn't you call me.

"We did," they said, "But you didn't answer. We're sorry but it was life or death, and you signed papers saying if we could not reach you we could do the necessary procedure." Evan was walking the hall, pacing, his hands locked behind his head trying to absorb their words. "Life or death?" How could that be, just yesterday they thought she was on the mend. It was all his fault he had forgot to recharge his phone. He had thrown himself across the bed and slept only a few hours troubled sleep before racing back. His mind was all a muddle was she sliding back when he left and he hadn't noticed?

"What's wrong now?"

"She has pneumonia and the feeding tube is to give her sustenance. Her body is starving, it needs nutrients. I'm sorry, Mr. Jacobs, we are trying to take care of your wife and others if you will excuse me."

He was ashamed. He had failed her. Was she dying? "We'll just roll her down the hall and get a few scans, thirty minutes work and we won't move her; she won't have to be out of her bed. Go get a bite of breakfast while you're waiting." The words circled his brain and meant nothing. He stumbled out to the Garden Chapel. Thankful no one was there, he sank on his knees and the sobs wracked his body.

"Lord, Jesus, I'm so afraid she will die. I've never had anyone love me before, Jesus. Could you spare her? I know I'm selfish. Heaven won't have the problems we have down here but Jesus, she has given me a glimpse of heaven…you know that. Could you spare her, Lord, and let us live the rest of our lives thanking you?" He hadn't slept enough, he was anxious to return to the hospital. Now on his knees he cried to the Lord and as peace settled in his heart, his body ebbed out and sleep took hold. They found him there, beneath the cross, the background music playing ever so softly as he lay on the ground.

✳ ✳ ✳ ✳ ✳

"My, my, my. Folks are busy tonight, don't you know?" The old sailor shook his head. "I wonder what's behind all this activity?" He had stood in the street studying the Gates house with all it's lights on, decorations for Christmas being hung in the garden. Even the sisters were there. Had they mourned enough their sibling that died? Leaving he drove by the Jacob's house; it was black as pitch. He wondered about the lights on at Harriet Becker's. She should be getting old enough to retire . And last there was the home of Will Martin. Through the windows he saw the grandparents holding the new baby. Ah, yes, and how does that leave the Coleman's. Sutton, my boy, is in jail because she couldn't take a little push or shove… my boy that was credited to Charles Landers, but it wasn't his, that's why he didn't marry Leona. I had a say in that. Then, what does she do, marries Sutton Coleman to save her name. "You wouldn't marry me," she says, "You always kept everything secretive, like if it mattered, Clayton and then you marry society's darling. We could have been happy but you were too busy climbing the ladder to what?" This made him angry; his conscience talking back to him, bringing up the past. Last he'd seen there was nothing happy about the Coleman's home. "So you married for stability, your precious Sutton Coleman and you're not happy. My boy's in jail, your girl pregnant and the other boy, Ben, following Fawk around as though he really will be a doctor."

He shoved Clayton Walden back inside himself. Tonight he was the crusty old sailor, the same one that followed the young couple to the beach, the one with the violin when Evan Jacobs was waiting to sign in to the Graves home front. It hurt; he received no recognition for all his abilities. He was a master. In his early life, perhaps something did go wrong. He often wondered if he'd made better choices.....why was he here wandering around by himself? His wife kicked him out. The law was after him. But he eluded them. He was responsible for people dying and he didn't care, if his plan went well more would die because he was tired of their living the good parts of life when he couldn't. The girl just as well die, too. He was particularly exhausted with the good person her husband portrayed. When he sent his thoughts her way his intentions seemed blocked. Unknown to him and to her husband, Harriet awoke with Evan and Jewel on her mind. She went to the window, her thoughts penned on the young couple as she prayed for them. Colton Coleman, tiny little person that he was, demanded his mother wake to feed him, the colic had ceased with the new medicine. Now as she held him Jewel's lifeless grip returned to haunt her. Penny began to pray in earnest for Jewel and Evan. So it went, as though the Holy Spirit was going door to door, waking the friends that they would pray. Their first thought was of Evan and Jewel. On and on, house to house, Andrew and Anne, Marigold and Matt, the Gipsons and Haley, and Si who had come to love them like family bowed before the Lord and prayed with tears running down his cheeks. Not one questioned why they felt the need to pray, nor the knowledge the couple was in need.

The people of Christ Church Congregation filed quietly into the pews, their eyes to the front where Pastor Joe stood. He appeared to be in prayer, his head bowed, his hands clasp together almost as a child would portray the childhood favorite, "this is a house, this is its people, open it up and there's the steeple." They had heard the news through the grapevine, "that new couple's going through serious times." The story followed about how they struggled to continue on in the two store end of town where someone destroyed their place of business and stole their inventory. Bits and pieces circulated, some true, others exaggerated but the ending was sad, "the wife now has pneumonia."

"Please be seated." Pastor Joe stepped down to walk among them, shaking a hand here and there, quietly assessing the group of worshippers. "I realize you have come to pray for Jewel and Evan. Our hearts are full as we have heard Jewel was struck down in her own home, whether by accident or intent." He paused by little Mrs. Henderson's side as she reached up a bony hand to touch him. "We have witnessed this young couple's love for each other, but more importantly for the work of this church and the faithful commitment to their Lord. Many of you have called and asked what they need." Tears slipped down his cheeks, "That makes me exceedingly proud to be your pastor, that you always think of others. Now I'm going to tell you what they need." He breathed an emotional breath. "They need the intervention of good people praying to bring Jewel from the brink of death. As I understand, her friends began vigil early this morning and have continued all day."

"Perhaps the Lord is using this to bring us all together to remind us, this is the holy season when he gave the world the greatest gift of His love, His son." One by one, his deacons came from different areas of the room. Dressed in work clothes, whether denims or suit, they dropped down on bended knee at the altar. Their pastor's heart was so touched, all he could say was, "thank you, Jesus. Now, let us pray and as we pray let us thank God for the blessing of life, the blessing of caring and sharing each other's burdens and let us pray His will in the life of Jewel Jacobs and her husband, Evan."

It was a time of prayer the church had not experienced in a while and when it ended, the quietness held, the whisper here and clasping of one in gratitude to one's chest done with reverence and as Mrs. Henderson was helped out she said, "Pastor, heaven came down."

✳ ✳ ✳ ✳ ✳

The balcony of Christ Church rose up over eight rows of seats on the congregational floor. The staircase began on each side coming together upstairs in a widespread u, that when the Christmas decorations were applied it was a beautiful scene and many families pictures were shot there each Christmas. The setting spoke to hearts and a wedding at that time of year was always considered one of the prettiest. Evan moved his legs as he sat sprawled feet out, slumped in the chair. She had called him twice but he was tired and didn't answer. He was at Christ Church, waiting for Jewel to appear and then she called his name. Softly, once, twice and on the third, "Evan," he awakened. He had slipped into that dark slumber of the first hours when the body is in charge to rest and the mind seems to have left the body. He glanced around, hoping no one saw him in that lifeless drunken sprawl. He had to smile. He didn't drink.

The dream was so real, as though Jewel was well; they were ready to do a concert for the church. He pinched himself. Yes, he was awake. Oh, if only it had been true that she called to him. As close as he could he pulled the chair to her bedside, but that didn't work and what did it matter? He pushed back the chair and lay beside her, her hand in his, one arm beneath her cradling her to his side as he whispered, "Come back to me, Jewel. I miss you. I was dreaming but I thought you called me. Are you making your way back? I pray it's so. I long for our times together. When you call my name, dear Jewel, that's when heaven and earth stand still." The longing to know she would stand by his side brought tears. "God in Heaven," he whispered, "please, let her come back to me."

She roused from the depth of darkness that pulled her down unmercifully. Wasn't she rested? Why must she struggle? She was fighting to rise but the darkness kept pulling her down. Someone's calling. I'm dreaming. I'm sleeping and I can't wake up. I hear you… I know you are calling….

It seemed an eternity as she tried to make her eyes open, her mind work, understanding must come. She was safe. She reached the spot she was searching, she knew that face. He looked haggard, his hair longer than she remembered, he was whispering her name. The smile built along with the joy that was coursing her soul. He was her earthly haven. Somehow she knew she was the reason he looked worn.

From the door worried voices ask, "What shall we do?"

"Nothing," Dr. Fawk replied. "Absolutely nothing. Let them rest. God has decided their need and we have nothing to do or say about anything." He closed the door. "I'm sure you can find other things to do." The nurses scurried down the hall and soon the hospital was abuzz, Jewel Jacobs has come out of the coma, but … Dr. Fawk gave them a disapproving glance, "I don't want to hear that she is asleep in her husband's arms, now. Keep that to yourselves." He smiled as he walked away.

✳ ✳ ✳ ✳ ✳

On the night it snowed, the Cape was the setting for a Currier and Ives Christmas card. Lampposts wearing bright red ribbon adornments shed light on the old brick road that run through the elite section that led into town, Christ Church had laid a blanket over the nativity's Mary, Joseph and Jesus and Si kept vigil at Evan's shop. It had been a bumper day. The lessons Evan and Jewel gave brought parents in for supplies along with others signing up for the future. If he'd had the instruments that were stolen he knew he could have sold every one. Without them, he and Evan had work for two years ahead. He had slipped out to check on his wife in the nursing home and returned to the secret chamber he'd constructed where he could see out but not be seen. He was not going to let anyone destroy Evan's shop, if he could help it. He wasn't a man of violence but his best friend's son was part of the Police force and they'd made agreement should anything happen, the son would be there on the spot. Si was to keep quiet and observe. Not thinking it would happen, but a possibility, Si, turned in for a good night's rest.

✳ ✳ ✳ ✳ ✳

The lights were dim in Christ Church, there would be no need for more, when the tree was lit up and the lights in the garland running up the staircase came on, the dark wood of the church would come aglow and the sanctuary would come alive with God's love and man's ability to fashion a place of holiness the congregation would remember and no matter the condition or weather outside they would come. It was in their hearts, tradition or ritual, call it what fit in one's mind, it was good, the reason to join brothers and sisters together, to tighten the bond, to bless and heal, the beginning and the end of celebration.

The time was set. By nine o'clock the families would have taken care of duties and come with hearts ready to celebrate the true reason of Christmas, Christ birth. It was Friday night with no school tomorrow, the children could sleep late. Hot chocolate and cookies would fill their tummies and keep them by their parent's side. Pastor Joe, stepped to the vestibule in case one arrived early.

At five minutes til nine, Orville Priest began ringing the bell in the tower of the steeple. He would ring for five minutes and then Carrie Green would be seated at the organ as the first majestic and joyful chord rang out and the excitement would press through the body of Christ people in one accord as they lift voices to sing. It happened as planned, the pews were full, a few coughs here and there, but for the most part families sitting together, an occasional sleeping baby, a hand on a toddler, his people were present and it was good.

With the two men serving Pastor Joe started to close the door when he saw the old woman out on the street. He hurried, "Madam, please, may I assist you. Let me take your hand." She seemed an independent sort, even his deacons noticed as they stepped back welcoming her but allowing her the dignity she claimed. As she settled into the next to last pew, Pastor Joe went forward. His men, Daniel and Andrew took the seats behind her.

"Welcome. Welcome. Our hearts are filled with the glory our creator has bestowed upon us tonight. Only He could give us the perfect setting, the beautiful snow, and the ladies of the church have coaxed and shown our youth patience as together they decorated our Place of worship. Isn't it beautiful?" He paused for the applause. "Of course our hearts are filled with joy hearing one of our own has come out of a time of ill health. If you haven't heard, Jewel Jacobs awakened from a time of walking through the valley of a terrible sickness. We don't know if it was coma or something else but I'm sure we will know in the future. For now, she still needs rest and cards would be appreciated but hold off on the visiting. Now as we lift our voices in song, let us give our best to the one who hears our prayers."

Gloria, appropriately was the last song and everyone's countenance portrayed joy as they entered the time for scripture. "Silent night, Holy night, all is calm all is bright," Pastor Joe began. "Our hearts are filled with the glory of God's love and the goodness of mercy and grace he has given us through the birth of His Son, Jesus Christ… Scripture tells us when Mary gave birth, she wrapped her baby in swaddling cloth and laid him In the manger because they had found no room in the inn. That was a humble beginning. God's son was sent to mankind, not the rich in a castle, not to only the poor but to mankind.

In those days, a shepherd was considered an outdoor person who was willing to work with the sheep, his place of work might be a hill or valley but it was outside, an humble setting, an humble person with hopefully an humble heart. Is it within our hearts to understand why he would send an angel to speak to shepherds watching their flocks out in the field? The Angel said, You will find the babe wrapped in swaddling clothes lying in a manger and to this announcement suddenly there was with the angel a multitude of heavenly host praising God and saying Glory to God in the highest and on earth peace and good will toward men. When the angels were gone away, the shepherds said, Let us go to Bethlehem and see this thing which the Lord hath made known to us. And they found Mary and Joseph and the babe lying in a manger. Their hearts were filled with wonder and they returned glorifying and praising God for what they had seen and heard.

As we conclude this service we set aside to open our hearts to the wonder of Jesus birth and a Savior who came to earth for us, let us think on these words. The wonder of it all that a baby would be raised up for our sake, the wonder of God telling humble men of the baby's birth and the wonder of the songs we sing to commemorate that baby in the manger two thousand years later. The next words I hope you will remember, He was born to bring peace and good will. We live in a world full of decisions we must make, sometimes difficult and full of turmoil but we long for peace in our heart, in our lives, among others and what better time than Christmas as we celebrate Jesus birth, what better time to have peace and goodwill as we consider He came for us…that when we leave this earth we can look forward to eternity with him if we make a decision to live for him. And that is the wonder of it all, that He made it all possible. He gave us a choice where we will spend eternity. It is up to us. Now as we open our hearts to the true meaning of Christmas, let us say the Lord's prayer together."

The organ prelude covered the excitement of children on their way to the main hall and the dining area where desserts of every kind graced tables and hot chocolate was in demand by young and old. Daniel and Andrew had opened their eyes from prayer, thinking to assist the old lady but she was gone.

Closing his eyes tight, Andrew felt a chill wash over his body. He had felt uneasy. Now, mentally he shook himself, tonight all was right with the world. He must not borrow trouble.

Chapter 15

Slipping quietly from the seat into the aisle she had made her way out of the church. Anger laced with malice toward herself caused her body to shake. She must gain control on these icy streets, even deified visitors could fall. She laughed at that. Were the devils cohorts deified, as the saints were sanctified and set aside? Staying in the shadows she slipped through the bramble of vine and into the solitude of home. Home. There, where handiwork of another kind was evident, evident in surety to put him behind bars and it was becoming more confusing each time as to how one should escape. Removing the wrappings of a woman he became himself, sick of that disguise in knowing he could no longer use it. Andrew Graves had sensed his presence, without realizing why he had known Christ Church's contender was in their midst and that was one reason why he hurried out. The other was he could not stand to hear the Lord's prayer. It was about him, deliver us from evil they said, lead us not into temptation, his purpose in the world so easily dismissed in words of a prayer. Of course his job was to lead into temptation.

Whose voice was he hearing? It did not have to be that way, you sold your soul to the devil for personal gain and now you wrack havoc on my people. I know you, he screamed…do you listen to my thoughts? You have taken what is not yours. You know what you must do. I have spoken. Walden clutched his head in his hands. Voices. Voices. They would destroy him. As a broken needle on an old record the words continued, you have taken what is not yours. You know what you must do. The words resounded until finally he lay prostrate on the floor. He did not have full reign to wander the earth tonight spewing hatred, nor taking possessions. Tonight was not his. The battle was not over but tonight the war was not waged. He did not win.

Broken he performed as told. Finished he lay down. Even if they found him there was no proof.

Si had heard movement, going to the place where he could look out but there was nothing, only a shield of darkness, still he dare not leave the safety of the compartment. Tomorrow would suffice.

✳ ✳ ✳ ✳ ✳

"Daddy, I need to see Jewel. I told Momma and she said I must tell you."

"Why do you need to see Jewel?"

"God told me. He lets me know when there's something I must do."

"And what is that, Ruthie?"

"I must sit with her and Evan. He will be there and his body is…" Ruthie paused as she searched for the right word. "He feels it's all tight but he doesn't know what to do. He's sad, Daddy, he's still not sure Jewel is going to get better. She's been sick such a long time."

"Do you know why Evan is sad? Is it losing the instruments?"

"No, it's not about the instruments, its losing Jewel. Jewel is the first person ever loved Evan."

"What about his parents?"

"The momma didn't love him and she didn't allow his father to give him attention."

"Let me finish jotting a few numbers in this book and I'll take you to see Evan and Jewel."

✳ ✳ ✳ ✳ ✳

Daniel went in with Ruthie to be sure it was all right she sit with Jewel and Evan. She fit in rather well, he thought, the two didn't talk a lot when he was there but he suspected they did at other times. Content as a betsy bug, he left Ruthie sitting between the two. A smile of satisfaction played across her face. Evan smiled back but Jewel was asleep, resting peacefully. "The nurse will remove the feeding tube after a while," Ruthie said. "And someone will be bringing you breakfast before long." Ruthie giggled. "I wish they'd bring me biscuit and gravy."

✳ ✳ ✳ ✳ ✳

"Can we come over?" Marigold's voice came over the phone, as Ellen laughed. "I'm as excited as a kid, Ellen. After Ruthie sit with Jewel and Evan the doctor checked her from head to toe and it is his thought that she should go home. He feels the Lord healed her all the way through, so he said." She giggled. "Old doctor Fawk said it was the prayers of the people and he wasn't sure what Ruthie's role in it was but where his patient's husband had been wound tighter than imagination, he was relaxed now."

"We'd love to have you over. I'll call Anne and see if they can come and of course, Harriet."

"We could change the plan and everyone come here," Marigold offered. "I just want to share the good news and give thanks for Jewel's recovery and poor Evan, he has lost weight and looks terrible." She sighed. "I know, I shouldn't say that…so what do you say, want to come here, instead?"

✳ ✳ ✳ ✳ ✳

Daniel was in high gear, enjoying every moment. "I have pigs in the blanket in the oven and S'mores. How do you like that, Momma of many?"

"Fine, Daddy of the year. I'm always proud you make snacks for our guests while I settle the twins."

Suddenly, though expected, the friends were coming through the door, hanging up coats and hats, shoving a tray of goodies on the counter and embracing each other as always. Harper and Dorothy arrived with Harper's voice overpowering everyone else and Dorothy shushing him to speak softly.

"Well, how do you do that when God gives you volume and there's no control panel?" He complained.

"Oh, your house is decorated beautiful. Ellen you are so talented." Marigold's enthusiasm had not waned. "So what do you think? Did God answer our prayers? I'm told she is being released."

"What else healed Jewel?" Daniel asked, as he was checking on a third batch of S'mores.

"Where do we go from here?" Andrew was lifting Adeline up from the floor. She was too small to be in the midst of the older children. "I've told Daniel, now I'll tell the rest of you. I believe Walden in disguise, as usual, was in Christ Church Friday night for our special service, but he disappeared which is his signature act, getting away unnoticed before we realized it was him. He was there for some reason."

"Where does it leave us, if it is as you, Daniel and Pastor Joe think he targeted our group because we stand firm on our love of the Lord and if he can trip us up, where just one of us forsakes our Lord then he will feel a job has been well done." Matt waited for one of them to reply. "It's that serious isn't it?"

"I'll tell you like I explained to a friend that ask me about this," Harper's voice boomed through the room "He had the gall to say he didn't believe the devil had enough power to go after someone with the intention to ruin their life when there were too many good men he could choose, why would he choose a man who had very little wealth, to begin with, and then was it coincidence his home was destroyed by flood, his instruments stolen and did I really believe God would allow the devil to tamper with one of his own's health, as in the case of Evan's wife?" Harper was warming to the subject. "Then he further explains to me if it's true the devil roams the earth why in the world would he start here in the Cape with his shenanigans?"

"Now what was your reply, Harper?" Daniel always enjoyed Harper's discourse.

"You ready for this? I told him where there's love and peace in the midst of God's people, that's where the devil begins to do his dirty work, he's not content with people working together, such as the kingdom of God we're part of. Well, he wasn't having that either. I just stopped talking and started praying." Attentive to Harper, the group barely realized the sisters had arrived and were listening.

"We've watched a lot play out, this past year." Matt took in the Christmas tree, all lit up with its angel at the top. "I think we, here, are as the shepherds. We know we have a Savior. We need his mercy and grace…otherwise how would we last through everything that happens…it all adds up and we either have peace to deal with it or unending turmoil. Marigold and I thank God everyday for watching over us, otherwise we might not be together because life gets difficult."

"Amen, brother," Andrew chipped in. "Anne and I have been pushed to the wall, too many times, some of it of our own making but God has pulled us through the muck and mire and we stand with you tonight and I can tell you Harper Gipson literally pulled me out of the muck and mire."

"Then," Harriet spoke up, "You are saying, you believe right here in our insignificant little city of the Cape, the devil could do his work, but because we believe our God is stronger and defeats him as we pray and ask guidance on our lives that is what our world needs, not that we are special but that our God is the authority for our lives; he truly has the key to world peace, it starts right here with us?"

One of the sisters spoke up, "a lot of what you say is foreign to us, though our mother believed. We have been out in the world, sometimes your plan of salvation doesn't work, and you can't always rely on it." Aldean looked at Harriet as if to challenge her question. "What makes it work for you?"

"We rely on God," Ellen said quietly. "It is by faith. We can't always look ahead and see what's around the corner. Faith truly is the substance of things hoped for and that faith is rooted in Jesus Christ. We cannot straddle the fence; we either are in or out. God has given us a choice. Walden, like each of us has made a decision. Yes, they tell us drugs he chose to use ruined his mind and practically destroyed his body but on the other hand he has stated publicly he serves the devil. God has allowed the devil to walk the earth and meddle in our lives, that is part of allowing us a choice whether to serve him or not. I don't know about you but when this life is over I want to know as a child of God Jesus will call my name and it all starts with whether I ask him in to my heart or not. It is that decision, again."

Everyone grew quiet as Ellen spoke and no one offered rebuttal or agreement; when suddenly the door swung open; everyone jumped and then quickly clapped hands as Evan carried Jewel into their midst.

"Welcome," Daniel said with a bow to the two as Matt gave up his chair and pushed it over for Evan. "In closing our discussion we've left a lot unsaid, but on the other hand, perhaps our bond strengthens us as we support each other. Let's greet Jewel and enjoy each other…because…"his eyes twinkled with merriment, "it is Christmas Eve's eve and for many reasons this year will be the best Christmas ever. What more can we ask for? Now, Evan how did you know we were all here, waiting for you two?"

"We saw the cars,' Evan began, "And nothing do Jewel but we stop in but we won't stay long."

"Merry Christmas," Jewel said in a voice almost inaudible. "I love you all so very much and I know except for your prayers I would not be here." Everyone clapped hands again as Ellen called "foods on."

Marigold come to sit opposite Jewel as Evan held her. "It wasn't so many years back I was in terrible pain and there were severe problems. Long story short, through the pain I realized I must fight to live. There are scenes in my mind of those moments, did anything happen to you…similar?"

"I thought I heard Evan call my name," Jewel whispered. "Before that I was in darkness struggling to reach the light I saw in the distance. That is still in my thoughts and concern over Miss Geri dying."

"I think what we were all involved in discussing before you arrived goes along with this. We are almost one hundred percent believers, the two remaining sisters seem to have a few questions, still just as you were struggling to find the light, and in my case the light found me, the Holy Spirit was working for us. Let us pray Aldean and Nina have peace in their hearts this Christmas because by her own testament Geri died at peace knowing our Lord." Marigold smiled. "Now that's a good Christmas, isn't it?"

✳ ✳ ✳ ✳ ✳

Christmas morning found three additional inches of snow on the ground. The landscape was a fairy tale surprise, long icicles dripped from the trees whose branches sagged from the weight of the extra snow. Everything was beautiful.

Cullum made his way to Harriet Becker's door. She was expecting him and welcomed him in with a hot cup of coffee in her hand. "Merry Christmas, Cullum. Come sit and we'll have a nice cup of coffee and a hurried discussion of last night's events. I know you want to rush back to your family."

"No, ma'm, I don't have family. My parents died last year and I have no siblings."

"Nor do I," She replied. "If you don't mind, let us get into the business of the hour. I have twenty some people expected for four o'clock dinner and if you aren't busy, please join us." She leaned forward, an interested expression on her face. "Tell me. I hear there's exciting news."

"It is strange," Cullum began. "You know we were able to thread a camera and audio into the area we thought was Walden's hiding place and you surely agree there's nothing visible to suggest any thing of importance in there. Last night amidst the thunder, which is unusual with snow coming down, we received an alert on the equipment. For a time, what we visibly saw was an elegant room with display cases. Now I'm talking elegant in a sense we don't see in the Cape."

"You're thinking he knew the place was bugged, so to speak, and gave you something to view but whether it was his surroundings or not…?"

"Exactly." Cullum's expression changed. "It is indescribable, to work on a secret operation, unable to discuss with your fellow workers and yet you wonder all the time who knows about this? Surely Walden seeks help, he couldn't possibly take care of all the little avenues of his own making, could he?"

"Andrew is convinced Walden's pact with the devil has entitled him to abilities we can only imagine."

"I've come to agree with Mr. Graves. I had such a sense of danger and darkness to my soul last night, it was as though evil and goodness were in a struggle and I felt it though I couldn't see what was happening. When I walked past Christ Church I felt a magnetism of being drawn into something I couldn't understand. But here's the most interesting part to me…and I'm hoping when Mr. Gates and you and Mr. Graves examine the tapes we have; you can shed light on this. You know the scripture in the Bible where Paul speaks to King Agrippa and Agrippa says, "Almost thou persuade me to be a Christian?"

"Yes," Harriet replied softly, not taking her eyes off his face, "Go on."

"Whether it is Walden or someone else or his own tricky way of trying to offset where we are going, we could hear discussion. It's on the tape. It is comparable to Walden's voice, he says it will require more than you have to bring me back…though I don't know if you allow one back who made tryst with the devil." Cullum paused, rethinking the next words. "We who were selected to listen, in secret of course, did not hear a voice at this time but down to a man these words entered into our conscious thoughts, "you have taken what belonged to a good and just man. Return it." Walden was as a spoiled child in tantrum and again, the words fed into our conscience, "you have taken what belonged to a good and just man. Return it."

"What can that possibly imply?" Harriet straightened to stare across the room to the world outside.

"Here's the kicker." Cullum blushed. "Forgive me, Mrs. Becker, I got excited. Here's what happened next. The same elegant room we had seen before, flashed on the screen, briefly, but the display cases were bare, the room was void of object. This morning Evan Jacob's man who works for him, called, I believe his name is Simon or Silas, they call him, Si. Well, he called and seems he had built a compartment of sorts to spy on those who enter the shop when it is closed, if anyone does he could hear the sound but there was no one there. The room was shielded by complete darkness."

"Another dead end." Harriet felt the disappointment.

"Today, Simon Nettler called excited as could be." Cullum grinned, "Funny how names come to you later, isn't it? Anyway, Simon said we needed to come to the shop right away."

"Oh, no, more problems? For Evan? I hurt for him."

"No, ma'am. The violins were returned, all except one. There was no evidence the door had been tampered with, the alarm was still on and yet those violins stolen months previous were on the shelves."

✳ ✳ ✳ ✳ ✳

Evan had awakened early to be sure the house was in tiptop condition. Now he sit across from Jewel, his bride, his helpmate the one God had found in an obscure household with strange parents that never showed themselves in society; parents to the one he felt God saved for him. Her heart was pure and nothing but goodness came from her, raised in a strict environment, God had given her biblical training. She believed the word and loved easily. The years of his young life had been lacking in the normal child's need of encouragement but with Jewel, life had taken a turn for the best. "Thank you, Jesus," he whispered. "Thank you, Jewel."

The house was quiet. He had turned off his phone. Dr. Fawk said for the next month Jewel must have continued rest. They had spent days in the hospital without time to shop for a gift but they had each other and they would celebrate Jesus birth. As he sit there, quietly not disturbing her sleep and somewhat out of her sight should she awaken, he could only be thankful for God sparing her life. She had brought joy and an expectation of each tomorrow, for him. His mind wandered to the many unanswered questions and trying situations their friends had to bear. Sutton needed the Lord, but no one knew his thoughts. What would happen to his wife and child while he was away and would Sutton begin to realize peace lay in knowing Jesus? He wondered about Sutton and often the sisters, his own heart ached that Geri was gone but to a better place. He would be grateful that one who resembled pictures of his mother was kind to him. On and on his mind rambled as he sat there waiting for Jewel to awaken. "Merry Christmas, Jesus. Merry Christmas, Jewel," he whispered. "Thank you." .

Once more Walden shot the lock, listening with satisfaction as it went through the rolling sequence of shutting down. Only the best. Now he studied the violin. It was probably Evan Jacob's best work. Seldom did he back down. It wasn't his nature. True, the warning light in his brain kept flashing, "Thou believest that there is one God: thou doest well; the devils also believe and tremble."

He had chosen his own path. In the end he had no friends or family and no God. He was alone. He knew the scripture, making agreement with the devil, as it was said "selling his soul," earthly gain had been his but now what was left for him, hiding from people like the friends of Ellen and Daniel Gates while making as much disorder in their lives as possible. Why had he decided to return the violins?

He chose Evan Jacobs to break from his belief in God. Walden shuddered as he said the most high's name; but he failed. Jacobs held to his faith. Still, he was not finished with Jacobs, nor any of them. For a moment a soft spot captured his brain, almost he wanted what they had but there was no going back. Was there? The words rang in his ears….thou believest there is one God? The devil also believes and trembles.

* * * * *

"Jewel."

Jewel stirred, opened her eyes, and smiled. She was home, with Evan. The little angel on the top of the chest of drawers beckoned she look further and there it was the nativity set the sisters said was handed down through their family for over a hundred years. The Christ child was in the manger, Mary and Joseph keeping watch and as if waiting just for her, the ornament she and Aidan found together.

Hope and joy, peace and comfort were wrapped in knowing God had truly sent his Son. Jewel stretched and then sit up in bed. It was good to be home. She remembered bits and pieces of her hospital stay but she would never forget knowing someone had fought the battle for her; whether her own angel, kept guard at times or when it was Jesus sitting by her side her faith was only strengthened. Whatever God had in store for her and Evan, they would do it together. Truly, this was the best Christmas ever.

Thank you, she whispered and if it were possible she felt a smile wash through her body.

"Merry Christmas, Jewel." Evan had watched her awakening and arose to go to her.

"Merry Christmas, my darling." She replied as her feet touched the floor and his arms opened wide. "I thought I heard you call my name."

The End

Betty invites you to join her on her blog

Forgiven by Betty Lowrey

on Facebook